# SPICE OF LOVE

## ANYA STASSIY

# ACKNOWLEDGMENTS

I would like to express my deepest gratitude to all the family members and friends who have been excited and so supportive of my writing adventure. Your interest in my journey as an author, as well as your reading of my debut novel, *Eyes of Amber*, and hearing your feedback inspired me and gave me fuel to write this novel.

I would like to say thank you to my beta readers, Monica Dolack and Gabby Drakh. I appreciate you taking your time and reading my draft when it wasn't perfect; your feedback helped me put final touches to the story, tying all the loose ends.

A special thank you goes to Krista Dapkey of KD Proofreading. I can't say enough how much I appreciate your sharp eye for catching all those missing commas and correcting all those misspelled words.

Michael Pilgrim, my editor, thank you so much for helping me polish this story. Your approach is the most helpful with both gentle delivery of the critique and firing up my enthusiasm about writing and finishing this novel.

The team of ebooklaunch.com has my deepest gratitude for creating the perfect cover yet again and formatting of this book.

To my husband, thank you for your endless support. You are my rock. To my kids, thank you for your "just because" hugs and kisses, I love you.

# 1.

## ANGELINA

I stare through the large window of the terminal, where the color gray dominates in low hanging clouds, wet pavement, and even faraway trees that have taken on the morbid color. My airplane outfit is simple, skinny jeans and an oversized soft sweater; my hands are warmed by a peppermint mocha. The planes taking off, landing, and being taxied on the tarmac of JFK airport is an elaborate movement performed with seeming ease. The October air of New York is cold and crisp, but I am escaping the coming winter on the 10:30 a.m. flight to Grenada.

My best friend, Jenna, is getting married to a wealthy Silicon Valley tech company founder. A destination wedding is a good reason to take a long-needed vacation and spend time with Jack. I look at my phone, it's 9:30 a.m., he's running late. He always runs late. I'm not surprised, but I hope he made his connecting flight and he doesn't miss the plane. Jack is coming back from his book signing in LA, he's had a long spell of not releasing any books. He is excited, he finally finished his trilogy. The last book has taken him two years to finish. I've known it would be a best seller since I read the first draft. The man has a talent for writing fascinating stories.

I dial him, he picks up the phone, but continues talking to someone before he says an elongated apologetic, "Hi!"

I know he is not coming on this plane with me. "Where are you?"

"I'm still in LA. I'm sorry. I met so many fans, and there was an impromptu welcoming party. I overslept. There's nothing I could do."

"Well, when is the next plane?"

"I don't know. I went back to the hotel. I have a few ideas that I must write down. I'll stay here a few more days. I like it here, the whole vibe. You understand, of course?" he replies. Of course I understand, I must always understand that when he is writing, nothing else matters. Not even me.

"I thought that we'd spend more time together now that you're done," I tell him, disappointed.

"I thought so, too, but the editor had some great input on my next manuscript and my fingers are already itching to type. I just don't want to lose my train of thought. I promise to meet you in Grenada. Be a darling, and when you get there, see if you can arrange for my flights."

"When do you think you'll be able to come?" I sigh.

"Let's talk when you land, and I'll give an exact date. Enjoy your time there." He sounds as if he's in a hurry to finish our conversation.

"I'd enjoy it if you came with me," I voice with sadness. Lately we have been spending little time together. I knew once the book was finished there would be a book tour and constant book signings that would intrude even more on our relationship. I realized I would be living in the shadow of Jack's talent when we started dating three years ago.

By then, at forty-three years of age, he was already a celebrated author of fantasy. I'd just finished college and was working as a publisher's assistant. At twenty-four years of age, I had written and published a few short stories, but finally had started to work on a book of my own. We met at a bookstore's night for local authors. He was eloquently spoken, funny, and charismatic. His success story was inspiring, and I wanted to get to know him. I was attracted to his talent and triumph. I stood out in that bookstore, the youngest person in attendance. I decided to seize the opportunity and told Jack that I would love to take him out for a drink. To my surprise, he agreed. He told me I was exciting, I was inspiring; but that was three years ago, and I feel Jack doesn't find me as exhilarating as before.

"Angelina, please don't do that. You know how important this book is to me. The vacation is ten days long. I'll see you there, and I promise we'll spend plenty of time together." I sense irritation in his voice and decide not to push him any further.

"Okay, I'll see you there," I reply agreeably.

"Have a good time, darling," Jack finishes our conversation and hangs up.

"Bye!" I say into the silence of the phone. It's all right, I will be busy with Jenna and maybe will have some time to go over my manuscript once more.

The female voice over the speaker announces that the flight to Grenada is now boarding. I patiently wait for my group to be allowed onto the plane and then orderly proceed to my window seat at the end of the plane. Gretchen is also running late. I might get to Grenada without my boyfriend and one of my best friends. Jenna, Gretchen, and I have been friends since middle school, yet we're completely different. I'd met Jenna in a hallway of our school when a bully knocked my books out of my arms and stepped on the essay I'd been working on for days. She tripped him as he was walking away from me, he fell and scraped his knee. She got called to the principal, but I defended her with a carefully crafted speech. We met Gretchen in the cafeteria, a shy girl, always dressed in pretty outfits and sparkly shoes. She, too, was picked on by a group of girls who made fun of her and called her Ms. Piggy for not being thin enough. Jenna and I looked at each other, took our trays, and sat next to her from that day on. Now, Gretchen is a divorced mother of an eleven-year-old girl, Jenna has decided to get married, and I, well, I'm still searching for my own life purpose.

My seatmate turns out to be a young woman in her twenties, she is dressed in layers of clothing that hide her body. I smile politely at her and she returns a smile and a cheerful "Hi!" as she clumsily moves into her seat. When she sits down, the layers of her clothing move and I spot a round belly. She looks pregnant, very pregnant, I want to ask her how far along she is. But what if I am wrong? Then it will be a very awkward plane ride for both of us. She puts her hand on the belly and then covers it with her clothes again. I think she spots me looking, she leans in and whispers, "I'm so nervous. Do you mind if I talk to you to settle my nerves?"

"Sure," I reply.

"Oh, thank God, you're nice. I was so worried I'd sit with someone strange or terrible," she continues in a low voice.

"I don't think I'm strange or terrible, you have nothing to worry about," I promise her.

4

"I'm pregnant, you know." She smiles at me and moves her clothes to show off her belly, but then covers it up again when she spots the flight attendant.

"How far along are you?" I inquire.

"Thirty-four weeks tomorrow." The woman rubs her belly, beaming with joy, her accent gives away the native Caribbean in her. "My doctor cleared me to fly, but I am hiding because I heard that sometimes the airlines don't let pregnant women on the plane," she leans in even closer, speaking low as her eyes get big.

"Oh, wow! You look great!" I compliment her in a low voice myself. "Don't worry, I won't tell on you," I give her a promise, feeling that we just formed a bond.

"Thank you! I can't wait to meet this little one already, he's been kicking up a storm. I'm Deja, by the way," she extends her hand for a shake, and I squeeze her warm hand in return.

"First time going to Grenada?" Deja asks while the rest of the passengers settle into their seats.

"Mm-hmm, my friend is getting married there."

"Oh, you'll love it. Make sure to try nutmeg ice cream." She smiles a wide, friendly smile while chatting with me. I appreciate the conversation; although I love being in airports, I get anxious during takeoff and landing. Her almost-singing, joyful voice steadies my heart and my breathing.

"Nutmeg? In ice cream?" I giggle at the odd flavor. "I'll make sure to try it."

Finally, the passengers settle into their seats, flight attendants pass by for the final check, and the plane starts taxiing. I hope Gretchen made it. I turn off my cell, close my eyes, and lean back into the seat. Deja pulls on my hand

and puts it onto her belly. "Feel this little soccer player." Her belly is firm, she moves my hand over it until I feel a soft nudge into my palm. The unexpected sensation of the baby kicking is wondrous, I wait for another kick. The life in the belly of Deja is active, he kicks again and again, the young mother giggles, and I join her laughter.

"This is amazing!" I breathe out. "Does it hurt?"

"Sometimes he kicks me really hard in my ribs, he tells me to roll over to the other side that way, and when I do, he is happy again. I will let you feel him again when he stirs."

"Sure." I look out the window and we are already in the air, climbing up high to the necessary altitude. We penetrate the blanket of fluffy clouds and glide along the clear blue sky. I ache with the feeling of sadness that Jack is not with me. In the past three years, we've shared a lot: his frustration with writer's block, and then his sudden breakthrough where he wrote nonstop for weeks, forgetting to eat. I had to put the plate in front of him and take clothes off of him, otherwise he would grow angry and stinky, and it would only prolong his writing.

I, myself, wrote only when he was asleep. The response to my short stories was positive, but I decided to switch from criminal suspense to fantasy with the encouragement of Jack. The creation of another world came to me easily. I've been waiting for Jack to tell me his thoughts on the new-for-me genre, hoping he will feed me with words of encouragement. But we'll have time in Grenada. He's a fast reader. I know he'll finish it in no time, I tell myself before I'm lulled to sleep by the humming of the plane engines and manage to doze off in the tight, uncomfortable chair. I don't know how long I've been asleep when I'm jolted awake by the turbulence and low humming that's coming from Deja. She's pressed into the seat, her eyes shut tightly, her nose is crinkled as she slowly breathes out air through her pursed lips.

"Deja, are you okay?" I rub her arm so she looks at me.

"The baby isn't enjoying this plane ride. My belly is getting hard," she tells me through her clenched teeth. I pass my hand over the roundness of her flesh and it feels rock hard.

"Deja, are you having a contraction?" I ask.

"I don't know, I've never had one before." She opens her eyes, full of worry.

"Do you want me to page the flight attendant?" I look at her and then look above the seats to see if a flight attendant is nearby.

"No, no, let's just wait. I'll try to relax and fall asleep." Deja waves me off and I see her face relax. She looks at me and smiles.

"Okay, but tell me if you need anything." I lean back, but keep my eyes on her belly that she hides under the clothing again.

She nods and leans her head back, taking a long, deep breath through her nose and letting it out through her mouth. I put on my headphones to watch a movie on the plane's TV to keep me from falling asleep, so I can keep a close eye on my seatmate. Turbulence prompts the signal to buckle our seat belts, which lights up above our heads. The calm, male voice of the captain announces that we are forty minutes from Grenada and will start our descent in twenty minutes.

I turn to check on Deja to share my excitement over our soon approaching landing. But my joy changes to deep concern when I see her pressed into the plane's seat, fingers squeezing the seat handles tight, little drops of sweat rolling down her face even though the inside of the plane is cool.

"Deja," I nudge her arm gently. When she doesn't respond, I shake her again. "Deja."

She turns her face to me, looking tired and scared. I understand instantly that for her, the time has come to have the baby. "We're almost there. Can you hold on a bit longer?" But Deja shakes her head no before she tenses, her body becoming still, her nostrils flaring fast and a low humming escapes her lips.

"The contractions," she takes a deep breath, "they are about a minute apart ... I'm afraid I'm going to have the baby on this plane."

"Okay, okay. Just hang on a minute, let me call the flight attendant, we'll need help." I press the call button, and a short woman in her forties with her hair pulled in a perfect bun appears instantaneously in front of us.

"How can I help you, miss?" she says, smiling.

"She, she's having a baby." I point to my deep-in-labor companion.

The professional smile of the flight attendant disappears before she vanishes to the back of the plane. Deja starts having another contraction and squeezes my hand instead of the seat handle, her moan is now louder, and the passengers across the aisle lean over to see what's happening. "Just breathe Deja, we're almost on the ground," I reassure her, not really knowing what else to say, ignoring the curious stares.

The overhead speaker crackles and a calm female voice announces, "Dear passengers, if there's a physician amongst you, please press the call button." I say a quick prayer, asking for a doctor to come help and for us to land as fast as possible.

The same flight attendant appears again, but now without her professional smile, and she is accompanied by a tall man with a baseball hat, dressed in jeans and a light sweater. His well-defined muscular arms are noticeable through the fabric. A sharp jaw meets a square chin and his full lips are framed by the stubble of his facial hair. I don't care what he looks like or that he looks a bit young, all I care about is if he can help Deja.

He kneels next to Deja and takes her hand into his. "Hi, my name is Dr. Gable, I'm an ER physician." Deja waits for the contraction to pass before she is able to speak.

"The baby ... it's coming," she manages to pronounce.

"How many weeks are you?" the man inquires as he concentrates his attention on Deja, and I stare at the details of his face, trying to decipher his inner thoughts about the gravity of the situation. As I peer into his blue eyes, I get stung by the feeling of knowing him; blue eyes are of his Englishman father, jet black hair inherited from his Brazilian mother. These eyes were the crush of my teenage years. I looked for them in the halls of my high school. They ignored my naive obsession, they disapproved of my childish hijinks, and stirred the feelings of my emotional, hormonal brain and body. This is the older brother of Jenna. I haven't seen him in ages, since he left for college and then medical school. He is five years older than Jenna and I, so he must be thirty-two by now. He is smart—no he is bright, super intelligent—and was popular in school. Everyone always crowded around him, wanting to be his friend. Jenna has been updating me on his accomplishments. He's been practicing emergency medicine in one of the best hospitals in New York City. He's now very rich because he created some application that he sold for many millions, and he has his own tech company. But despite the riches, he continues to work. Jenna says he really loves being a physician. He also has a girl that he loves, Kai is now engaged. My heart sank into a puddle of disappointment for unfulfilled youthful romance when I'd heard about it, but my brain quickly plucked me out of the sorrow and reprimanded me for holding onto things that were not meant to be.

"Kai?" I call his name. He looks at me, and a smile of recognition spreads over his face.

"Angelina?" His brows raise in surprise. "Jenna didn't tell me we'd be on the same flight."

"She's been too consumed by this wedding. You know how she gets," I reply. Jenna has a tendency of diving into whatever venture is right in front of her, forgetting to validate the existence of other people until she wants to pull them into her new adventure. Deja lets out a loud grunt, and both Kai and I turn our attention back to her.

"Deja, your contractions are close together, you might have this baby on the plane, but we need to get you on the floor so I can check you." Kai switches his friendly tone to a more professional one. Deja only nods in agreement.

"Angelina, come with me, I'll need your help," Kai prompts. "Miss, I need blankets and gloves," he delegates to the flight attendant.

I help Deja up and shuffle behind her with my arms stretched in a protective semicircle around her.

We slowly manage to move to the back of the plane, where I sit at the head of Deja when she lays down, Kai positions himself between her legs, and the flight attendant turns her back to us, creating a fence between us and the rest of the plane.

My oversized sweater comes in handy as a hastily made pillow. Kai checks his new patient and tells her that the baby is crowning.

"Deja, look at me, you're going to have this baby now. With the next contraction, I want you to bear down and push while I count to ten. Okay?"

She nods, acknowledging her understanding. "It's coming," she growls, putting her chin to her chest. The sound of her pain transforms into a monstrous, deep, animal moan. I count quietly along with Kai, squeezing Deja's hand.

She relaxes as the count of ten escapes our lips.

"You're doing great, Deja. I can see his face, and he has lots of hair. A couple more pushes, and he'll be out," Kai informs. The soon-to-be mother nods and bears down again, starting the new count. The change of pressure in my ears tells me that we are descending, and I wonder how long we have been down on this floor as I wipe Deja's forehead.

"You're almost there," I say.

"... nine, ten," Kai finishes the count. Deja grunts loudly, her face is tense, eyes shut tight. But when Kai puts the small, pink, crying baby with skinny outstretched arms and legs on Deja's chest, she relaxes, instantly cooing with the little one. She wraps him in the plane's blankets, kissing his headful of black hair. This moment of life coming into the world is sweet, and I bet most people would tear up, but I haven't shed a tear in years, and even this wondrous event can't make me squeeze any drops of salty substance from my eyes.

"It's a boy!" Kai announces to the universe and to his mother. The plane bounces as it softly hits the runway. As soon as we're done taxiing, the local medics rush in, finishing the delivery of the placenta, cutting the umbilical cord, and wheeling an exhausted Deja out. I trail behind her with the baby in my arms while Kai helps with the luggage.

Once Deja is in the ambulance, I hand over the baby to her. "Your son is beautiful."

"Thank you, but he's not my son," she replies. Before I get an answer to this revelation, the doors of the ambulance close, taking her away and leaving me wondering what she meant.

# 2.

# KAI

I look around the apartment that I have been sharing with Candice for the past four months. Early light streams in through floor-to-ceiling windows, and the gray skyline of New York City covered by the low, rain-filled clouds stands in a motionless picture outside. My place looks like it belongs on the cover of a magazine, each piece has been picked out by my fiancée with absolute precision to show off its expensive and exclusive nature. I gave her free rein to choose whatever she needed to be comfortable in my apartment, but as the weeks have gone by, her taste and her things have overtaken my own, and now I am the one who looks completely out of place in my home. I shake my head and rub my tired eyes; I haven't slept all night. I have come back to New York to end this relationship. My plane leaves in a few hours, and I still haven't finished packing. Candice follows me from room to room; an annoying shadow whose presence I detest.

"Kai, please, let's just talk about it. I made a mistake. It means nothing," she nags.

"Sleeping with Dave. My … my best friend," I hit my chest with my fist, "who … who also happens to be my partner is not a mistake. What were you thinking? No, you weren't thinking, not about us at least. Shit! This week wasn't supposed to end like this," I reply while going from bathroom to bedroom, packing what I think I will need for the next few weeks in the Caribbean. "You cheated on me. While I was building something for us in Grenada, you were here just demolishing it, and you weren't even trying to hide it." A bitter taste of bile comes up in my throat as I say it.

"It wasn't my fault," she pleads. "I was just confused, and he came on to me! Ask him. Have you spoken to Dave?" She runs up in front of me, blocking my pacing.

"Is that supposed to make me feel better? I don't care whose fault it is. Move." I tower over her. Frankly, I blame both of them. My friend has betrayed me and I wanted to punch his face bloody for destroying the friendship, the partnership, and my relationship. I want to push Candice aside, but the thought of touching her is nauseating. I step aside and walk around her, wiping my hands that feel suddenly sticky and dirty on my jeans.

"Stop, just pause for a minute. Look at me." Candice pulls my sleeve, forcing me to turn around; when I do, she puts both of her hands on my cheeks, making me look at her. This girl is beautiful, but like overeating sweets, she makes me nauseous. I hardly recognize her. Her full lips have become plumper over the last few years, her hair has gotten longer and blonder, she is batting full eyelashes that are not hers, there is little of her appearance that is natural. Has our relationship been fake?

"You know what was a mistake?" I ask her a question that I know she will not have an answer to. She cocks her head to the side and waits for me to answer it myself. "It was a huge mistake to ask you to marry me. I don't think

I've ever loved you. This, this engagement, it was a temporary excitement." I know my words are harsh, but I don't think they sting her as much as her cheating hurt me.

"You're lying," she calls my bluff as she glances at her phone and scrolls with her perfectly manicured finger. I know she is looking at one of her social media accounts. That's all she cares about, her social media world. It's pink, full of beautiful destinations, new purchases, and beautifully plated meals. She has been consumed with projecting an image of a carefree, happy, luxurious lifestyle rather than working on the substance of the world that she is in, and I've obliged her for too long. "Wait." She presses her lips and grabs my hand.

I stare into her eyes. I don't want to reveal my emotions to her. "What? What more do you want to tell me, Candice?"

"I love you," she puckers up her lips and bats her eyelashes.

"Oh, for fuck's sake. Just shut up. You should've thought about that before." I pull away from her, the bile is bitter in my mouth just thinking that her hands touched another man.

"I was lonely. You left me. I felt like you were making all these decisions about us, about me, and I just got scared," she continues.

"Candice, I was gone for two weeks. I went for a job interview so we can build a beautiful life together. We spoke every day. Don't you dare blame me for what you did. If you were scared, you should've told me, we could've talked about it." I walk away from her.

"I was afraid to lose you!" she screams out in a fake high pitch in a last-ditch effort to keep me.

"Oh my God! Your logic is fucking insane! But honestly, this is all for the best. This relationship was built on pretty fluff. But no more. And you know what? You're perfect for Dave, you both have commitment issues, he ran away from taking care of his own daughter and you ... you just care about yourself ... I'm done." I finish packing my bag and order an Uber to take me to the airport. I will figure out how to deal with the apartment, and all my things, and how to manage the partnership with my former best friend later.

The car arrives shortly after and when I get inside, I contemplate not going, imagining how awkward the wedding is going to be for me. But my sister and my mother would never forgive me for not showing up. I will just have to explain what has happened with Candice. I rub my eyes, the sleepless night is catching up to me, and I am fighting the urge to fall asleep in the car as it drives me to the airport. Maybe it will be a good getaway. It'll be a fresh start. The hospital in Grenada is a large one, plus St. George Medical School has been growing, it will be great to teach the residents, certainly a challenge. I will have time to concentrate on my new software. I close my eyes and drift off into a restless nap rocked by bumps, twists, and turns of the road. At the airport, I pull my baseball hat low over my eyes to avoid eye contact with people. I find a seat in the far corner of the gate waiting area, put on my headphones, and tune out to the thumping beat of techno. I board the plane as a first-class passenger as soon as boarding is announced. Sleep overtakes me as the plane takes off, but the sleep is restless. I am uncomfortable in the tight space, my knees pressing against the seat in front of me. It's certainly a disadvantage to be six feet tall when flying. Grenada is just about forty minutes away when I hear an announcement requesting a physician. What could have gone wrong? They couldn't wait to land? I hesitate for a moment to let them know I am an ER physician, but I know I'll regret it and think incessantly of what I could have done. I press the call button. A smiling flight attendant appears and whispers that there is a woman in labor who needs assistance. I haven't delivered a baby since medical school, but since no other physician is present, I'm her best chance to have this baby safely. I run through the files of my knowledge about what to do in this situation, I hope the baby is in the right position and we have no breathing issues, everything else can be handled.

The girl is definitely in active labor, she can't even speak through the contractions when I come up to her. I introduce myself, and between contractions she tells me her name is Deja. I get her pulse and count her breaths while she is having another contraction. We probably will have to move her to the back of the plane. Thirty-four weeks is not a full-term baby, I just hope it's not in distress. Who is the bright fuck of a doctor who allowed her to fly, I wonder. I start speaking to the girl, but in the periphery of my vision I sense a presence of someone staring at me. I take a quick look and recognize a girl that I haven't seen in years. She is the best friend of my sister. They had been attached at the hip, annoying me with their antics in high school. She is no lanky, awkward teenager anymore. The oversized sweater looks too big on her, her dark brown hair is tied at the back, she has no makeup on, and looks like she just woke up. Her blue eyes light up, recognizing me after a few moments—do I look that different?

It's good that she is here, I'll need help, I hope she doesn't panic in these kinds of situations. I direct both women to the back of the plane and ask the flight attendant for towels, gloves, and blankets.

Angelina sits at the head of her in-labor seatmate while I check Deja's cervix dilation, hoping that she is not fully dilated and will be able to deliver in the hospital and not in the back of the plane behind the bathrooms. But my hopes evaporate when I discover that the baby is already in the birth canal and will be delivered in the next few minutes. I look up, and both women stare at me. Deja looks scared. Her breathing is fast, drops of sweat roll down her face and she holds onto Angelina's hand tight as she lets out a scream, and I know another contraction begins.

"Breathe, Deja, I will count to ten and you push," I instruct her as Angelina looks up at me. Her big blue eyes reveal no panic; she is calm, whispering something to her friend, and then sends me a reassuring smile.

Deja follows all my instructions, she tolerates the contractions and makes good progress, and as I say, "...ten" the little human falls into my hands.

"It's a boy!" I announce his arrival. Rubbing his back vigorously, his purple color turns pink, and he lets out the whimpering cry of a small kitten. I put him on Deja's chest, who puts him on her breast which he latches onto right away, and his mother looks completely content. He is small, barely five pounds. Angelina surprises me with her calm demeanor, not everybody would be able to step up like she has no tears that I have to tend to. Thank God we're so close to landing, I think to myself just as I feel a soft bump, and I know the plane has touched the ground. I leave the cord attached to the placenta until the emergency personnel rush in and give me the instruments to clip and cut the umbilical cord. I let them take over and deliver the placenta. Angelina is still sitting by Deja and holding her hand, softly speaking something indistinguishable to her. Her oversized sweater is gone, revealing her slim, but surprisingly muscular arms; she must be working out. I help place Deja in the wheelchair so she can be transported to the hospital, and take Angelina's bag while she is carrying the baby. I'll have to go and visit my accidental patient in the hospital, I make a mental note. Outside, Angelina passes the baby to his mother, and the ambulance takes off with sirens wailing, leaving Angelina looking puzzled.

"Are you all right?" I touch her bare arm. She folds both her arms across her chest and shrugs her shoulders.

"That was some in-flight entertainment," she stifles a giggle, but I pick it up and burst out laughing. The stress of the situation gets released into the air through our outburst. We must look ridiculous to the passengers passing by.

The weather on the island is sunny, the warm rays bathe the lush tropical greens which cover most of the island. The clouds are resting only over the mountains. The rainforest produces a lot of humidity even in October. But by the coast, the air is pleasant without the sticky, suffocating thickness.

"Let's go get our bags. Jenna will love to hear about this one," I suggest. Angelina nods and we walk to the terminal. I've never spoken much to her; I wonder if she is always this quiet.

"How have you been?" Angelina asks me.

*Shitty* I want to say, but instead I reply with a meaningless, "Good, good. You?" I kick it back to her.

"Good, busy with work, you know, just the usual," she replies.

"What do you do?" I ask as we walk across the hot tarmac.

"I'm an assistant to a publicist," she tells me. I pause, not knowing what else to say. I have no idea what the assistant to a publicist does, but don't want to be an ass and ask. "I just prepare statements and press releases," Angelina specifies, probably sensing my ignorance.

"I see, I see." I scratch the back of my head.

"I heard you got engaged," Angelina continues to chitchat. Fuck, this is an uncomfortable conversation. I guess I'll have to explain it anyway, she'll just be the first one to find out.

"I was, I was, but we broke up." We walk into the small airport pavilion with several belts for the baggage where some of the bags have already slowly started to arrive.

"I'm sorry," her cheeks turn a pretty shade of pink. I think I made her feel more uncomfortable than I, myself, felt.

"It's all right, we weren't right for each other," I explain as we stare intently, looking for our luggage. I want to tell her that I am raging inside from the betrayal, but Dave is the ex-husband of Gretchen, Angelina and my sister's best friend, and I didn't want to bring this news into my sister's wedding getaway. I didn't want to hear his name mentioned anymore.

I get my bag first, she spots her small suitcase shortly after. I go in to help her get it, but she stops me, "It's okay. I'll get it. It's not heavy." She picks up her luggage, pulls out the handle and looks towards the exit. "Let's go," she nudges me.

"This is it? This is the only bag you have?"

"Yeah," she shrugs her shoulders. "We're here for just ten days and it's warm," Angelina replies, staring at her luggage. That never stopped Candice from packing at least three suitcases for a few days' trip.

"You're right, you're right." Fuck, I have to stop repeating myself. The annoying habit comes out when I am nervous, but why the hell am I nervous right now? I've known Angelina since she was like twelve.

We follow the signs directing us to the transportation for the resort. A little white van that looks like it could tip over with a slight blow of the wind slides its doors open, and we climb in. The trip is short, down mostly dirt road. The resort is convenient, three minutes away. The cars travel on the opposite side of the road from the US, and it makes me dizzy, my brain is confused.

Angelina stares through the window, her eyes are open wide, consuming the new images in front of her.

"Look at the color of these houses, they're so bright!" She points at the yellow, pink, and blue colors of the local buildings. They certainly add to the cheerfulness of the island.

"You should see the capital, it's like each house tries to outdo the next one in the brightness of the colors," I tell her.

"Jenna planned a boat trip there tomorrow, so we can do just that," she replies.

"Jenna planned something? Well that would be a first," I chuckle.

Angelina takes her eyes from the window and looks at me giggling, "Well, actually, she didn't, I did. Jenna is always good at coming up with adventure, I'm the one who's better with planning. I created the whole itinerary."

We pull up into the resort, framed by the beautiful Caribbean plants. Its orange walls stand out amongst the greenery. We are welcomed with cool towels and cold champagne that feel refreshing.

"Welcome. My name is Tonya," a middle-aged woman with slicked back hair dressed in all black greets us from behind the counter. "I will assist with your check-in. Is this your first time in Grenada?"

"Hi! No, I've been here before, but not to this resort," I reply to the hostess who has a big toothy smile.

"I haven't, first time," Angelina adds.

"Welcome to both of you. What is the occasion of your visit? Honeymoon? Anniversary?" she proceeds down a memorized greeting.

Angelina lets out a giggle. "He is not ... we are not ... together." She looks at me, blushing again. "We're here for a wedding ... not our wedding. His sister is getting married." Angelina gesticulates with her hands, hitting me accidently on the nose.

"Fuck," the accidental smack is painful. I pinch the bridge of the nose and check if I have a nosebleed.

"I'm sorry. I'm so sorry." Angelina freezes, her eyes are full of concern, her rosy cheeks light up again. I shouldn't have cursed. I really have to rein in the habit.

"It's nothing, don't worry about it. How's my nose, is it straight? Will I live?" I tilt my head back so Angelina can take a look. She takes a step closer, peering inside my nostrils. "I'm kidding, I'm fine," I laugh, hoping to erase the look of concern from her face.

She lets out a nervous laugh. "Are you sure?"

"I'm fine, don't sweat it." I give her a nudge. She relaxes and smiles, letting out a sigh and wiping her forehead.

"Here are the iPads. Please fill out the empty fields and we'll take you to your rooms," the hostess chimes in. We grab the thin tablets and take a seat on the nearby couch. It seats just two, and my leg and arm touch Angelina ever so lightly. She smells of pleasant warmth, strands of her dark curls have come undone from her ponytail, but she doesn't rush to fix them, there is a quiet confidence in her that is refreshing to see. My observations are interrupted by a shrill that I know too well. My sister always manages to intrude at the most inconvenient times.

"You're finally here!" She rushes to Angelina, hugging her and the girls jump up and down, squealing together.

"Hi, Kai!" she greets me without the same excitement.

"What? You're not happy to see your older brother?" I tease her.

She comes in for a quick hug before she asks the inevitable, "Where is Candice?"

"She's not coming. We broke up."

"Shut up," my sister's eyes grow big.

"No, you shut up," I fire back.

"You're lying," she punches my chest as Angelina laughs, looking on.

"No, I'm not." I shake my head.

"Finally, you came to your senses. That girl was a total bitch."

"Now you tell me." My sister never voiced her opinion about Candice, though I never really care to hear one from anybody about who I date. My stubbornness has never been my best quality.

"I knew you'd come around," she squints at me and chuckles, then throws her arms tight around my neck and gives me a quick peck on the cheek.

23

"Go see your rooms. I'll meet you for dinner. It will be in the restaurant by the beach."

I am exhausted and happily oblige. We are escorted away from the lobby, passing the party pool where sunburned bodies of men and women play water volleyball or sit by the bar where the bartender hands drinks right to them while they are submerged in water. Our bellboy points to the restaurants and the gym. "And you are staying at the lover's lagoon," he stretches the insinuation. The rooms were booked while I was still with Candice, there will not be much love happening. I glance at Angelina who blushes at the name. She's alone, I wonder if someone is joining her.

Our rooms turn out to be right next to each other. The small patio is furnished with a wicker table, two chairs, and a freestanding bathtub. It looks odd, but I am sure Candice would have used it, just to take pictures for her Instagram.

"That tub is odd," Angelina says aloud what I have been thinking.

"It really is," I add.

"Here is your room key, miss, and here is yours," the bell boy passes us the keycards. I turn to Angelina and extend my hand, letting her go past me to her room.

"See you soon," her voice is soft and gentle.

"Looking forward, looking forward," I inadvertently reply. Why did I say that to her? That sounded weird. Of course I'll be happy to see her, but looking forward? She's just my sister's best friend that I've known for years.

She looks up at me from underneath her dark long lashes, her blue eyes look straight into mine, "I am, too."

# 3.

## GRETCHEN

The insistent doorbell rings announcing the urgency of the visitor's intentions.

"Sorry! I'm coming!" I yell to quell the impatient guest. I open the door, chastising the person behind it in my head, but it's my daughter who rushes past me, almost knocking me off my feet while my ex-husband, Dave, leans on the railing of the porch. He looks good: rested, fit, I bet he has time to go the gym. He wears jeans and a gray sweater under a trendy jacket. His dark hair is gelled into tiny spikes, a clean-shaven handsome face has no wrinkles of stress or a hard life. His green eyes stand out against his tanned Italian skin. No one would think he is a father of an eleven-year-old girl at his twenty-seven years of age.

"What happened?" My motherly brain goes through the list of accidents that might have occurred while our daughter was with him.

"I can't do it," he replies matter-of-factly.

"I'm sorry, but what do you mean you can't do it? You had her for not even two days." My vocal cords tighten, and I am only able to whisper as my eyes swell with tears, the asshole is ready to abandon her during a vacation that she has been looking forward to for weeks.

"You'll take her with you to Grenada. I bought her a ticket," he informs me calmly, not showing any concern about disappointing his daughter. I was wondering why he was texting me with questions about the flight, the jackass was already planning to get rid of her yesterday.

"I'm sorry, but do you understand how devastated she'll be?" I stare into his eyes trying to find any wavering, but he looks away—as always—his jaw clenched tight. "She's already been through enough with the divorce. You can't do this to her," I plead with him. I wish I could squeeze his neck tight to strangle and shake him, but I am a girl who was afraid to play basketball in school for fear of being hurt. My body's response to any challenge or offense are tears and apologies, I would never imagine laying a finger on anyone.

"She'll understand," he replies, unbothered by my appeal to his decency, and now I am punching him hard—but only in my head.

"She's eleven. You can't expect her to understand that her piece-of-shit father ..." I take a deep breath and wipe a tear. "I'm sorry, her father, is choosing a week without her because he's not used to the responsibilities of fatherhood," I manage to finish with my voice cracking.

"I can't do it. I just can't. You're her mother. You're made to handle all this," he persists in an uninvolved manner.

"I'm sorry, but I'm a person just like you. I need a break. Are you upset that you haven't been invited? Jenna just wants a small wedding, she is not trying to offend you." I feel I am losing grip of my emotions and they are about to spill out in a hysterical breakdown in front of the person who I least want to see me cry.

"I don't care what Jenna wants. I don't care about that whole family anymore. I can't have Hailey with me. I can't handle it. I can barely handle my own shit," he continues without apologizing.

"Can you hear yourself? Kai has been your best friend forever, what happened?"

"Gretchen, it's none of your damn business. If you don't take Hailey, I'll hire a babysitter," Dave says through clenched teeth.

"She just wants your attention and you can't even give her that. You'll come to regret this one day, and it'll be too late."

"Gretchen, I don't know what you want me to say. We shouldn't have had her when we did. We were too young," he says, shrugging his shoulders and looking at the ground.

"But we did have her, she's here and I'm her mother and you're her father. This is our job that we'll have forever," I try to plead with him, but he says nothing, staring at the ground and then looking to the side, avoiding my eyes. "You found money quickly enough for her ticket, but I have to beg you to pay child support on time. I haven't seen a cent from you in months."

"I put it on my credit card," he explains without apologizing for the late child support payments.

"Jesus, Dave, you're such a liar." I stop myself from speaking any further. "I'm sorry. I didn't mean to say that. Fine, do what you need to do with your life." I don't care about his money, we can do without it. He makes his own choices now, he should be the one worrying about the consequences. I have my own problems to worry about.

"Just go. Okay? I need to speak to our daughter." I slam the door shut and the windows shudder in comradery of my disappointment and anger.

Before I go face my girl's likely devastated, sad, raging disposition, I dial my mother.

"Hi, Gigi, honey! How are you, sweetheart?" she chirps.

"Sorry to bother you, Maaaa," my voice trembles, and I take a deep breath to stop myself from crying.

"What's wrong, honey?" she lowers her voice that now is full of concern. I wish I were a better daughter. I've disappointed my parents so much. Getting pregnant at sixteen was not something they had in mind for me, but still they supported me. They helped with Hailey so I could graduate high school. My mother and father paid for nannies when they couldn't babysit themselves so I could finish college. They attended Hailey's school events and picked her up when I was busy in medical school. Their love was unconditional. My parents did everything for me to succeed. But I think they've been growing tired of my escapades. When I'd announced my decision to switch from ER medicine to psychiatry, my father got up from the table and poured a drink for himself and my mother, which he finished in silence, then went outside. "If that'll make you happy, then do it," my mother had said and gave me a hug.

"Dave brought Hailey back, he says he can't handle it," I complain to my mother.

"So?" my mother replies.

"'So?' So, he disappointed Hailey. I'm afraid to even go upstairs now to talk to her because she's devastated and will take it out on me," I sigh.

"Gigi, you know what?" my mother replies, and I hear background noise full of voices. They are probably having guests over, after all, they escaped New York to Boca to enjoy themselves.

"What, Mom?" I ask, pressing the phone closer to my ear expecting her to support me in my misery of having a terrible ex-husband.

"You need to go buy yourself some pretty lacy under-wear," she advises me.

"Huh? What do you mean, Mom?" I am bewildered by her reply.

"People who have pretty underwear, they are happy. Gigi, really honey, enough with being upset with Dave. Accept him the way he is and just be happy. Just go, go buy the undies," she insists. I think my mother has had enough of my problems. I hear her cover the phone while laughing and talking to someone.

"It's okay, Mom, go enjoy your guests. I didn't mean to intrude," I reply to her.

"Gigi, honey, go speak to Hailey, and enjoy your time in Grenada. Love you!"

"Love you, Mom," I reply and hang up the phone.

I drag my feet up the stairs, going over the words I'll have to say to my daughter to make her feel better. I knock on her door and open it just slightly before coming in. The wrath she can unleash on me from walking into her room unannounced can last for days.

"Go away!" she barks at me.

"Hailey, honey. I'm sorry Daddy brought you back, but it'll be fun to go to Grenada together," I suggest.

"I said go away!" Something is thrown, making the door slam against my forehead. I rub away the pain, and the insult, and open the door to Hailey's bedroom. She is sprawled on her bed, facedown. Her pillow is laying on the floor, a missile that was used to prevent me from walking in. I sit on the edge of the bed, rub my child's back, and move her hair to one side so I can see part of her face.

She is sobbing into a blanket, the blotchy skin on her neck gives away her distress.

"Please don't cry," I whisper softly. "Daddy will take you next time."

"It's your fault he didn't let me stay!" Hailey raises to face me. Her pretty face is red, with tears pooled in her eyes, and her jet-black hair sticks to her sweaty face.

"Honey," I try to hug her little, resisting body. "Dad has to go in to work. He'll get you next time," I make up a lie.

"He has to work so hard because you told him to leave!" she screams through the sobs, pushing me away. "He has to do everything now, go shopping, cook, and wash his clothes. You just don't want us to spend time together." She thrusts right to my face, the heat of her breath on my skin. "I hate you! I wish you weren't my mom!"

It hurts. I wish I could just let her know that her dad was not a good husband and not the best father. He has a cleaning lady and orders takeout, he doesn't even know how to operate a washing machine. But she probably won't even believe me, her immature mind will twist it as lies against her perfect daddy. The therapist said I just need to give her time and be patient. Maybe this trip will be a good way of spending time together. I say a silent prayer for everything to go well and for my daughter to love me again.

I don't show her how much her words affect me. "I love you, Hailey. Rest up, we will have to get up early tomorrow."

"Get out of my room!" Her sobs erupt again, and she throws herself facedown on the bed.

I'd feared that the separation would affect her, but I couldn't have imagined the level of rage she would experience. Of course, she blames me. All she knows is that Dad left one day. How could I explain to the eleven-year-old that her father had been a cheating scumbag? He had been cheating for years, I don't even know how many women there have been, but there was one whom Dave left too scorned. She'd sent me texts and the emails between them. I felt dizzy, nauseous, and short of breath.

I'd loved him for so long, since I was a child myself. He was the only man I knew. Dave got me pregnant at fifteen. It was exhilarating to have the most handsome boy in the whole school pay attention to me. My own parents were preoccupied with having their parties and traveling, and I'd frequently had the house all to myself. I was so in love, I'd thought that this was it; this was the love that I had been reading about in books. We will be happy forever, we will have our own little family, I'd thought. I'd hoped that the tribulations of young parenthood would make us stronger. I'd blamed sexless months on his work and exhaustion. But he'd spent his energy banging everything else. Dave had come home only to eat and put on clean, ironed clothes.

I decide to give Hailey space to calm down. The psychiatrist said that I can't force myself on her, she will come around, she just needs time. I lean in and place a soft kiss on her head from which she jerks away.

"I love you, call me if you need anything. I'll bring you your suitcase, would you like me to help you pack?"

Hailey breathes out a forceful, annoyed sigh and I know her patience is running short.

"Okay, I'll be in my room." With a sigh, and the weight of constant failure as a mother, I get up and walk out of her room. I shut the door to my little girl's room and squeeze a fist against my chest to stop myself from crying. I pass by the mirror, and I pause, not recognizing the girl in front of it. At twenty-seven, I look matronly with twenty pounds of extra weight bulging and jiggling. I don't look curvy, at least not in any attractive way. I strike a pose, pop a hip, and put my chest forward, but I look ridiculous, worn down, uncomfortable. I haven't cut my hair in over a year, it's the color of rust from the home attempts at coloring it. Even my outfit is wrinkled, my T-shirt stretched out with small holes that I haven't bothered to take care of. What has happened to me? I am in a body that I don't recognize, seeing a reflection that I hate. I really need to pull myself together, I have to be better than this for Hailey.

In my bedroom, clothes are sprawled on the floor and on the bed. The luggage is still empty, nothing so far has made the cut of making me feel good about myself, it's either too tight, the wrong shape, or the wrong length. I am so used to being in scrubs at work, and at home my wardrobe consists of mostly black yoga pants and oversized T-shirts that are also black. The mess of my clothes makes me dizzy. I realize just how much this monochromatic pile is the reflection of how comfortable I've gotten in life and in clothes that are not making me happy. A wave of anger starts to rise in me. I need to put an end to the unfitting comfort of just existing. I run downstairs, grab a garbage bag and shove the tight and loose garb into it.

"Hailey, honey! Let's go!" I scream out from the hallway, riding the wave of anger with a purpose of taming it and arriving on the shores of self-love. Not hearing a reply back, I run up to her room, my smile and a burning from exertion face is met by her furrowed eyebrows.

"C'mon, we're going to the mall," I tell her.

"Why?"

"I need to get some new clothes."

"I'm not going shopping with you." She refuses to be seen with me, even when I drop her off at school it has to be where her friends won't spot me.

"Well, how about you text your friends to meet you there to hang out?" I suggest.

"Okay," my daughter breathes out an annoyed answer and feverishly types texts a call-out to her girl squad for a get-together.

• • •

Once we get to the mall, I drop Hailey by the fountain where several of her girlfriends squeal with excitement at seeing her. I give her forty dollars to spend on a movie and a snack and send her off. The stores are already displaying shine and sparkle for the holidays. But, tucked in the corner is a small boutique, Forever Summer, which I know will have everything I need. I'll have to pay more than I'm used to, but I know that the money spent now will be a new beginning of a better, fresh look.

The girl in the store looks me up and down, and greets me with a rehearsed, "Hi! How are you? Welcome to Forever Summer. Is there anything I can help you with?"

"Yes, please. I'm sorry, but I'm leaving for a vacation. I left my husband a while ago, and I need to get out of the yoga pants." My plea must really touch the sales girl, she comes up to me, gives me an unexpected hug and leads me to the dressing room.

"Stay here, I'll help you have a *Pretty Woman* experience." She shuts the curtain, leaving me in the booth with three mirrors that I can't hide from. I plop on the thin bench in the tight booth, seeing my reflection from different angles. The light throws shadows on my face that make me look even more tired than I already am. Now I remember why I hate shopping. I fiddle with my fingers, staring at the ceiling and then the floor, avoiding looking at the unattractive reflection seeking me out.

Five minutes later, my sales girl knocks and walks in with an armful of clothes for me to try on. I would never have imagined that my body shape would have so many options, there are sundresses, rompers, shorts, and, I gasp, swimsuits with cutouts.

I will not be afraid to try these on. I am done being afraid. Afraid of what my ex-husband will say. Afraid of what my daughter will think about me. I am done prioritizing everyone else and losing myself in the process.

All the clothes are bright blues, greens, yellows, pinks. The gamut of the palette alone is elevating my mood. The white shorts magically round my butt and hide my gut. Sundresses give me a waist, and I even look cute in the rompers.

The swimsuits, that I haven't worn in ages, slim me down in all the right places, and lift my breasts to heights I am not used to.

"I'll take it all," I breathe out to the sales girl who quietly nods with approval. Before she rings me up, I spot a stand with lacy underwear. I grab several G-strings to add to my pile.

I pay with my credit card and march down the mall with the bags of new clothing, looking forward to wearing it all in sunny Grenada.

The see-through windows of a hair salon attract my attention, and I enter, hoping they can fit me in for a cut and color.

"Welcome to Zen salon," a pretty receptionist with perfect long hair greets me. "Do you have an appointment?"

"Sorry, but I don't, I was wondering, though, if you can take me now for a cut and color?" I ask and the pretty girl stares into the computer, clicking the keyboard with fingers adorned with long, sharp, red nails. Her brows furrow, and I start to lose hope that this makeover can't be completed today.

Her brows part, the corners of her mouth go up. "You're in luck, Jennifer has a cancellation and will be able to take care of you. Take a seat. Would you like water, tea, or a cup of coffee?"

"If it's not too much bother, a cup of green tea, please."

The beauty tosses her hair back, and walks off to the back of the salon. I perch myself up on the edge of the seat and look through the magazines, looking for inspiration for my new 'do. The receptionist comes back with a cup of hot water and a packet of green tea. I sip the warm liquid, still surprised by my spur-of-the-moment courage to remake my appearance. I wonder if Hailey is even thinking of me. She's probably glad to get rid of me. What am I going to do with this girl? How can I show her that I love her and want only the best for her?

My thoughts are interrupted by a young man who walks up to me, swinging his slim hips wider than any model walking down the catwalk.

"Hiiii! Cut and color?" he purrs.

"Yes."

"Okay, sweetheart, follow me," he turns wide, arching his back and motioning with his finger to follow him. I prance behind him, giddy with excitement.

I almost fall asleep during the shampoo, it's been a while since I enjoyed another person's touch. It's relaxing and calming.

"Okay, sweetheart. Come here. Jennifer will be with you in a minute," he winks at me and struts away. I sink into the chair and face the image of myself in the huge mirror. I look terrible with my wet hair laying in flat strings down below my shoulders. The shadows under my eyes are even darker in this mirror than in the store. The wet look doesn't really suit me.

"Hi! Gretchen?" A petite girl, probably my same age, greets me. She is dressed in all black, tight pants and a thin sweater. Surprisingly, she is wearing high heels at this job where most of the time she is standing.

"Yes. Hi!"

"My name is Jennifer. So, cut and color?" she questions, lifting my wet locks, disapproving of the length and color.

"Yes. But not too short." I show her the length just above my shoulders.

"And what about color?'

"Sorry." I cringe. "I don't know? What do you think?" I look up at Jennifer hoping that she can come up with a different color than my usual rusty red. Her own hair is perfectly curled in loose waves of a rich, caramel color.

"I think you'll look great as a strawberry blond with some highlights." She starts to brush my hair back.

"Okay," I nod to her suggestion, not really able to imagine what I'd look like.

She puts on a black apron and starts with a haircut. My look worsens when Jennifer colors the hair and puts it into the foils. The wet dog look is what it is. I hope I look better once my hair is done.

Three hours later, Jennifer finishes the cut, color, and blow out, and I am pleasantly surprised by what I see in the mirror. The girl staring back at me looks like she's in her twenties with fair skin and rosy cheeks. The hair is a warm honey color with highlights framing my happy face. Sparkles shine in my eyes that I haven't seen in a long time.

I check in with Hailey via text, she responds that she is hanging with her friends at the food court. I get myself and my bags there, excited to show off my new look. When I spot her, she looks at me quickly and turns away, not recognizing me.

"Hi, honey! Ready to go?" I call out to her. My daughter slowly turns back to face me, her lips part and her brows go up and then come into a deep frown.

"What did you do?" she asks disapprovingly, leading me away from the table of her friends who giggle loudly.

"Oh, just a cut and color. Do you like it?" I chirp, ignoring her dislike of my new look.

"No. I hate it." Hailey's reply is short, she turns away and shushes her friends. The girl has disrespected me long enough, the new look demands a new parenting attitude.

There will be no more back talk or ignoring my requests. I am a new woman through and through.

"Okay, missy. Let's go," I order with unusual sternness in my voice.

"What do you want?" Hailey turns to me, rolling her eyes.

"I said let's go, unless you want to spend the night here," I put my face close to hers, speaking through my teeth.

"I will call the police and tell on you."

"Try it and they'll take you away, you can see what life you'll have without me." I sound so harsh, I can't believe that I've just said that to my daughter. What will she think of me, will she despise me?

"Fine." She starts walking towards the exit. I'm shocked, there is no back talk, there is no stomping of the feet or angry outbursts, she does what I ask her to do. I'll have to try to be stern more often.

We get into the car and start our ride home in complete silence. Our dispositions are polar opposites, I am cheerful and confident, and my daughter is angry with her brows furrowed and her hands folded tight on her chest.

"I am looking forward to our trip together …. Really, I think it'll be fun for us to get away. Don't you think?" I try to draw Hailey out in a conversation.

"Why did you change your hair? I don't like it. You didn't even ask me." Her voice gets quieter and she begins to sob.

"Hailey, honey? What's wrong? Why are you crying?" I am confused by her sudden tears.

Her sobbing makes her words unintelligible, her face and neck are covered in red blotches as she gasps for air.

I pull over and unbuckle so I can face my distressed child. She throws her long thin arms around me, and her body shakes against mine. I pat her back gently. I have no idea what has brought this outburst on, but I am enjoying the moment of physical contact that has been initiated by her, something she hasn't done in a long time.

"Everything is ... it's, like ... it's changing, and no one is, like, asking me," she reveals and it makes this outburst completely understandable. Her childhood has been turned upside down, and she's been trying to keep control of all the things to prevent further change. In her mind, change is a collapse, a deterioration, and not a way to be reborn.

"Oh, honey! I am so sorry that you've had so many changes. I know it's been very difficult. But Dad and I, we love you very much." I have to say that about her dad, he is still a man she looks up to and he is a perfect dad in her eyes. "I promise, I'll do everything in my power to make you happy, to keep you safe. My haircut and the new clothing doesn't mean that I've changed. I am the same Mom. I just did it for myself, not to upset you. I need to look in the mirror and feel happy about my reflection. I believe if I'm happy, I'll be a better mommy to you." Hailey's sobs quiet down. I pull her away from me so I can look into her pretty blue eyes. They are full of innocence. Her world is small and full of only white and black colors, even the smallest change leads to an earth-shattering collapse. She looks up at me with her face red and swollen from crying. I know she needs a lot of reassurance that life will be okay, and I know that my love for her has no limit. I'll be there for her in an instant. I'll wipe away her tears. If only my kisses could take all her hurt away, I'd spend endless hours covering her little face with them.

Hailey nods her head and sinks back into her seat. I stare at her for a few seconds longer, my girl is becoming a teenager, but she's still my baby.

We get home and have a peaceful dinner. I enjoy the return of my little cheerful girl who responds in a calm manner to my questions without rolling her eyes. She tells me about her friends, her grades, and how she would love to learn an instrument. Our evening ends with me tucking her into bed, and giving her a kiss on her forehead. I wish I could take all her worries away; but tonight, her allowing me to kiss her reminds me that my little girl is not gone. She's still there, she's just hid herself from all the changes that came her way.

I go to my bedroom and when I pass the mirror, I flip my light new hairdo, and I tell myself that there is so much more out there for me. I am only twenty-seven, my life hasn't ended, it's just beginning.

I pack my new wardrobe into my suitcase and look through the things that Hailey packed for herself. She is minimalistic, just a few shorts and T-shirts and a couple of bathing suits, black and gray are the only colors of her recent clothing. I lie down and spread my blown-out hair above on the pillow so I can preserve the shape for tomorrow, and fall asleep with a smile.

I wake up to the morning light filling my room. I jolt to the seated position, realizing that today we are supposed to fly to Grenada. The alarm clock shows eight o'clock. Shit, this cannot be happening.

"Hailey!" I holler. "Hailey, honey, get up, we are late!"

# 4.

## MITCHEL

The memory of my last vacation has faded. It was somewhere warm, but I don't remember which of the Caribbean islands it was, or maybe it was Mexico. I think it was about fifteen years ago. Rita was still alive, we'd made plans for the future, we'd wanted to start trying for a baby. But it was all gone, taken away by the diagnosis of breast cancer. Our small family was destroyed. She stayed strong until her last day. I should've been the strong one, but I'd collapsed under the weight of grief, even before she took her last breath. It was hard to watch her suffer, she was in such pain; the seizures convulsed her body, then her eyesight was gone, and soon after, she was too sedated to even respond to me. Life without her was unimaginable.

I'd cried inconsolably on the day of her funeral. Our few months old puppy licked my face. If not for his need to be taken care of, I would've been completely consumed with grief.

My nephew, Brian, had just turned thirteen when Rita died. He was so lanky and pimply, and now I am flying to witness him become a husband. I hope my sister will be able to handle seeing her ex-husband with a new fiancée. It's going to be a very awkward family reunion.

I settle into my seat. The two other seats, one by the window and one next to me in the middle, are still empty. I wonder if I'll have anyone to share this flight with. On the other hand, it could be nice to stretch my legs and arms out in the ever-decreasing personal space of the airplane.

The last of the passengers shuffle onto the plane, they stuff the overhead bin with their bags before scooting and plopping down in their seats. I guess I'll have three seats all to myself.

I watch out the plane's window as men feed the luggage to the airplane's belly before we takeoff. A pleasant, smiling flight attendant comes down the aisle, checking if all the passengers are buckled, and closes the bins above us. She disappears to the front of the plane as I glance at my watch which indicates that we are on time. I look to the front and see an out-of-breath, blushing woman walking towards me, apologizing quietly along the way. Her strawberry blonde hair is thick and wavy down to her shoulders. She is pleasantly plump with almost alabaster-white skin and blue eyes that are sad with a look of worry. She looks like she is crying, she probably had been worried about missing the flight. A young girl of about ten walks in front of her staring at her phone, oblivious to the people around her, large headphones covering her ears. I wonder if the two are mother and daughter, but have doubts since the woman looks so young. The little girl has the same pale skin and piercing blue eyes as the woman walking behind her, but her hair is raven black. She's dressed in dark clothing, not the usual pinks and purple sparkles and ruffles I see so often on my students; it's as if she doesn't want to be noticed, doesn't want to see or hear anyone. I bet they will sit by me.

The two young ladies inch closer to me, the older one looking up to read the numbers above the seats. She stops right by me and looks down.

"I'm so sorry, but can we get in to our seats? We are A and B," she says softly, the little girl doesn't take her eyes off her phone.

"Of course." I get up, and step back into the aisle allowing them to slide into their seats.

"Hey, watch it," a man across the aisle barks at the woman as she accidentally bumps him with her daughter's backpack.

"I'm so sorry," she apologizes, her face turning red. She gently pushes her daughter to take the seat by the window and taking the one in the middle.

"Fat ass," he mumbles, just loud enough so she can hear him. Her eyes well up with tears, but she still repeats, "I'm sorry."

"There is no need to be a jackass, young man," I address the insult-hurling man.

"Are you talking to me?" The man's attention turns to me now. The woman and her daughter squeeze by into their seats, and she tugs me on the sleeve. "It's okay. Thank you."

I stare into her sad, defeated eyes, and I have an unexplained desire to defend her. "It's not okay." I then turn to the man across the aisle, "Yes, I'm talking to you. She didn't mean to slap you in your face. But, judging by your insensitive response, you deserved that. So, why don't you tuck away your bruised, manly ego and apologize to the lady." The man's nostrils flare, he squeezes the handles of his chair and attempts to get up, but is interrupted by the flight attendant who is passing by, checking that everyone has their seat belts buckled.

"Is everything all right, gentlemen?" She looks at both of us, the smile not leaving her face.

"Yes, thank you, everything is great," I reply. She looks back at the confrontational man who stays silent.

"Are we going to have a trouble-free flight? Or I can always have the TSA agents resolve any issues, and of course you'll be able to take the next flight to your destination once the issue is resolved."

"Yes, everything is fine," the man forces through his clenched jaw. I sit back, satisfied with this unexpected encounter and its result.

"Hi. My name is Mitchel," I extend my hand to the woman next to me.

"Hi. I'm Gretchen, this is my daughter, Hailey. Thank you for what you did." She nods in the direction of the jerk.

"Don't mention it. Off on vacation?"

"Yes. Kind of. My friend is getting married, so my daughter and I have decided to make it into a little getaway."

"Don't lie," her daughter says under her breath, not looking away from her screen.

"Honey!" Gretchen looks back at the girl, her neck erupting in red hives. "I'm sorry. She's mad her dad wasn't able to stay with her," she turns to me to explain before looking down at the floor.

"It's all right. Don't apologize, I work with teenagers. I know they have a black-and-white understanding of the world at this age."

"Oh," Gretchen relaxes her body and looks up at me. "What do you do?"

"I'm a high school principal." I feel odd saying this out loud. I'm still not used to the title. 'Teacher' rolls off the tongue much easier. I love teaching, engaging with the teenagers, especially. They develop such tough personality shells, they judge the world so harshly, but what I've realized over and over again is that behind all that seemingly unbothered harsh exterior will be a vulnerable child who needs a lot of love and attention.

"That's wonderful! How long have you been one?" Gretchen leans in.

"Two years."

"And before that?" she asks, her blue eyes draw me in.

"I was a teacher, history teacher." I swallow hard and look away, not able to hold her gaze.

"Did you hear that?" she nudges her daughter. "He's a teacher."

"Whatever." The girl rolls her eyes, concentrating on her phone screen.

"Kids, they're not easily impressed," I try to make light of the grumpy attitude of the little girl. The plane pushes off the ground and we are pressed into our seats. We sit quietly until cruising altitude is reached. Gretchen pulls out a magazine, and I take out the chess set I always carry with me.

"Do you play?" I ask her. She pulls away from the magazine and stares at the miniature board. "This is a queen, a king, a rook," I continue.

"I remember! This is the knight, and the bishop, and these little guys are pawns," Gretchen interrupts me, giggling from the excitement of remembering the names of the rest of the figurines. Her laughter is pleasant, genuine, and warm. I smile back at her, "That's right. You remember correctly." I observe how the corners of her mouth go up and small crinkles develop by her eyes and on the sides of her nose, this woman is beautiful. I stop the thought, feeling guilty for finding her attractive. Am I betraying the memory of Rita?

I cough to collect myself, and bring back the tone of the tough school principal that I've been practicing. I don't want to make Gretchen think that I'm interested in her. No other woman can take the place of Rita.

We play chess, and I beat Gretchen a few times. She no longer giggles, but instead yawns and apologizes.

"I think I'll take a nap, plane rides always make me sleepy," she tells me.

"Of course." I collect the chess and put it away. Gretchen leans back and puts her forearms on the armrests, when I sit back my hand touches hers. She doesn't jerk away, but smiles and slowly moves her arm to her lap. I want my hands to be all over her. I swat the thoughts away. I cannot think that. Gretchen closes her eyes and her body relaxes, after a few minutes she is asleep. I browse through the movie content offered by the airline, but turn it off realizing that I have either watched them or have no interest in them. I open my tray table and take out the chess again. I put all the figures on the board and make my first move with the black pawn. I turn the board around and move a white pawn. I turn it again to play the black side and after a couple of moves I take one of the pawns with my knight.

"Are you playing by yourself?" a child's voice a seat away from me asks. I turn and see Hailey watching me play.

I clear my throat, "I am."

"How do you play against yourself? You already know what you're thinking, so there's no way you can trick yourself," she speaks almost in a whisper not to disturb her mother.

"It's not really about tricking. It's actually a good exercise. It trains your mind to see into the future and decide on all the possible outcomes if you make a certain move," I try to explain as simply as possible. She continues looking intently at the board.

"Would you like to try?" I move the board slightly in her direction. She looks at her mother who is sound asleep and nods, stretching out her hands. I pass the chessboard to her, and she places it on the tray table in front of her.

Hailey stares at the board and then grabs her phone, but puts it down after glancing at the screen. "I wanted to look up the rules, but there's no internet here."

"You don't know how to play?" I ask, and she shakes her head no.

"All right, rookie, I'll show you." I'm happy to show her the game. The teacher in me gets excited at the opportunity to pass on knowledge to an eager mind. I look over the chessboard and make sure all the figures are in the right spot. I go over each figure's name and the move that it makes. Hailey watches the board, her feet are folded on the seat in a yoga position. She looks up at her mother once in a while. I wonder if she doesn't want her mother to witness this. Will playing chess make her uncool?

Hailey takes her time making the moves. She puts a drawstring from her hoodie into her mouth and chews on it before deciding to make a move, when the move is made, she folds her lips in, waiting for my countermove. When I don't take her figure, she blows out the air and gives a small smile, but when her move is not successful, she begins to chew the string faster, her eyes moving across the board, deciding what to do next. As we play, her moves become more confident, the string gets chewed less, and she smiles more.

"You're good at it. You should join a chess club," I encourage.

"Ha, no way."

"Why do you say that?"

"I'm not a geek."

"Am I a geek?"

"Yeah, you are," she states without hesitation. I laugh loud enough to wake up Gretchen. She looks confused for a moment.

"Hailey and I are playing chess. I hope you don't mind," I explain. She looks at her daughter smiling. "You play chess? I didn't think you'd like it."

"Whatever." Hailey rolls her eyes, puts the hood over her head and tightens the strings so only her nose and her mouth are seen. She leans back on her chair and puts her headphones on to listen, or pretend to listen, to some music.

Gretchen turns to me and shrugs her shoulders. "Sorry, I'm having a hard time connecting with her."

"Don't worry. It takes time. Kids always test their parents. She'll come around."

"Do you have any kids?"

"No, I don't," I shake my head.

Gretchen pauses. "I'm sorry, I didn't mean to pry."

"You didn't." I don't speak much about Rita's death to strangers, but for some reason I feel at ease with Gretchen. "My wife died a few years ago, we never had a chance to start a family."

"I'm so sorry to hear that. That's terrible. How long has she been gone? If you don't mind me asking."

"Five years." It has been *years*, how strange it is to say that. It doesn't feel so long. "She had breast cancer."

"And you never remarried?" Gretchen leans in closer, and I get to smell the pleasant perfume emanating from her porcelain skin. She tries to keep her voice low, so her daughter doesn't overhear us. She looks back at her girl who sits with her face still covered, bopping her head to an unknown tune.

"I didn't," I confirm.

"May I ask why? I'm sorry. I know you probably think that I'm this crazy woman who is so nosy, but I'm divorced and I just want to hear something positive about marriage so I can have hope, you know?"

I nod, not at all offended by her nosiness. "I just loved her so much. I couldn't imagine feeling again what I felt with Rita. It almost feels that I will tarnish her memory."

"Was your wife against you marrying again?"

"Ha-ha, no, quite the opposite. She insisted that I start dating again after her passing. I just never felt the urge to get to know someone again." My gaze meets hers, and her blue eyes pierce mine with an inquisitive naïveté, her mouth parts as if she is studying my face. I realize I want to get to know Gretchen better.

She smiles at me and sits back in her chair, seemingly satisfied with my answer. A flight attendant passes by offering snacks of peanuts and pretzels. Gretchen and I both go for peanuts, Hailey just tightens her hood more and shakes her head, refusing any snacks. Another pair of flight attendants pass by with drinks, and we both get tomato juice. I smile at the coincidence. I get the courage to ask Gretchen a personal question as well.

"You're young. At what age did you have Hailey?"

Gretchen takes in a long, deep breath before she says, "Sixteen. I know what you are going to think. 'Stupid girl, what was she thinking?' But I thought I was in love, that I would be with my boyfriend forever, that we would be a happy family. I guess I watched too many Disney cartoons. But I love my daughter, I can't imagine not having her, you know?"

"Sure, and I don't think you're stupid. You made a very tough choice to have a baby at a young age, it was brave of you."

"Brave? I haven't heard anyone say that to me before. Thank you," she replies. The rest of the flight we stay quiet. I drift off to sleep. I dream of Rita, she is standing on a shore across a river. I try to swim, but the current is too strong. I try to build a boat, but it sinks. I wave, I scream to her, but she doesn't move. I fall to my knees, and when I look into the reflective waters, I see the face of my wife. She looks happy, she smiles at me. The water brings her reflection to me and I taste the cold on my lips when she kisses me. "It's okay, Mitchel. I'm okay. I'm happy. Now it's your turn to be happy," her reflection speaks to me. I try to caress her face, but fall in and the water pulls me under. I tumble and fight the force that takes me. When I come up ashore, I'm on a beautiful sandy beach, the sun is shining, and something is calling me to go forward.

When I wake up, the captain announces that the plane will be landing soon. I look across Gretchen and Hailey at the window which allows me to see a small corner of the blue ocean, the sky is clear and the sun is shining brightly.

This, for some reason, feels like it's going to be an exciting trip. Out of the corner of my eye, I see Gretchen asleep, and my eyes drift over her face, down to her lips, beautiful neck and soft, high breasts. I look away quickly, ashamed of my own desire. I press the back of my head into the seat and close my eyes. The plane shakes slightly, I feel the pressure pressing against my eardrums, we are descending. The flight attendant who was previously beaming with a smile, rushes passed me, bumping my elbow and not apologizing. The announcement asks if there is a doctor on the plane, and a few minutes later a tall young man walks past me from the first-class section. I look back to see where he is rushing to and see him and another young female help a heavily pregnant woman move to the back of the plane.

"I think there is a woman who is about to have a baby," I mumble, but Gretchen doesn't wake up and Hailey is preoccupied with listening to her music with her headphones on. The flight attendant rushes passed us again to the front of the plane. I catch her by the arm, "Is everything all right? Does that pregnant woman need help?"

"Are you a doctor?"

"No," I shake my head.

"Stay buckled up, we're landing soon, we already have a physician helping her," the flight attendant replies and then rushes off.

The plane lands softly and our bodies are pulled forward by the plane's powerful brake system. Before anyone is allowed to stand up, emergency services board the plane to take the woman out first, behind her trails the young man and a young woman with a baby wrapped in a blanket. She stops by our seat just when Gretchen wakes up. The girl with the baby smiles at Gretchen, "Hi! I'm so

51

glad you made it. Look," she tilts the baby towards us, "I helped deliver a baby. I'll see you at the resort," and she continues walking down the aisle towards the exit. Once she disappears out of our view, the rest of the passengers jump to their feet and crowd the aisle, pulling out bags from the overhead bins.

I always like to sit in my seat and wait for the rush of impatient passengers to pass. I look over to Gretchen who stays in her seat, patiently waiting for her turn to get up and leave the plane.

"That was my friend with the baby. I can't wait to hear that story. Isn't it exciting?" she tells me.

"I don't know if the lady who had the baby found it to be so," I point out another side.

"You're right, sorry. How terrible of me to say that. I can't imagine delivering a baby on a plane. I would be mortified."

I get up after the rush of passengers and the rude man have gone. He'd kept staring at Gretchen, mumbling something indistinguishable. I'm glad she hadn't noticed since she was preoccupied with her daughter. I let Gretchen and Hailey get out of their seats, and help get their bags from the overhead bins. She walks in front of me, and I enjoy looking at her curvy figure from behind.

I like walking next to these women, the three of us. Somehow it feels comforting to walk in numbers instead of all by myself. Gretchen gets her bag from the baggage carousel first, "I'm sorry if I'm asking too much, but which resort are you going to?"

"Grand Escapes," I tell her.

"Us too." Her lips stretch into a smile. "I'll wait for you, and we can take the same car. If you don't mind, of course," she tells me.

"I don't mind, that's very nice of you," I reply. After my bag arrives, we pass security without any problems, and follow the signs to the transportation to the resort. Outside is sunny and pleasantly warm. I glance at my phone which already displays local time of three o'clock. A hill of lush green trees is in front of us, and the sparkling blue ocean is to the left. Across the street, a small café blasting music displays a sign for beer to the arriving passengers. A small white van, already packed with travelers, has just enough space left for the three of us. We give the driver our bags to be put in the trunk and take our seats. The little white van takes off effortlessly down a narrow, dusty road. Both sides of the road are covered in green tropical plants with a scattering of bright walls from houses peering between. The van takes a sharp right and starts climbing a steep hill, it stops at the very top at the entrance to the orange-walled resort. We climb out, refresh with cool towels and champagne, and proceed to register to get our room keys. The joy of the arrival is tarnished when I spot the angry guy from the plane also checking in at the front desk. Gretchen doesn't see him, and I hope their paths don't cross. She stays nearby, and I bet we look like a family to the strangers who pass by. I wonder what it would be like to have a family at my age. I am just too old, I would look pathetic at forty-five with someone as young as Gretchen. I look at her, and she waves to a blond girl who's squealing as she runs to her and they hug each other tight.

"I'm so happy you're here. Angelina came just before you." I recognize Jenna, my nephew's fiancée.

ANYA STASSIY

"I know, I saw her on the plane, she helped deliver a baby, can you imagine?" Gretchen informs Jenna.

"And who's that young woman behind you?" Jenna peers at Hailey. "Hailey is that you? O ... M ... G, girl you look dope, love the headphones." I guess Hailey really likes Jenna, as she gives her a hug and a smile.

"Jenna, this is Mitchel, we sat together on the plane," Gretchen introduces me.

"Hi! You're Brian's fiancée, right?" I ask because Brian only showed pictures of this girl to me.

"Yes, and you are his uncle," she squints and points at me.

"That's right. It's my pleasure to finally meet you." I stretch my hand for a shake, but she gives me a hug.

She pulls away and claps. "I'm so excited you guys. Everyone is almost here. Go, go to your rooms. Rest, go to the beach, and we'll have dinner tonight." Jenna ushers us off, the girls hug, and Gretchen gets her keys first, while I still have to wait for mine.

As my new acquaintances walk away with the bellboy, Gretchen turns and waves goodbye, "I'll see you tonight."

I wave back and happily reply, "See you tonight." Indeed, I am looking forward to seeing her again, strange, the feeling of guilt is not there. I haven't felt so giddy since ... since ... I think, I was still young.

When Gretchen looks away towards something that the bellboy is showing her, Hailey turns around and gives me a quick wave, but turns back swiftly before her mother is able to see the sweet gesture.

54

# 5.

## ANGELINA

The room is spacious with a king-size bed against a partial wall that hides a huge walk-in shower. It's definitely too much for just one person. I check my cell phone, there is free Wi-Fi, but Jack hasn't called yet. I dial him, but my phone call goes directly to his voicemail. He is probably working on his novel. I take a shower, and dress in shorts and a T-shirt that are more appropriate for the warm weather of Grenada. It's four o'clock, and there is plenty of time before dinner to explore a bit and take a dip in the ocean.

When I'm done, I grab a beer from the fridge, my headphones, and my laptop and go to the small patio with the odd freestanding tub. Who in their right mind would decide to take a bath while others are passing by? I sit in a wicker chair, put my feet on the chair across from me, and open my laptop. Cold beer pleasantly goes down my throat, I take a breath in and close my eyes. My solitude is interrupted by the voice of Kai from the patio next to mine. I can't see him, as the wall separates our small outside space, and I can't make out the conversation but the tone gives away that it's not a pleasant one. I decide that it's best not to intrude, so I put my headphones on and turn up Bon Jovi.

I stare at the page of the Word document on my computer. My novel has been complete for two years. I come back to it once in a while and add minor changes. A fantasy tale of 110,000 words, I am still amazed I've written this much, but I am terrified of letting it go out into the world. I want Jack to give me his blessing first, but he is too busy with his own writing to give the proper time my manuscript requires. The only readers who have given me positive—but I am sure very biased—feedback are my two best friends, Jenna and Gretchen, although they only read a few chapters. I'm not convinced I can trust their excitement about my writing. I close the document and stare at the lush green plants and bright flowers growing along the property across from my room. A large iguana lays still, warming its cold-blooded body in the sun. I pick up my phone and take a picture. The first picture of this Grenada trip.

Kai walks from his patio over to me and waves. I take my headphones off, lift a beer up and return the greeting, "Hey. Do you want a beer?"

"Sure," he responds.

I get up and grab one more from my fridge. I hand it to him, and he opens it with the bottle opener that is conveniently affixed to the patio wall.

"Did you hear my babbling on the phone?" Kai asks and takes a sip of the drink, looking into the distance.

I shake my head no and point to the headphones while gulping my beer. He nods his head and takes a long sip himself. The man is certainly easy on the eyes. He has changed, as well, into a T-shirt and swim trunks. His skin is tan, making his blue eyes stand out. I shouldn't think like that, I probably should try to avoid him, the past attraction from my high school years is still there, and I don't want to lead myself into temptation.

"It was my fiancée, ex-fiancée. Sorry, I don't know why I'm telling you this," he shakes his head and takes another sip.

"It's all right. I can lend an ear if you need one," I reply.

"She's been blowing up my phone, and my sister's phone, I had to call her."

"Why don't you just block her?" I suggest the obvious.

"It seems a bit too drastic, I guess." He shrugs his shoulders and leans back in his chair.

"Why did you break up?" I take a sip of my beer.

"She cheated on me, while I was here in Grenada. I was offered a position at St. John's Hospital."

"Oh wow, congrats, that would be so great to live here." How lucky is he to work and live in a permanent vacation spot, I think.

"That's what I thought."

"Do you still love her?" I decide to be direct since he feels comfortable enough to bring up the subject himself. He shakes his head no and takes a sip, squinting his eyes, then looks directly into mine.

I look away, the stare seems too intimate, I don't want him to see that I'm attracted to him.

"I don't know if I ever loved her," he offers the unexpectedly sincere reply.

"Why would you get engaged?" I look at the ground and finish my drink as I ask.

"Habit, it was time, all our friends were getting married or engaged," he shrugs his shoulders.

"We all make mistakes. But isn't this a great place to be—to just get away, to have a break, to recharge?" I offer words of wisdom, but there is something that doesn't feel right when I say those words. A feeling stirs in my chest. A question that I've ignored for too long. Did I ever love Jack? Was I calling it love—my admiration for him, for his work? Did I love his writing and then tricked myself into loving the man who put the words on the paper? I push away the thoughts and put the empty beer bottle on the table.

"Do you want to go to the hospital to see Deja later on?" Kai asks.

"I'd love to." I wonder how the baby is and why Deja said it wasn't hers.

"You want to hit the beach?" he offers.

"Yeah." I jump to my feet. Kai follows my lead, and we stroll down the narrow path that is adorned by palm trees, banana trees, and beautiful flowers. We walk by the party pool that has music blasting, the water bar occupied by a loud, talking and laughing crowd, and then the restaurants and the reception. We walk through the outdoor palapa that has a bar, a billiard table, and curved couches, and then pass another pool that has a sunken fireplace in the center of it that certainly would be great to sit by in the evening. We finally make it to the beach, and what a sight it is. The water is a perfect clear blue, across the beach, the tropical mountains of Grenada rise out of the water with sail boats floating on the calm waters like large white seagulls. I take off my flip-flops and step onto the hot sand. Kai follows me, he then takes off his T-shirt, throws it on the beach, and runs into the water yelling indistinguishable, excited sounds. He dives and disappears under the water for a minute. When he reappears, he shakes the water from his head and with a beaming smile yells, "Get in! What are you waiting for? The water is perfect." This reminds me of the days we'd spent by the pool at Kai and Jenna's house. We'd splashed, jumped, and dove. Kai was funny, and I'd made sure he found me when we played Marco Polo. Oh, what the heck. I take off my shirt and shorts and run into the water just as I used to when we were kids. I squeal and laugh when my body hits the water. It feels cold on my sun-warmed skin but once I am submerged under, it feels warm and pleasant. I walk on the sandy bottom and stare at the little, light-blue translucent fish swimming close by, unafraid of my presence. Kai swims up, humming the tune from *Jaws*. He makes me laugh. I splash him in the face. He dives down, grabs me by the waist, lifts me up, and then throws me back into the water. I resurface and laugh.

"Let's swim to those floats," I point to the large orange floating rings farther away from the beach. Kai nods and heads in that direction. We first swim with a relaxed stroke, but when I sense him speeding up, I increase my pace. He glances at me wickedly and begins to swim front crawl. I am not to be outdone. I love a friendly competition, so I start front crawl as well. I come up for air every few seconds, Kai and I are head-to-head. We reach the rings quickly. I think I touch it first.

"I win!" I yell.

"No, you don't," he splashes my face. "I felt bad and went easy on you."

"Oh, shut up. You're just too embarrassed to admit that you lost to a girl," I splash back. Kai throws his head back and laughs for a second. He puts both of his hands on the ring, pulls himself up, and throws his upper body over it. I follow him and do the same. I am able to see my feet dangling in the clear water. Little fish swim up closer,

I wonder what they think seeing humans floating in their world. I look up at Kai who is staring at the fish as well. His body is defined by muscles, droplets of water glisten on his skin. He doesn't look like the boy I used to know, he is a man that turns me on. I dive down under water, to drown out the thoughts. "I'm going to head back to the beach," I tell Kai when I come up.

"Okay. I'll hang here for a minute," he replies. I nod and begin my swim towards the beach. When my feet feel the sandy shallows, I walk against the resistance of the water, there is no wind and the sun dries the water off my skin almost immediately. I get our clothes and find two loungers.

"I always wished that the two of you would get together," says a woman on the lounger next to me. I look in her direction and recognize Mrs. Gable immediately; she wears large sunglasses and a wide-brimmed straw hat, looking elegant in a brightly colored caftan, she's sipping a drink with a straw, her lips lined with red lipstick.

"Mrs. Gable!" I get up and throw my arms around the woman whose house I've spent endless hours in. She was the only adult who spoke to us like we mattered. She'd made me feel that my childish problems were important and deserved the time of a grown up. I'd once witnessed her confronting a stranger at a store who decided to comment on the way we were behaving. "You don't talk to those kids. If you have a problem you speak to me. Do you understand?" She'd stood guard, as we hid behind her back. But, boy, did we get a lecture about our behavior from her later on.

"Good to see you, honey! And, please, no more 'Mrs. Gable.' You make me feel too old. It's Nina from now on."

She hugs me back tightly and takes off her glasses, giving me a look over. "You look absolutely wonderful! Was Kai behaving?" She looks at me from under her hat, biting on the handle of her sunglasses.

"Mrs. Ga … Nina, Kai and I are just friends." I wave her off. "Plus, he just broke off his engagement, he needs time."

"Oh, I'm so glad he finally did it. That girl was nothing more than pretentious sausage water who wanted to be a delicacy." The expression is a familiar one, Nina often used it to describe people who have nothing special about them. It's always made me laugh.

"You're too funny. I hope you don't think I'm 'sausage water.'"

"Angelina, child, far from it. I just wish my Kai would see that." She looks into the distance where her son is still hanging out on the floating ring. I shake my head and sit back on my lounger.

"I'm in a relationship with a wonderful man," I say and it sounds like I am trying to persuade myself.

"And where is your 'wonderful man'?" The question zings, but I know Mrs. Gable is just curious and doesn't mean any harm.

"Working," I offer a short explanation.

"Well, I hope I will get to see him soon," she replies with a side-eye. I nod and smile at Kai's mother. I hope he actually makes it here. I check my phone and there are still no messages from Jack. I'll call him in a little while, he needs to give me the date of when he is coming.

I look at the water and see Kai coming towards us. As he wades through the shallow water and reaches the beach, water droplets run down the muscles of his abdomen which are defined squares that narrow into slim hips. I shift in my chair, uncomfortable from the desire that stirs deep inside of me.

# 6.

## KAI

I feel embarrassed that Angelina might have heard my conversation with my ex. Candice has been blowing up my phone, and since I've been ignoring her, she's started calling and texting my sister. If I hadn't picked up, who knows who else she would have called. I change into swim trunks and a T-shirt and dial Candice, but all I can hear is her sobbing. I decide to stay quiet to see what she has to say, after a few moments the sobbing ceases and she calls out my name, checking to see if I'm still listening.

"What do you want, Candice?" I say, clenching my teeth.

"I'm sorry. I love you." She starts crying again.

"Candice, I don't fucking care. Don't call me. Don't call my sister or my friends, we're done."

"You have to forgive me," she begs, ignoring my demands.

"What's wrong with you, Candice? We're done. I don't love you. Move on."

"But I don't want to move on," she continues whining annoyingly into the phone. "I want to be with you."

"Candice, listen, I'm done. We have nothing else to talk about. Bye." I don't wait for her to respond, and hang up the phone.

I don't even pay much attention to my surroundings during the conversation. I pace the room, but the walls feel like they are closing in on me, trying to trap me within, so I push the sliding door open and step outside onto the patio. I should have considered that Angelina might hear everything, she is sweet not to admit otherwise.

But when did Angelina become so damn attractive? She is calm and unpretentious, her quiet confidence is a complete turn on. We chat over beer. For some reason, I open up to her about my relationship and break up. I am not used to a girl like that. I don't want her to linger over that conversation and decide to change the scenery and ask her to go to the beach. But, after a few minutes in the water she leaves me. I wonder why she runs off to the sand, did I make her uncomfortable? I stare at her toned back and perky butt. Damn it, the girl is fit.

I'd better control myself with her, or Jenna and Mother would never forgive me. Hanging in the water feels lonely, small fish don't mind me at all and start pecking at my legs. I think Jenna mentioned that she arranged for a scuba diving lesson tomorrow. I've always wanted to learn. I wonder if Angelina has ever done it?

I decide to swim back to the beach and see what she is doing. I find her sitting by my mother.

"Hello, my son," my mother greets me.

"Hi, Mom. How was your flight?" I lean down and give her a kiss on the cheek.

"Too long, but this place is marvelous. A bit of discomfort is so worth it. I'm glad you'll be working here. A change of scenery will be good for you. Angelina told me you broke up with that girl, what's her name again?"

"It doesn't matter. She's no longer important." I glance at Angelina to see her reaction, she looks up at me and mouths, *I'm sorry*.

I smile and give her a wink to make her feel more comfortable. I'd imagined the conversation would have gone quite differently, so I am thankful for Angelina being here.

"When is Dad coming?"

"He'll be here … let me see … in four days. You know how he is, always needs to finish all of his business before he can relax." My mother sips the last bit of her cocktail.

"Do you want a drink, ladies?" I ask.

"Please, darling, a glass of champagne for me," my mother requests.

"I'll have the drink of the day," says Angelina, and I walk off to the bar. Once there, I order the drinks and the energetic bartender prepares them swiftly. I go back and find my mom and Angelina chatting while still lounging in the same positions that I'd left them. Angelina looks up at me and gives me a wide, beaming smile.

"Thank you," she says as I pass her a tall glass full of light blue cocktail with a pineapple slice perched on the edge and a small umbrella. Her fingers touch mine as she grabs the glass and I linger to let go of it.

"You're welcome," I reply. "This is yours, Mom." I pass her the champagne.

"Thank you, Kai. Put on some sunblock. Here, I have it." My expedient mother passes me the tube. "The sun is very strong, you'll burn." I take the tube and begrudgingly start applying the thick white paste.

"Angelina, can you help him with his back? My hands are sore today, otherwise I would do it," my mother requests lying perfectly still, her large dark glasses covering her face.

"It's okay, Mom, I'll put on a shirt," I reply. My mother is a smart woman, she always has a reason for asking something. This request reeks of a set up.

"You'll burn, and skin cancer runs in the family," she persists, staying in character as an innocent, concerned mother.

"It's all right, I can do it. Give it to me." Angelina sits up and stretches her hand. I pass her the tube, giving my mother the stink eye, but her facial expression doesn't change, she looks away towards the ocean and takes a sip of her drink.

Angelina loudly squeezes out a dollop of the sunblock, giggles and smacks the cold concoction on my back. My chest arches forward from the unpleasant sensation, but once she starts rubbing it fast over my back, I relax and enjoy her touch. The swift movements slow down as her small hands glide over my shoulder blades and then down my back. The skin of her hands has a few rough calluses, and the scratches send pleasant shivers through my body. I look down at the sand, enjoying the moment, hoping that it will last just a bit longer. I feel Angelina's gaze on me. I glance at her and our eyes connect. She turns the color of deep red and pulls away. She gives my mother the tube of sunblock, "All done. I'm going to check on our scuba diving lesson for tomorrow," she tells us and gets up from the lounge chair.

"I'll come with you," I blurt and spring up. She looks back at me, but doesn't say anything, and I have to take a few strides to catch up to her. She keeps her head down, looking at her feet sinking in the wet sand as the warm, clear waves come and go, washing away her imprints. She walks fast and I trail behind, "Wait up, where are you running to?" I call out.

"Sorry. I didn't realize I was walking fast," she slows down her pace, and I am finally able to walk next to her.

We keep strolling along the edge of the beach. The sand is fine and warm with white seashells peeking from underneath. We pass by a pier leading up to a platform with a large wicker chair. The sand turns black, volcanic. I lean down and pick up a fistful and show it to Angelina. "Black sand."

She stops and pokes her finger around in the sand while it's in my palm.

"That's so cool. I've never seen it before." Her head leans over my palm, and I am able to smell a faint scent of grapefruit that is pleasantly hitting my nose. She looks up at me and smiles, I return the smile and then wash the sand from my hands. We start walking again. I remember where I'd heard about black sand and decide to tell Angelina about it.

"Last year, I read a cool book. It was about this earth god that was drowned by the ocean, but he loved the sun so much he was able to send pieces of himself in the form of dark sand so the sun would warm him with her touch. Very well-written fantasy."

Angelina stops suddenly and turns sharply towards me. Her brows are furrowed. "Where did you get the book?" She sounds angry.

"My sister had it, it was just laying around. I read it in a few days and left it for Jenna. Why?"

Angelina shakes her head and now smiles. "I wrote that book. I gave it to Jenna so she could read it and give me feedback. She was one of my beta readers."

"What? You wrote that? That's so awesome! I didn't know you write."

"It's more of a hobby." She shrugs her shoulders.

"Did you ever publish it?"

"No."

"Why not? I'm telling you, the story is great!" I nudge her.

"I don't know. I'm just not sure if it's good enough. Maybe I'm just scared to take the step towards querying and people judging me. I want to get my boyfriend's opinion first, maybe then I'll submit it to agents," she rumbles. Oh yes, she has a boyfriend. I'd better stop liking her.

"Well, I think it's great. You should just send it to the agents and not be scared. If you want, I can read it again and give you more feedback?" What the fuck, why did I just say that? She has a boyfriend, I don't want to come on to her.

"Sure, I'd love that. I'll send you the second part," she offers. I nod and we start walking up the beach to a large hut that has the sign *Scuba Diving* over one of its windows. We go up the steps, I let Angelina walk ahead of me, as my mother has taught me. Angelina checks with the tall, lanky man regarding scheduled scuba lessons for tomorrow, and I walk around checking out the equipment for scuba and souvenirs. My gaze concentrates on the new objects for a few seconds, but then drifts off to find Angelina. God damn it, god damn it! I am like a fucking creep around this girl. I'd better leave her alone before she thinks the same.

"Angelina, I am going to head to my room. I'll see you later tonight."

"Okay, Kai. Is everything all right?" Angelina asks.

*No*, I want to blurt, *I am starting to like you, so I have to stay clear of you*, but instead I say, "Yeah, yeah, just need to check my email, unpack. You know, you ..." I stop from repeating myself, turn, and swiftly walk away from Angelina.

# 7.

## GRETCHEN

I couldn't have imagined that my plane ride would be this exciting. Mitchel certainly made an impression on me. I'm shocked to find that Hailey enjoyed playing chess. I had to fake being asleep to see my girl enjoy the game. I never thought she would like something like that. My phone-obsessed angel actually has likes beyond chatting and viewing the lives of others on social media. She would have never done something like that with me. I wonder if she is afraid to be vulnerable with me, to show joy, maybe she thinks she will be hurt again. I have to find the right moment to talk to her.

Mitchel is nice. I thought men like him didn't exist. He is smart, attentive, patient. He looked interested in the game himself; I guess it makes sense, he is a teacher after all. My ex never enjoyed spending time with us, twenty or thirty minutes is all that we would get, and then he was off to tend to emails, texts, and God-knows-what on his phone. I hope I get to chat with Mitchel again, I really enjoyed his company.

We get to our room on the second floor. Across the room is a large sliding door leading to a balcony, it overlooks the palm trees and the perfect blue of the

Grenada sky. Two queen-size beds are there for Hailey and I, but a large open shower might be a bit tricky for the privacy.

"Ewww, an open shower. How am I supposed to wash myself?" Hailey has been shy lately over her developing body.

"If you need privacy I'll stay on the balcony or step out of the room when you need it," I reply preemptively so she doesn't get upset any further. I really want to enjoy my time here, and I hope she will recharge with some positive vibes.

"Let's change and walk around, check out the resort?" I open my luggage and decide what to wear as my first outfit. I pull out a white romper, beige sandals, and a navy blue bathing suit that promises to make my figure look slim in all the right places. I look over the outfit and decide that it's quite perfect for a stroll on this Caribbean paradise. I hear Hailey sigh loudly, she probably rolls her eyes as well, as she opens her bag and gets a pair of black shorts and a tank top out to change into.

"All black? Really honey? You will be so hot. Why don't you put on something a bit more colorful?"

"This is fine," she snaps and disappears into the closet. I decide not to push her on the outfit, she might decide to stay in the room for the rest of the day and not come out at all. I have to pick my battles. When she comes out, I grab a beach bag with hats, sunglasses, and sunblock, and we head downstairs to start our exploration. Narrow, picturesque trails take us downhill to a wider path that leads through the reception area. We then pass a large, roofed area with comfy couches and egg-shaped hanging chairs and swings, and then find ourselves by a square pool with an infinity edge.

"Do you want to stay by the pool or go to the beach?" I ask Hailey.

"I don't care," my daughter replies.

"Then beach it is, follow me, missy." I grab a couple of towels while Hailey trails behind me, her eyes transfixed on her phone screen. She doesn't lift her head even when we start walking on the sand. Once I find two beach chairs, I set up the towel for her while she feverishly types something into her cell.

I pull her down by the arm so she sits, and then I sit in my chair. The weather is perfect, it's warm without the overwhelming humidity. I'm glad that Jenna picked this island for her wedding. I've never even heard of it, but I bet Jenna did some adventuring here before. That girl is fearless. I am actually surprised she is getting married so fast. She had known the guy only for three months before they got engaged, it took another three months to plan the wedding, but their relationship has been going strong, and my friend chirped happily about her upcoming nuptials over the phone. I am excited for her, but my own failed marriage makes me a pessimist about relationships.

"Why don't you just date a bit longer? Why are you rushing to get married?" I'd pressed my friend.

"I know you probably think I'm crazy. But I've never felt like this before, and he is so supportive and he loves me and I love him. We just can't wait to call each other husband and wife," Jenna explained.

"But you realize those are just words. Husband, wife, who cares? They will not define your relationship," I'd persisted.

"Oh, Gretchen," my friend laughed. "Of course, listen, I love you and I am sorry I'm selfishly chatting about my wedding when you just went through a divorce. I'm happy, and I want you to be happy for me. Okay?"

"Of course, Jenna, I am happy for you." I've never questioned my friend again about her quickie marriage set up. I hope she's not making a mistake by rushing it.

"Hello, ladies," a deep, familiar voice calls from behind. I turn around and see Mitchel walking slowly towards us, carrying three ice creams in his hands. "Do you want to try some nutmeg ice cream? I was in the bakery shop over there," he points behind him. "And saw you walking towards the beach, so I figured an ice cream would be a perfect treat."

"Sure, it's perfect! That's so sweet of you." I take two ice creams out of his hands while he pulls a beach chair next to ours. I nudge Hailey who lifts her head from the screen and grabs her ice cream from my hands.

"Hey, Mitch, thanks," she blurts.

"'Mitch?' Hailey!" I get embarrassed by her familiarity, but she ignores my elevated tone.

"Don't worry about it." Mitchel touches my arm lightly. Although it is hot outside, the touch raises goosebumps throughout my body, a man's touch hasn't caused this reaction in a long time. I smile at him and dig into my ice cream. I take a bite and an unusual flavor sends my brain into confusion, the blend of sweetness and the spice of nutmeg is unusual, but after a few slow chews, I realize I like it. Mitchel laughs loudly at my reaction, taking a spoonful of the ice cream into his mouth.

"Unusual, right? But in a good way." I nod, returning the laughter.

"Yuck, what kind of ice cream is this?" We turn around to watch Hailey spit the ice cream out of her mouth.

"It's nutmeg. It's delicious," I explain to her calmly. She stares at the container for a second, smells it and then pulls it away from her face.

"I'm not eating this, it's so disgusting."

"More for me then." I take it out of her hands and put it in the sand by me. "Sorry, her taste buds haven't matured yet," I tell Mitchel.

"She's a kid. Don't worry about it. She probably eats chicken nuggets, mac and cheese, and pizza, right?"

"Pretty much," I reply. All my attempts to introduce a variety of fresh produce have failed in the past. Although I'm learning to hide veggies in sauces, meatballs, and meat loaves, I have tricked her into believing that my homemade chicken tenders are store bought.

"Like most of the kids at my school. She will learn to be more adventurous with food soon."

"You're so positive, it's really nice to hear that."

He stares out at the ocean as I look him over. He is older, maybe early forties, but still in great shape. Gray hair dusts his sideburns, short stubble covers his face, but his brown eyes sparkle with curiosity or maybe just energy. He looks happy, kind.

"Ha, thank you, I'm afraid I keep talking like a teacher. I can never give up on a child, there's always hope."

"I often feel like I'm a terrible mother. When I gave birth to my child, I also delivered a bundle of parental guilt. It's just always there. A constant doubt, wondering if I'm doing everything right."

"You don't do everything right," Mitchel blurts, and I look up at him in a panic. "Don't get me wrong," he laughs. "That's completely normal. You're human, it's impossible to be perfect. But children are very forgiving, they're resilient. They teach us how to be better, we just have to pay attention."

"Your wife was a lucky woman to have you."

"Thank you. We were both lucky to have each other." He takes a bite of his ice cream and looks towards the calm water. Then his gaze travels to me, he smiles and says, "Do you want to check out the water?"

I glance at Hailey who hasn't changed her position and nod to him eagerly. He takes off his shirt to reveal a very muscular chest and defined abs. I turn away from Mitchel and take off my romper, shy about my body and how imperfect it is. He takes my hand and we stroll slowly, sinking our feet into the warm sand. When we get close to the water, Mitchel bends down and picks up something from the ground.

"What is it?" I ask, and he gives me a cone-shaped white shell, which is twisted into a perfect rosette. "This is so pretty. Thank you. I'll keep it as a souvenir." Mitchel smiles and treads into the water first. I follow him right away into the clear, warm ocean. I can't swim, so I stay just knee deep. Mitchel looks at me wickedly, dips his hand into the water and splashes a little bit at me playfully.

"Don't, don't you dare," I warn him before he can splash me again, I kick my foot up and splash him. The resistance of the water throws me off balance and I fall back into it. I disappear under the rolling waves and struggle to get up, the current pulling me under and farther from the shallow water. I panic, my arms flail looking to grab onto something on the surface. My feet fail to find firm ground. Am I going to die like this in waist high water, will my daughter have to grow up without her mother? I have little air left in my lungs, and I feel I am being pulled deeper under the water. I say a prayer and promise God that I will do anything as long as he saves me. As soon as I finish, my hand is grabbed and I am pulled upwards. I gasp as soon as I come up and start coughing up the salty water with an ugly, choking sound. I gasp again, Mitchel holding me tight against his chest, patting my back.

"It's all right, that's it, that's it, cough it all up."

I finish the bout of coughing and take a deep breath of air, slowly filling my lungs.

"You can't swim, can you?" he asks me, looking into my eyes. I only have the strength to shake my head no. "I guess we'll have to put a life jacket on you anytime you approach water." He tries to laugh. I smile coyly and nod, I feel embarrassed by my lack of swimming skills. Mitchel probably thinks I am a complete moron. He is so smart, and I am so stupid.

"Let's go get you dry." Mitchel takes me by my hand and leads me out of the water towards our chairs. Hailey is still glued to her screen when we come up, she looks up at me, squinting her eyes, shielding them from the sun. "You're back already?"

"Yes, your mother had a little accident in the water, so we decided to come back," Mitchel explains. Hailey giggles, looking at Mitchel first and then back at me. "Mom, when are you going to learn how to swim? It's so embarrassing."

"Yes, Hailey, I'm aware of that, thanks for reminding me," I answer her smart-ass remark.

"I can teach you," Mitchel offers. "I used to be a lifeguard in high school and college."

"You should totally learn, Mom." Hailey lifts her head from her phone.

I've been afraid of water for as long as I can remember and have always found excuses to avoid swimming, but now that Hailey is approving of me taking lessons from Mitchel and him being so kind offering, I guess I have to face my fear and go for it. "Okay, I'd love for you to teach me how to swim."

"We'll start tomorrow, then." Mitchel glances at his watch. "I'd better get going, Jenna and Brian have a dinner planned at six."

"What time is it now?" I ask.

"Four thirty," Mitchel replies.

"We'd better get going, too. Hailey, let's go honey." I nudge my daughter. Mitchel springs up from his lounge chair as Hailey and I rise from ours. I pause for a moment, dumbfounded by this gesture. He stretches out his hand, and I give him mine. I wasn't expecting a handshake, why would he want to shake my hand, it's so cold and official. But instead of a shake, he brings my hand to his lips and gives it a kiss. I don't expect it at all. There are men who do this kind of thing, but I've only read about it in books, and now here I am experiencing it. My skin erupts in goosebumps. I smile at Mitchel, I like him, no one has done so many gentlemanly things like this for me before. I can't even remember one. Hailey giggles. Mitchel lets go of my hand, he then looks at Hailey who stops her laughter and stares keenly at him. He bends slightly at his waist in another unexpected gentlemanly gesture towards Hailey. She smiles and surprises me by doing a curtsey. I stare at her, not recognizing my little girl. Where did she learn how to do that? She looks up at me and shrugs her shoulders. Mitchel stares at both of us, and we all erupt in laughter.

"This is so sweet Mitchel, and you, Hailey, where did you learn to curtsey, missy?"

"This is nothing Gretchen, it's my pleasure to pay you ladies some attention."

"I read books, Mom."

"Do you, now? Well that's news to me, but I absolutely loved that you did it. You have to teach me sometime. Okay, let's get going now. Bye, Mitchel!" I wave to the man who made me feel special and saved my life today. I am curious to get to know him more.

"See you, ladies!" he replies.

# 8.

## ANGELINA

Kai looks like he's running away from me. Have I said something that made him upset? It felt great to hear that he'd read and actually liked my writing. I'd given my manuscript to Jenna, Gretchen, and Jack, and none of them finished it. I'd felt discouraged assuming that my writing was so bad that no one had any interest in finishing the story. Gretchen apologized and said that she was overwhelmed with the divorce and Hailey acting out, Jenna was busy in her new relationship, and Jack was finishing his own writing. I didn't want to press them, so I'd just put it away.

I finish making arrangements for the scuba class tomorrow and get back to my room. Jack still hasn't called, so I dial him and he picks up right away.

"Hi, Angelina! How is Grenada?" he says it in one breath, and I sense that he is not really interested to know about it.

"Hey! It'd be better with you here. Where are you?" I walk slowly across the room, then back towards the glass sliding door.

"Oh, you know, writing." He keeps his answer short and vague.

"How is it going? Are you almost done?" I keep pressing for details.

"No, not done yet." His answer sounds cold, and he doesn't reciprocate with any questions back.

"So, do you think you will be able to make it here? The rooms are very quiet. I'll leave you alone so you can work."

"Angelina, I'm sorry. I can't do this." His voice gets deeper.

"Oh. Well. It's okay. I guess. We can spend time together when I get back." There is silence on the other end. "Jack?"

"Angelina. I can't do *us* anymore. It's over." Somehow, my body finds a chair and collapses into it. I've been preparing to hear that our relationship is over. Jack has finally decided to voice what I've long suspected. I feel relieved, I'd been so blinded by meeting this man's needs that I'd completely lost myself and forgotten about my own needs.

"How long have you felt like this?" I ask, my ego demands to know so it can recover and move on.

"Angelina, it's not important," he tries to pacify me.

"No, it is important—to me." I slam my fist on the nearby desk.

Jack sighs heavily into the phone. "I don't know anymore, Angelina, a few weeks … maybe … maybe a few months … I haven't been keeping track of time."

"'A few months?' A few months? Are you kidding me? I knew this was coming, but you've left me hanging for *months*?" My bruised ego picks itself up and ignites into a rage, feeling used and lied to.

"Angelina, please don't be dramatic. I want this to be a civil separation. I was just looking for the right moment to address it."

"I wish you would have told me months ago," I yell into the phone. I fell for his confidence and was always impressed by how direct he was in addressing any issue head-on, but now he has revealed that those seemingly positive qualities are just well-masked selfishness and a disregard for the feelings of others.

I hear a forced sigh on the other end again, and Jack then monotonously tells me, "Angelina you are a lovely girl, but our relationship ceased to be exciting, and I need that as a writer, as an artist. You just don't inspire me anymore. We really had a good run, but let's stay friends. I'll collect your things and ship them to your apartment. I really have to go. I hope you have a good time at the wedding. Bye, Angelina." And without giving me a chance to say anything else, Jack hangs up the phone. I look at the screen which tells me that the phone call lasted three minutes and twenty-two seconds, and that it has ended. I sit there on the chair, staring at the dark screen and then I catch a reflection of myself in the large reflective glass of the phone. I look so sad, with a blank stare into nowhere, I feel drained and empty. My chin starts to tremble, and the inside of my nose begins to itch and gets stuffy, but instead of tears, a loud sneeze erupts. I am not overly sad because we broke up. Somehow, I've known that we would not last forever, but I am disappointed because I lost myself in this relationship. I'd built this man up at the cost of my own growth. I'd persuaded myself that he needed me, I'd made myself into his crutch so his life was easier. I'd worked jobs so I could be available when he needed me. I'd only write when he was traveling. I'd been buying groceries that he would eat, and failed to buy the things that I enjoyed because he didn't like them. He hadn't asked for any of it, but to be with him I'd morphed myself into someone else. I'd become someone else for him, and now he doesn't want me. I am angry over the lost time of living my life the way I wanted to live. I know that it isn't the end, that this sadness will pass. I need to concentrate on the wedding. This is Jenna's week. I need to make sure she is having fun. I will pull myself together. I get up and go to the large mirror near the sink. My eyes and nose are red, I look tired. I wash my face in cold water and then take a shower. When I am done, I climb into bed and close my eyes. I don't remember falling asleep, my brain just shuts off from the exhaustion of travel and the break up. I don't know how long I'd been asleep, but I am jolted from my nap. When I open my eyes, I don't move. Lying quietly, I listen to the sounds around me. It's perfectly quiet, it's still light and sunny outside. I realize that I am in Grenada, and I am not dreaming. I remember the phone call and the break up with Jack. It still hurts deep down, but it is not debilitating. I know life will go on, and I will feel better. I sit up and hug my knees. I watch the large palm trees through the sheer curtain that gently rock back and forth in the warm wind. I've read somewhere that palm trees are perfectly designed for surviving storms; their thick trunks are flexible, their thin roots are a spider web network that spread wide in the soil, and even the leaves are designed to collapse under the strong winds, sparing the tree itself from major damage. Not the prettiest tree, but the best survivor. The break up with Jack is my storm, but it will not uproot me. I swing my legs to the edge of the bed and look at the clock. It's 5:30 p.m., and I need to get ready for dinner with all the guests that have arrived today. My hair is still damp from the earlier shower, I blow it out and put on mascara and a bit of blush. Makeup isn't my forte, and I prefer to keep it to a minimum. I get a long, blue dress out of my luggage and put it on. The fit is perfect, the two high slits show off my toned legs, and the lace back gives it an interesting detail. I put on my nude pumps and finish off with a touch of lip gloss. It takes me just twenty minutes to get ready, and then I look at my computer to pass the time.

I scroll through emails, none require my instant reply. I then go into the documents and open the file with my manuscript. It's been sitting there complete, waiting to be read by someone other than me in its entirety. Jack will certainly not read it now, and my girlfriends are busy with their personal lives. I figure there is no one better than Kai to send the rest of the manuscript to since he has already read part one. I find his email address in my electronic address book and attach my manuscript to the email. My heart beats faster as I press send. Will he like the end of the story? Will he like my writing? I figure it is better to hear any critique so I can make it into the best story it can be. I cannot be sensitive to people's opinions if I want to succeed in this business.

I close my laptop and head outside. The dinner is in the restaurant by the beach. The space has a beautiful view, unobstructed by windows or walls, the sun is bathing everything and everyone in its golden hour glow. A light, warm breeze brings in the salty smell of the ocean. Gretchen and her daughter are already sitting at the table talking with a good looking man that I haven't met. Jenna and her fiancé are standing at the head of the table, him whispering something into her ear that she clearly enjoys, responding with laughter and wrapping her hands around his neck. Kai's mother is by the bar sipping champagne and chatting with the bartender, laughing loudly over something. The parents of the groom are divorced and each has come to the wedding with their new significant other. They manage to keep their relationship cordial, although Jenna told me that Brian's mother feels hurt that his father is dating someone younger. Brian's best man, his fifteen-year-old brother who is an awkward, lanky teenager, sits at the table staring at his phone. Brian's best friend, Doug, is already married, and his wife, Elaine, is pregnant with their first child. They are sitting opposite Gretchen. Doug rubs the small rounded belly of his wife. Only one person is missing. I stand at the entrance wondering why Kai is late.

"Boo!" Kai whispers into my ear, coming up from behind me. I startle from this unexpected little prank, but I quickly relax hearing Kai laugh and apologize, "Sorry, sorry I didn't actually want to scare you."

"You didn't. Looks like everyone is here." I am happy to see him. I hope the topic of my relationship doesn't come up. I don't feel like explaining the breakup to everyone present here.

"Do you want a drink?" Kai asks me. "I need a bit of a confidence boost if I'll have to make a toast."

"Good idea. I don't love public speaking myself. I'll have a mojito." Kai nods and heads to the bar. I go to the table and greet everyone. Jenna runs up to me. Her greetings are always full of passion, as if we haven't seen each other in ages. She squeals and gives me a big hug. "Hi! Maid of honor, Angelina. Your job is to keep me in check because I think I already drank too much," she laughs throwing her head back. Brian comes up and pulls her close to him, giving her a quick peck on the cheek. He and Jenna are nothing alike. She'd never went for his type before, she'd always gone for the bad boy who led an exciting life and then would end up hurting her. But Brian is very smart, master's degrees in computer engineering and math, he has a house, and a retirement account. Jenna attempted to go to college, first for nursing, then to study architecture, but dropped out because she didn't feel the connection to those professions. She'd always loved photography and travel, so she combined her two loves and became an Instagram influencer. She's amassed one and a half million followers and is making a lot of money from advertisements. I still don't quite understand who and what she is influencing, she says I don't get it because I don't have any social media presence, that I'm out of touch. The artificiality of that kind of communication scares me, and I resist it.

Jenna and Brian met in an unexciting line at Starbucks while both ordering soy lattes—he is lactose intolerant and she was on a health kick. She took him on her trips, he taught her how the world is one big mathematical problem. They're each fascinated by the other. Jenna realized that she was in love when he said her face corresponded to the golden ratio of phi, he told her he loved her when she took him to a cenote swim in Mexico. Jenna's mother met her daughter's suitor and welcomed him into the family, understanding that he is the ballast her daughter needs. Her mother always let Jenna and Kai make their own decisions and rarely intervened. She didn't object to their quick engagement and a spontaneous decision to marry soon after. Jenna confided in me that not everything is as great with Brian's parents, or rather his mother. She isn't happy that her oldest son is marrying someone who doesn't even hold a bachelor's degree, and she'd lectured her son on how marriage to Jenna is a huge mistake, all while Jenna was sitting in front of her. She'd calmed down when her son threatened to disinvite her to the wedding. The woman is a gaunt, tall, blonde, sipping red wine while staring at the soon-to-be married couple through squinted eyes. She radiates displeasure. Her ex-husband sits at the opposite end of the table with a younger-looking copy of his first wife. Her skin is smooth, her blond hair is bouncier, but she has the same look of displeasure while staring at the woman who was the missus before her. It will be an interesting pre-wedding meshing of the families.

Jenna takes my hand and leads me to my seat. The table is long, decorated with low arrangements of brightly colored tropical flowers. I am sitting next to Nina on one side and Kai on my other side. Brian's friend and his pregnant wife are across from me. Gretchen, Hailey and Mitchel, who Jenna introduces as Brian's uncle, are between the exes and their significant others. Kai comes back with my drink and gives a peck on his mother's cheek before he sits down next to me. Our arms brush lightly against each other, his skin is warm. I take a long sip of my mojito to distract from the pleasant sensation of his touch.

"You look lovely, Mrs. Ga … Nina." I turn myself to Kai's mother. "Love the turban."

"Thank you, dear." She touches her headwear and flashes me a wide smile framed by red lips. She leans towards me and whispers, "Have a shot of tequila with me. I really need it to help me tolerate my soon-to-be new in-laws." I give an agreeable nod and a waiter appears as soon as Nina throws her arm into the air. "Kevin, dear, please bring two shots of Don Julio for me and this young lady." The waiter smiles and rushes off towards the bar.

"I can't stand hard liquor," Brian's mother starts speaking to us, "I just don't understand the appeal." She scrunches up her nose.

"Donna, dear, drinking hard liquor in good company can be great fun, sipping wine in bad company can be a complete misery. I choose my liquor like I choose my company—by the way it makes me feel. Cheers, Donna, to good company!" Nina raises her glass towards Brian's mother who forces a smile that stretches her already thin lips into a barely visible thread. Our tequila shots are brought by the waiter, Nina clinks my shot glass with hers and takes the gulp of the fiery liquid. I follow her lead and throw my head back, helping the alcohol go down my throat.

Brian gets up and gently taps on his champagne glass with his fork. The guests quiet down and everyone looks at him.

"Hi, everyone! Jenna and I would like to thank all of you for joining us in Grenada for our wedding. Each one of you is extremely important to us and we appreciate your love and friendship. When two people get married, it's not just a creation of the union between the two of them, but also the coming together of two families. We are happy to be gaining new family members and new friends. Jenna and I would like to raise a toast to all of you. Thank you for being in our lives. Cheers!" He raises his glass.

"Cheers!" Everyone picks up the toast and meets his glass. We sit down and the waiters bring out salads with grilled octopus.

"Hey!" Kai nudges me. "I got your email with the book. I started reading it already. Great first page. I had to force myself to stop, that's why I was late."

Goosebumps erupt on my skin in the warmth of the evening air. "You started reading already? Thank you. That's so nice of you. Please don't feel obligated to read it all now."

"Are you kidding me? I'm honored, plus I absolutely love fantasy," he tells me as we finish off the salad and then indulge in fresh mozzarella and tomatoes drizzled with a thick balsamic vinaigrette over shredded basil leaves. This time, Jenna's mother gets up to make a toast.

"I promise I will be brief. I'd like to raise a toast to these two young, brave people. I'm very happy for you that you've decided to take the plunge and commit yourselves to marriage. The commitment is serious enough that not many young people decide to follow through. I wish for you to always remember the early days of your relationship. The butterflies and the anticipation of excitement. These feelings will not always be there. Marriage is like a fire you always have to tend to, don't forget that. Love each other, and don't ever go to bed angry! Cheers!"

"Cheers," everyone echoes.

Jenna runs up to her mother and kisses her cheek. Both women wrap their arms around each other in a tight embrace.

"I just hope this decision is not too rushed. You are right, marriage is a serious commitment, you cannot take it lightly," Donna says loud enough for everyone to hear, but no one decides to engage her.

"To the happy couple," Nina says loudly, drowning out Donna's further comments. Everyone picks up the cheer loudly.

"That's right!"

"Cheers!"

"To you guys!"

"Angelina," Gretchen calls out to me. "How's your book going?"

"It's finished. I just need to get a few more eyes on it before I send it out to agents," I reply.

"This is so exciting. Mitchel, Angelina is a writer, isn't it amazing that she wrote a whole book?" Gretchen addresses Mitchel who stays quiet observing everyone.

"It's quite an accomplishment indeed. Congratulations! What's it about?" he asks.

"It's a romance slash fantasy. I haven't quite worked out the synopsis. But it's about a girl who doesn't know she is part goddess until her father is dead, and she gets to find out her divine purpose as she discovers the realm of gods who live in our modern world, and of course, she is the one who holds the key to saving the world from destruction." I try to explain in a few sentences a book that is a few hundred pages long.

"That sounds very interesting. I actually minored in English and if you need another beta reader, I'd love to read your manuscript," Mitchel offers.

"Thank you so much! Absolutely. Give me your email address and I will send it." In one day, I've found two willing beta readers, and it feels absolutely satisfying.

"Isn't it a bit of a cliché? A chosen one, gets to save the world from destruction." Donna cloaks her rude attack with a sweet and calm sounding philosophical question.

"It's a common plot in fantasy, yes. But people like to read about heroes who save us. It makes us believe that we might be special, that we might have a bigger purpose in life," I reply.

"Oh. I never thought about it that way. But I don't read books, anyway," she cackles.

I feel Kai nudging me, and I look at him. He whispers, "Are you okay?" I nod and smile, I won't let this woman bother me.

"I've actually read Angelina's novel, I think she's quite talented." Kai unexpectedly speaks up. "I think you'll give your boyfriend quite the competition in the fantasy department." I feel a wave of heat rise up, burning up my cheeks. Everyone at the table, all of a sudden gets quiet and turns their attention to me. Why did Kai have to say that? Now I'll have to explain my relationship status to everyone here.

"Who's your boyfriend?" Brian's mother mutters, sipping her wine through a straw.

"Oh, he is Jack Wilson!" Gretchen chirps. "I've read all of his books. I'm such a fan." I smile at my friend and keep my eyes down hoping that everyone will find something else to talk about.

"Oh, yes. I've heard about him. I heard he is quite a charmer. Why isn't he here with you?" The dreadful woman managed to come up with the worst question of the evening, was she doing it on purpose? I sink deep into my seat, clench my hands, and take a long breath, thinking of the answer that will soon have to escape my lips.

"All right everyone, be quiet!" Kai's mother interrupts. "This is my favorite song! Shhh. Listen. Kai, please be a sweetheart and take Angelina for a dance it would remind me of your dad and I dancing to this song." Nina has a wonderful sense for turning the most unpleasant encounter into an unexpected opportunity. Knowing I might not get another chance to escape the table, I push myself away and grab Kai by the hand, tearing him from his drink. I really need to escape this awful woman. A statuesque singer with long braids ending in colorful beads belts out Etta James's "At Last" as we join other couples on the dance floor that was covered by lounge chairs during the day. Kai's hand slips around my waist and pulls me in closer to him, his other hand clasps mine and takes lead of the slow movement of our dance. It's easy to follow him, there is no effort, no guessing where he will step or which way he will turn. I'm not thinking about stepping on his toes, and he masterfully avoids stepping on mine. There is an ease in our movement, and I really enjoy it. With Jack, I was always cautious, we didn't dance so much as he pushed forward and I followed in his steps. I was not a partner who danced to a melody with him, he didn't care if I was there at all, I just made his movements easier so he could march ahead.

"That woman has no filter," Kai murmurs, chuckling.

"I felt like she was drilling me," I say about my frustration as we sway slowly to the music.

"May I ask why Jack isn't here?" Kai asks and I feel his hand clasp mine slightly tighter.

I take a deep breath, thinking over if I should tell him. "We broke up." I decide to be partially honest and not reveal that Jack is the one who broke up with me.

"I'm sorry, I'm sorry that happened. Are you all right?" He looks into my eyes.

"Yeah. I'm fine. It was a long time coming." I shake my head looking at the ground as I feel his gaze drilling into me. "Really, I'm fine."

"Good, good. I'm glad. Not glad that you've broken up, I mean, I'm glad you are okay," he stutters, and I wonder if I've made him uncomfortable. I hope I haven't revealed too much. His arm around my waist draws me closer, so that my cheek almost touches his neck. I breathe in the smell of his skin, and a wave of desire stirs in the pit of my belly. I can't be attracted to him. What will he think of me?

"Let's go back to the table. That woman is leaving." I pull away from Kai's hands and avoid looking into his eyes. I know if I look, I'll blush and make my attraction obvious.

He nods and we go back to the table where Brian's mother has gotten up and loudly announced that her stomach is not used to all this food and she'd better get some rest. Nobody objects, not even her son who is preoccupied with Jenna. He finally notices his mom leaving when she loudly moves her chair. He raises his eyebrows and opens his mouth to say something, but she cuts him off. "You don't need to get up. My arthritis is not so bad today." Her boyfriend leans in and whispers something into her ear. She purses her thin lips and forces a smile, she then wraps her arm around his, and when he says goodnight, they walk away towards their room.

"Who wants a shot of tequila?" Kai's mother breaks the silence.

"Me!" Jenna throws her hand into the air and nudges her fiancé who throws his arm up as well.

"What the hell," Kai chimes in. "Me too."

"Count me in," I add.

"One for me," Mitchel throws in.

"I'm good," Gretchen declines.

Nina places an order for all of us, and when the drinks are brought, we follow Kai's mother's instruction: lick the salt that we've sprinkled at the base of our thumb, then take the shot, and then bite into the lime. Tequila goes down with a pleasant warmth, and once I taste the sourness of the lime, I scrunch my face and shake my body. The band starts playing a fast, rhythmic Caribbean beat, and two female dancers appear from somewhere. They are dressed as if they are going to a carnival. Little two-piece red bathing suits are covered in rhinestones and beads, and their heads are adorned with tall feathers. In the back, the feathers are arranged in a large, colorful semicircle making the women look like exotic birds of the rainforest. Their bodies move rhythmically to the fast beat, their white tooth smiles spread wide across their faces, as they cheer and start coming up to the tables, pulling everyone up to the dance floor. Kai's mother doesn't need an invitation, she throws her hands into the air, gets up from the table and starts dancing to the music. She grabs Kai and I by our hands and pulls us up to follow her. Tequila affects my body fast. I join in on the dance, and soon Gretchen, her daughter, and Jenna are by my side. We are all dancing and hollering and hugging each other. From somewhere, more tequila shots appear. I take one and throw my head back, allowing the fiery liquid to go down my throat. The drums start to beat faster. The dance floor gets crowded. The air is thick with humidity and the breath of people who are letting go of their mundane lives. I run to the table to grab a drink of water, an ice cream is brought out, and I take a big spoonful of it. I close my eyes as I suck on the spoon, letting the ice cream melt in my mouth. Nutmeg flavor is sweet and at the same time spicy, the cold of the ice cream cools me. I open my eyes and see Kai staring at me from the dance floor. He is handsome, he licks his lips as his eyes drill into me. The heat wave washes over me. The hold of his gaze is broken when Jenna runs up to me with another shot.

"Drink with me. I am getting married soon! Woo-hoo!" She shoves the glass into my hand. I don't object and take the shot. She pulls me to the dance floor where we dance again. My body feels light. The music reverberates through me. I'm glad Jack never came. I wouldn't be this free with him around, we would probably just sit at the table observing everyone dancing.

The room starts spinning, the beautiful women with long feathers are all around me. The faces become blurred. I need fresh air. I try to get through the sweaty, moving bodies of the people on the dance floor, but the crowd is closing in on me tighter. I feel my heart picking up the pace, and my lungs are not able to expand and fill up with air fully before I gasp for more air. The humidity pushes down on me and the lights start to dim. My legs refuse to carry my weight, and I know I will hit the floor. The long bright feathers and the fast-moving, sweaty bodies crowd in around me. I try to find a familiar face, but my eyes can't focus. I am embarrassed to scream for help, and the heat of my body is drowned by a cold wave of sweat, the room goes dark and I start to float. I'll hit the floor any second, but instead I am picked up by something and carried out into the night where the air is fresh and easy to breathe. When I'm finally able to look up and make sense of my surroundings, I see Kai's eyes looking at me. He wets a cloth, places it on my forehead and puts a glass of icy water to my lips.

"Hiiiii, Kaiiiii!" I stretch in my drunken voice. "You saved me. You are so nice." I feel overwhelming happiness that he's right next to me. Tequila releases the brakes on my attraction and I blurt, "I like you. I really like you, you know? Like, I've had a crush on you since we were kids."

"No kidding," he replies and smiles. "Here, have some more water." He puts the glass to my lips again and forces me to take a sip. "Waiter, can you please bring a cup of coffee for this young lady," he tells the waiter who comes to check on me.

"I'm fine. I'm really fine. I'm just so happy." I flail my arms, my body feels weightless. I smile and all my gestures feel like they occur in slow motion.

"Do you feel dizzy or nauseous?" he questions me.

"No, I feel happy," I reassure him and put my hands on his shoulders. "You have muscles." I squeeze my hands over the well-defined musculature under his dress shirt. "I have muscles, too." I show off, trying to flex my right arm. The bulge of my bicep is small compared to his, and I laugh at myself.

"Yes, you have very nice muscles. Here, have a sip of coffee, it will sober you up a little." He brings the cup to my face.

It's black, I take a sip and shake my head, pushing the cup away, "I don't like it."

"Don't be a baby, Angelina. You almost passed out, this will help," he presses softly.

I like that he is looking after me. My body sways, and I almost tip and fall forward, but manage to catch myself and sit back. "I am drunk," I say out loud.

"Yes, you are," he chuckles.

"Don't laugh at the drunk, that's not nice," I scold him.

"I promise I won't if you drink some coffee."

"Okay." He brings the small cup to my lips and I take a few sips of the bitter hot liquid. I pucker up my lips and shake my head again when I've had enough.

"Are you feeling better?" Kai asks me again.

"I'm still drunk," I giggle. "But I won't fall down. Do you know why?"

"Why is that?" He keeps entertaining my drunken conversation. "Because you put me on a chair!" I throw my head back laughing, but my body fails to support itself and I fall off the chair.

"Ouch! I fell down!" I announce the obvious. I sit down on the floor like a petulant child. Jenna runs up to me from the dance floor, giggling, and sits right next to me.

"Hiiii! What are you doing on the floor?"

"Jenna, I'm drunk and I fell down," I complain. Finding the situation completely hilarious, I start to laugh.

"Aw! Kai, help her and help me." My friend reaches to her brother who pulls her up. She disappears onto the dance floor as fast as she's appeared. I stretch out my arms, Kai grasps my hands firmly and lifts me towards him. His strength pulls my drunk body into his. My face presses into his defined, firm chest and I breathe in his fresh scent. I feel my eyelids getting heavy and my breathing slows. I am able to carry my weight for a few seconds before my legs go soft and I know they will start to buckle under me. Kai picks me up and throws me over his shoulder as I start sliding down to the floor again.

"I'll take her to the room," he tells someone, and I want to object, but the thought of objection never materializes into a verbal one. The floor starts spinning again as I hang over his shoulders, and I feel that I am dozing off.

# 9.

## KAI

I wake up as the sun streams in through the sheer curtains of my room. Another sunny day in Grenada. I look at my phone, it's only seven in the morning. Yesterday was a wild one. I delivered a baby on the plane, I left Candice, I met Angelina—a grown up and gorgeous Angelina. Last night she was stunning. That dress hugged her body in all the right places. I imagined taking it off her and having sex with her somewhere on a secluded part of the beach, if only she had asked. The thought hardens my morning erection. She'd said she broke up with her boyfriend. Maybe I should stop thinking with my dick and get to know her. She's unlike any girl I've been attracted to. Her body is lean and strong, even muscular. She doesn't wear layers of makeup. She is smart. She has written a book, a damn good book, at that. I reach out for my laptop and open the Word document she sent me yesterday. I am almost halfway through. After I'd put her to bed, I couldn't fall asleep, or rather, couldn't stop reading and go to sleep. She's invented such a colorful world—the details, the smells, were described so beautifully I almost sensed them. I have to tell her she really needs to publish it. Maybe there is something I can do; I have a friend that might help.

The girl is talented. I read twenty more pages of her manuscript, and the clock shows 7:40 a.m. I get up, wash, get dressed in shorts and a T-shirt, and walk outside. I'm hit by the warm air. The resort is quiet, most people don't wake up this early on vacation, only the birds squabbling over something disturbs the quietness of the place. I take a brisk walk to the gym. The space is rather big, with many machines available for the physically active. The weights and the Swiss balls are organized by the wall. I put my headphones on and turn on Armin Van Buren. I step on the elliptical and start a pace that gradually increases until I am exhausted and have to stop to catch my breath. Armin changes to Tiesto as I start working out my legs. I hate leg day, but it makes me stop obsessing over Angelina for now. My muscles are burning, the workout is exhausting and invigorating. I feel the blood pumping through my veins. I take a deep breath and since there is no one in the gym, I strike a pose checking out my arms, legs, and then lift up my shirt to see that my abs are looking mighty defined. All right, my personal life is in shambles, but at least my body is rocking. I leave the gym energized and satisfied. I circle the small man-made pond on the way to my room, the windows of Angelina's room are still closed, just as I'd left them last night. I'd put her to bed and took off her shoes. I'd decided it was best to leave her in her dress. I didn't want to make her feel vulnerable when she woke up, probably not remembering the end of the night. I'd stared at her face as she slept, her breathing calm and deep, her lips soft and full, calling me to kiss them. I'd moved the strands of hair from her face before rushing out of her room feeling pathetic for ogling the girl that I've known since she was a kid.

I get to my room and take a long, cool shower. Somehow the proximity of Angelina just behind the wall is keeping my body on fire. My mind plays over the images of her face, the curves of her body, the details of her smile that I've never noticed before. I turn the water all the way to cold and gasp as the icy shower makes me shiver. I can only handle a few seconds of this temperature and shut it off so I can get dressed and head to the hospital to handle some paperwork.

I knock on Angelina's sliding door. I am just checking to see that she is okay after falling so drunk last night. When there is no answer and I don't hear any sound, I knock again. There is no answer again. I begin to worry, maybe I shouldn't have left her all by herself. I knock again, and this time call out, "Angelina, it's Kai. Are you okay?" But still, there is only silence. My concern for her well-being grows faster than my accelerated heart rate, I decide to enter her room through the sliding door, the only entrance available into each room on the ground floor. I have her key card in my pocket from when I had to get into her room last night.

I push the door to the side and enter the dark room. The smell of alcohol is heavy in the air. "Angelina," I call out, announcing my entrance. There is no answer coming from the bed. It takes me just a few steps to reach it. Angelina is laying in a cloud of blankets in the same position I'd left her in last night. Certainly, she would have moved by now, this is not normal. "Angelina?" She doesn't stir, I can't see if she is breathing. Fuck, I shouldn't have left her by herself. I climb by her side and shake her shoulder, she doesn't respond. I take my fist and rub it firmly over her sternum. This is painful, but it would wake anyone up if they were alive.

"Ouch," she stirs and her face scrunches, but she doesn't open her eyes and rolls to the side away from me.

"Thank God, you're alive. You gave me a fucking heart attack."

"What? Where am I?" Her voice is raspy and confused.

"You're in your room."

"What happened?" She covers her eyes with her palms, pressing them in.

"You got drunk last night."

"I did?" She pauses, lying completely still. "Oh my God! I did. This is so embarrassing." She buries her head under the blanket. "How did I get to my room?" I hear the muffled sound of her voice.

"I brought you back."

"You did?" She pulls her head out from under the blanket and sits up. Her hair is a complete mess and her eyes are covered in smudged mascara, but despite it, she still looks pretty. She looks around the room and then looks over herself. "I'm still dressed."

"Yes, you are. It would have been easy to take advantage of you last night, but my mother raised me right," I tease her, and her cheeks blush as she swallows hard.

I walk over to the mini fridge and get out a bottle of water, she must be parched after last night's drinking. "Here, drink the whole thing, you are probably dehydrated." I hand it to Angelina, and she puts the bottle to her mouth, taking long, deep gulps until the whole bottle is empty. The thin plastic crackles in her hand, a few drops drip from her lips, to her chin, and cascade down to her chest, disappearing between her breasts. I want to slide my hand there and follow that drop. I get up from the bed and walk towards the sliding door to distract myself. "I am going to head to the hospital in a little while. I wanted to see if you'd like to come with me to see Deja."

"Yeah," she replies slowly, looking around the room. "Let me take a shower and get dressed. I think I can be ready in twenty minutes." She slowly climbs out of bed and goes in the direction of the shower, massaging her temples, swaying.

"This is so embarrassing. What does your mother think? And Jenna? I'm the maid of honor, and I had to be carried out of the party," she mumbles.

"Don't worry, everyone was letting loose, including my mother and Jenna. They won't think any less of you." I hear Angelina turn on the water in the shower, and I decide to give her privacy to get ready. "I'll wait for you by the Captain's Deck, they are serving breakfast there today. We can eat, and then head out to the hospital."

"Yes, sure. I'll see you there," Angelina replies and I head outside. I get a table on the veranda of the restaurant, and she meets me in twenty minutes as promised. I am surprised to actually see her make it on time. Candice would say she was almost ready, and it would still take her an hour to actually be ready. Angelina has pulled her hair into a ponytail and dressed in a simple tank, gray shorts, and flip-flops. She is wearing aviator sunglasses, protecting herself from bright sunlight, but as soon as she reaches me, she takes them off. She squints and moans, the light probably seems harsh in her hungover state.

"Come, you'll feel better after having some food." I get up and pull out a chair for her.

"And coffee."

"Yes, and coffee," I chuckle.

The Captain's Deck is a quaint place on the second floor of a French Quarter-looking building. The veranda doors are wide open and offer a view of the ocean. A pleasant, salty scent is refreshing, no air conditioning is necessary. Angelina orders coffee, and I get myself orange juice. While the waiter is getting our beverages, we go check out the food and fill our plates. When we get back to the table, I am surprised by the amount of food Angelina has on her plate. The girl is certainly not on a diet. She has eggs, bacon, hash browns, a few pastries, and a bowl of fruit. Candice would always complain that she needed to lose weight and would follow some crazy diet of eating something weird or very little. Angelina keeps surprising me by how different she is from my ex. It feels good to be around her.

"What?" she questions me, as I probably spend too long staring at her plate.

"You've got a lot of food on your plate. You're going to eat all of it?"

"Yeah." She takes a bite of her bacon strip. "I love breakfast. I could probably have breakfast food for any meal. Couldn't you?"

"I guess I could."

"I do like lunch, too. I have to have a good breakfast and lunch, and I rarely have dinner, unless there is really good dessert, then I'll eat in the evening as well." She picks up a forkful of scrambled eggs and puts it in her mouth. This girl is something else, I have never met a girl who enjoys food so much and doesn't comment how it will affect her figure.

"I can take you to the Turtle Cove for lunch, then. It's right in the center of town, and they make great chicken there. It's not far from the hospital, we used to go there all the time when I was a student in medical school."

"That's right. Jenna told me you went to school somewhere on the island." She nods her head and takes a sip of coffee. Closing her eyes, she lets out a very loud moan. "I really needed this coffee."

"That's why she decided to have the wedding here. She visited me a few times and really loved Grenada." I try not to smile watching Angelina eat, I don't want her to think I am laughing at her, but she just looks so happy.

"I actually can't believe that Jenna is getting married. She is so adventurous, I never thought she'd settle down," she quips.

"Well, Brian is an amazing guy. I think he is an anchor that she really needs in her life."

"I agree. They make a cute couple." She halves a cupcake horizontally, then puts a bottom half on top of the icing, making the cupcake a sweet sandwich.

"What are you doing, you crazy person?" I inquire in fascination.

"What? The icing always gets on my nose and this way it doesn't." She shrugs her shoulders at her common sense eating of the cupcake and then takes a bite.

"You're a weird girl, Angelina. I like you, I like you," I repeat myself, a nervous habit that I can't seem to control when I am around this woman.

"Okay, I am done," she announces when everything she had on her plate has been eaten.

"Let's go to the hospital, then," I say and we leave the restaurant and go to the front desk where I request a taxi.

"Are you going to the hospital just because of Deja?" Angelina inquires.

"No. I need to pick up my contract," I explain.

"I'm jealous you'll be working in this paradise." She looks at the surroundings and then puts on her sunglasses. The receptionist motions us to come to the driveway where a compact white van pulls up and a short skinny guy rushes out to open the sliding door for us. I let Angelina get in first. She smiles at me, then looks out the window.

"I'm excited," she tells me.

"Me too, me too." Damn it. She will think I am a complete idiot for speaking this way.

The van takes off slowly, rolling down the steep hill out of the resort. We pass by the airport, and the dirt road finally changes into a paved roadway that takes workers and tourists right into this first all-inclusive resort on the island. Angelina keeps looking out the window, taking in the view of the tropical greens and the little houses that are covered in bright paint colors trying to outdo each other. There are no tall buildings on the island, nothing is competing with the natural beauty of this rain forest paradise. It takes us half an hour to reach town, the streets are busy with natives, tourists, and medical students. The van follows the curved road around the marina where the ships come in to unload their cargo.

"Look at that boat," I point to a gray superyacht that looks like a spaceship. "That belonged to Steve Jobs. His wife keeps it here for now."

"Wow. It looks so ... so futuristic ... and so large." Angelina stares out her window. I linger over her shoulder, breathing in her pleasant scent. When she suddenly turns to face me, I cannot take my eyes off of her lips. They look red and soft and like they want to be kissed … right now … by me. My illogical thought is interrupted when we hit a speed bump. Angelina jerks up with the van and then laughs at the unexpected bump in the road. I pray she didn't notice my desire to kiss her. That would be too weird for both of us. She just broke up with her boyfriend. I don't want to push myself on her, she would probably think I am taking advantage of her.

We pay the taxi driver after he stops at the entrance to the hospital. The light orange building with a coral pointy rooftop doesn't look so large from where we are, but when viewed from a boat it's a massive fortress, sitting in a mountain wall of the island.

"Come this way. We can go to obstetrics first to see Deja and I'll stop by the office to grab my paperwork." I want to reach out and touch her, but hold myself back and instead just nod my head in the direction of the elevators. She gives me a small smile and then follows me. When we arrive on the maternity floor, we are met by the smell of babies. The receptionist by the secured doors takes our names and records which patient we are visiting before buzzing us in where women are recovering and where the babies are introduced to the world or in Deja's case where he is already an experienced newborn.

We walk down the hall and find the room where the receptionist told us Deja is located. When we enter, Deja is sitting up in her bed with her baby nursing at her breast. She quickly covers up as I look away, I feel embarrassed seeing her engorged breasts even though I helped deliver her baby not twenty-four hours ago.

"Hi!" she says softly, gifting us a wide smile. "This is Gabriel." Deja stretches out her hand to Angelina and pulls her closer.

"Aw! He's beautiful!" I hear Angelina coo, softly touching the little one's head. Deja then waves for me to come closer. When I come up closer, I take a look at the human I helped bring into the world. He is small and has a lot of hair, so much that his mother was able to comb it and part it. His lips are still puckered and trying to suck on the breast that is no longer there, a drop of milk slowly moves down his cheek. He must have realized that his meal was cut short, he scrunches up his little face and lets out the tiniest of cries. His toothless mouth opens up and the cry becomes louder, demanding to be fed immediately. The women giggle.

"He has been feeding nonstop. That's why he probably came out so early, so he can eat." Deja sighs, lifting the gown and putting the baby to her breast. He quiets immediately.

I understand that nursing is completely natural, but it makes me uncomfortable, not because the breasts are somehow sexual. Not at all. This is a very intimate moment, and one I am not supposed to be a part off.

"Congratulations, Deja. I am happy you're both doing well. We just wanted to stop by and see if you needed anything."

Deja lifts her smiling face and looks at Angelina and I.

"Thank you, from the bottom of my heart. I'm so happy you and Angelina happened to be on the plane with me and helped me bring this child into the world. He'll be baptized as soon as we leave the hospital, and my family and I want to ask if you can join the celebration?"

Angelina and I look at each other. I have never been to a baptism before.

"It would be an honor for us to have you with us as this child is introduced to the Lord," she presses gently.

"Are these the two angels who helped bring my son into the world?" a voice questions loudly behind us.

When I turn around, a smiling woman who is the carbon copy of Deja is staring at Angelina and I. She then comes up and gives a hug to me first and then embraces Angelina. Angelina and I look at each other first, she shrugs her shoulders, points to the woman and then to Deja, both look-alike women break out laughing.

"This is my twin sister, Clarice," Deja explains. "Yes, sister, this is Doctor Kai and his friend Angelina, who helped bring this hungry child into the world." She smiles at the baby who stops nursing, his head thrown back lightly, eyes closed, he is full, at least for now.

Clarice comes up to her sister and stretches her arms out. "Come here, my son." She picks up the baby and puts him over her shoulder, patting his back. In a few moments, the child lets out the loudest of burps while still staying asleep. The women let out a synchronized, "Aw!"

"Do you want to hold him?" Clarice asks. I shake my head and my hands vigorously. I've never held a child before, and he is so small. But Angelina nods agreeably and stretches out her arms. Clarice places the bundle into her hands. This woman keeps surprising me. There is a peaceful aura around her, she is confident in who she is, there is no pretentiousness. I enjoy her drama-free personality.

"He likes you," Deja tells Angelina, commenting on how quiet the baby is in her arms. Angelina smiles while rocking the baby gently.

"He's just precious. It's quite a story he'll have for the rest of his life, being born on a plane," says Angelina while staring at his face and all the women laugh.

"He's a true gift, this child. I thank my sister for giving him to me," Clarice comes over and takes the baby out of Angelina's arms. "My sister and I have one difference. I can't have children of my own. We've tried everything, my husband and I. Doctors, acupuncture, healers, prayers, medications, and all for nothing." She strokes the cheek of the baby with her finger. "My sister saw my suffering and desire to be a mother, so she agreed to be our surrogate. Isn't it the greatest gift of love?" She looks at Deja, smiles, reaches for her hand, and gives it a tight squeeze.

"It's beautiful. I had no idea," Angelina says softly, clasping her hands over her chest. "I was so confused, Deja, when you said that he was not yours, but now it makes perfect sense. Kai, isn't it amazing?"

The surprising revelation is truly touching. I nod to Angelina and smile at the sisters.

"Deja, I'm happy you are doing well and truly grateful for inviting me to Gabriel's baptism. Here is my phone number, please reach out at any time. I have to go, I have some business to attend to. Ladies, congratulations. Gabe, buddy, you stay awesome," I gently rub the baby's head.

"Angelina, do you want to come with me, or do you want me to get you once I am done?" I ask.

"I'll stay here a bit longer and then wait for you down-stairs, okay?" she replies.

"Sure, sure." I leave the women and head to the third floor to collect the packet with my contract. As I walk the halls of the hospital, I struggle to decide if I should tell

Angelina about liking her. I'd better talk to my sister first, she surely will be able to make things clearer.

The young secretary in the main office is pleasant, she smiles when seeing me, "Doctor Gable! How are you today? When are you starting here, already?"

"I just have to sign my contract and then I'll be able to get my schedule."

"Here you go, then." She passes me an orange manila envelope. "We are all excited to have you here."

"Thank you! I'm looking forward to it, as well. Have a great day!"

"You as well, Dr. Gable." She waves to me and gets back to typing something on her keyboard.

I roll up the envelope and head downstairs where Angelina is already waiting for me. She beams when she sees me.

"What an amazing relationship those sisters have! Can you imagine doing something like that?"

"Ha-ha, no, I can't imagine getting pregnant for my sister."

"You're so stupid," she nudges me.

"I mean, I guess, if my sister—God forbid—ever needed a kidney or bone marrow transplant, I would do it without hesitation."

"That's just amazing to me. I wish I had a sibling to share that kind of love and connection with." She looks down at her feet and rubs her arms as if she is cold. I want to hug her tight in that moment, so she feels loved, but would she want that hug from me?

"Come, I'll take you to the place where they make the best chicken on the island," I give a quick rub of her shoulder. She nods and we step out into the sunny day.

The small restaurant is a few streets down from the hospital and we reach it within a few minutes. The place is two stories tall. The first floor is occupied by a grocery and the second floor, with a large wraparound veranda, is taken up by the restaurant. It's a common gathering place for medical students and hospital staff. The menu is small, and the food is simple with a homemade feel and local flavors.

"I love this place! Look at the view!" Angelina gasps, grabbing my arm and squeezing it tight. "Can we sit right over here?" She points to the table right against the banister overlooking the ocean.

"Of course, of course." Her touch is pleasant, and I want it to linger longer, but she lets go and moves effortlessly between the chairs to the table that promises a beautiful view. I pause, letting her go ahead. She is graceful, effortless, hot—fuck, I want her.

"Let's go! What are you doing?" Angelina startles me from my convoluted thoughts.

"I'm coming, I'm coming, sorry."

The waiter appears from the kitchen as soon as we take our seats. He gives us menus, I order a Coke, Angelina asks for sparkling water.

"So, you're saying they have the best chicken here?" she asks me, looking intently at the menu.

"Yes. It's definitely a must try." I offer my advice as my mouth becomes watery remembering the flavors of the juicy meat.

"Okay, I trust you. I'll have chicken. What are you going to have?"

"I think I'll have a burger with cod."

"Ooh, that sounds delicious, too." Angelina licks her lips, and I can't help but stare at her mouth. I want to reach over the table, pull her towards me, and kiss her.

"I'll share, so you can try it." That is as close as her mouth will get to mine. Why am I so attracted to her?

The food comes out fast while we chat about the beautiful weather.

My burger is accompanied by sweet potato fries, and her chicken has a side of coleslaw. Angelina tears off the drumstick and starts eating. "Mmm, this is the best chicken," she confirms after she puts the bone down and licks her fingers.

"Here, have a bite." I pass her my burger, before I've taken a bite.

"Are you sure? You didn't even try it yet," she hesitates.

"Yeah, go ahead, have the first bite." She grabs the burger and takes a bite. I can't help but chuckle. I enjoy watching her eat.

"This is delicious, too." She passes the burger back to me. "I wish I had more time to explore the island and try all the different restaurants. I really like it here." Angelina looks at the ocean, propping her chin up with her hands. Wind gently blows the strands of hair from her face. "I wish every day was like this." She picks a small piece of chicken and puts it in her mouth.

"Like what?"

"Simple, fulfilling, hopeful."

"Stay here, then," I blurt out unexpectedly. She transfers her gaze to me, staring intently, she then takes a deep breath and replies, "I wish, but what would I do here?"

"Write." I take a bite of my burger.

"Ha-ha," she throws her head back, "maybe if I were a best-selling author I would."

"You will be. I'm telling you, submit your manuscript, there are a lot of people who'd love it."

"Even if that was so. I don't have anyone here."

"I'm here." I want to get to know her, not just like a friend, but more. If only we had time, more time.

Her cheeks blush, she wipes her mouth with a napkin, takes a long sip of her water and then looks at me, her eyebrows pressed together. "Don't play with me, Kai."

"I'm not, I'm really not. It's weird, I know …. I've known you forever, but seeing you now, it's different … I like you … I really do." I decide to come clean. This girl doesn't deserve any games. I know I can be straightforward with her. She is staring at me, quiet … what is she thinking?

"Kai … I was drunk last night … and I told you things …." I swallow hard as the walls of my throat suddenly feel dry. "I said, I liked you … but …"

"Ha, you're using past tense quite a bit … hmm … I understand … I'm sorry, I'm sorry I said anything, let's just forget it." I take a sip of my Coke, little bubbles of gas erupt on my tongue, evaporating as fast as my confidence. Just as I am about to call for the waiter to bring the bill, she reaches for my hand and takes it into hers.

"I'm sorry, I just don't think it's the right time for us. You're staying here, I'm leaving, and as much as I'd want for us to have a chance, I don't think it's in the cards," she says.

"Don't worry. I told you, just forget about it." Hell, why did I decide to bring this up? She is totally right, what was I thinking? I will have to avoid her now for the rest of the time here, as to not make her uncomfortable. The waiter comes with the bill, I pay in cash, and we go downstairs to find a cab to take us to the resort. She avoids looking at me, and I am embarrassed to face her.

I hail a cab, and a small, beat-up sedan pulls up next to us. A smiling driver asks where we are heading and waves us in to get inside. The cab is clean with the seats covered in colorful, custom-made covers, the Caribbean music playing on the radio brings an atmosphere of vacation joy. The driver volunteers information about the island as he drives through the streets.

"All these buildings were destroyed by Ivan ...." He points to the homes which were rebuilt after the devastation caused by Hurricane Ivan. The streets that are now lined with colorful homes would never give away that there was any destruction in 2004. "Did you try oil down yet?" He looks at me in the rearview mirror, grinning from ear to ear. I've heard of this national dish cooked in coconut milk.

"No, I haven't had the chance," I reply. I don't know if Angelina is listening to him, she is looking out the window. God, she doesn't even want to face me now. She must hate me for spoiling this trip for her. I am such a shmuck.

"You have to try it, it is reaaaal good," he chuckles. "All the beaches are public in Grenada. Yes, it is true, you can go to any beach and no one will say anything. And all Grenadians know how to swim. It is true." He punctuates just in case I don't believe him. "Did you go diving yet?" He keeps chatting. He doesn't wait for my reply, instead continues to inform that, "We have the first underwater sculpture park." He lifts his right index finger into the air and wags it, accentuating the importance of such a tourist attraction.

"We are getting certified tomorrow in scuba. I hope we will get to see it." I glance at Angelina, but she still sits completely turned away from me, staring out the window. The driver keeps up his free tour guide accompaniment as I stare out my window at the blue ocean that disappears into the horizon. I'll probably hear from my sister regarding this blunder. I'll have to talk to her so she doesn't say anything to my mother, I couldn't bear her getting on my case about this. We soon reach the resort, I pay the cab driver and tip him for his entertainment. He smiles big, revealing white teeth with a gap between the top two front teeth and waves goodbye.

Angelina opens her door and doesn't look at me, I can't see her eyes through her dark sunglasses. "Thanks, Kai for the lovely morning and lunch. I'll go rest in my room." She backs away, and then walks off rapidly before I am able to say anything else to her. You really screwed up this time, buddy. I frequently have girls fight for my attention, but none have ever run from me, until Angelina—and she is the woman I want to stay.

I ponder for a moment what I should do, the sun is still high and it's too hot to lay out at the beach. I need to talk to someone, and my sister is always able to talk sense into me. They're staying at one of the villas, I decide to try my luck and see if she is in.

When I knock on the door of her villa, I immediately hear fast steps that I know belong to my sister.

"Who is it?" she asks at the same time as she opens the door.

"Don't you think you should wait to hear the person respond before you open the door?" I tease her, but she rolls her eyes at me. "What do you want?" She stands in the doorway, not inviting me in.

"Nothing much, just wanted to chat, see how things are. What, you don't want to talk to your older brother now?" I try to sound upbeat. She squints her eyes at me, folds her arms over her chest, and taps her right foot. After a few seconds she nods for me to come in. Brian is lounging by their private pool outside, a bottle of beer stands by his side.

"It's just my brother," Jenna yells as she leads me outside. She lays down on the lounger by her fiancé and takes a sip out of his bottle.

"Hey, buddy," her soon-to-be husband greets me with a firm handshake. "Beer?"

"Sure." A cold one would feel nice in this heat, and I can pace myself better taking sips instead of stuttering through what I want to talk to Jenna about. My sister makes an attempt to get up and go inside to get my beer, but her fiancé stops her. "Don't worry, honey boo, I'll get it."

"Love you, honey bear." She gazes at him and scrunches up her nose. When he leaves, I can't help but tease her, "Honey boo? Honey bear?"

"Oh, shut up. You're just jealous." She sticks her tongue at me.

"Ha, of what?"

"You have no one who calls you anything cute." She stings me, and I won't admit it to her, but it does hurt. Brian comes out with a bottle of Corona and hands it to me. I hesitate to bring anything up about Angelina around him. I've known the dude just for a few months. As if feeling my hesitation to speak up, he takes off his shirt and jumps into the pool.

"Are you guys ready for your nuptials?" I start off with a topic that is far away from my interest.

"Why are you being so weird?" Jenna looks at me from under her brows. "What happened? What did you do?"

"Why do you say that? Can't I be interested in the wedding of my sister?" I take a sip of my beer, trying to appear relaxed and truthful.

"No, I know you ..." She points her finger at me and squints again. "You want something. Spill it."

"I just have been thinking ..."

"That is a dangerous activity." She takes a sip of her beer, giggles and rolls her eyes.

"No, wait, really. I'm very happy for you and Brian. And since breaking it off with Candice, I've really been thinking about my own future. What do I want in a relationship? You know?"

"That is one smart decision you've made, dumping that plastic chick. Why do you always go for these shallow pretty girls? I just don't get it." She lights up when Brian sends her an air kiss, and she blows one to him and then waves. "Hi, honey boo! How is the water?" she calls out to him and he splashes her lightly as she squeals loudly.

"I don't know why ..." I take another long gulp of my beer and then continue. "I understand that these pretty girls are empty. They are just great to look at. I want to change. I want to have a meaningful relationship. I think I found a girl that I want to try and have a real relationship with, one that would lead to something meaningful."

"And who would that lucky gal be?" she turns towards me, smiling, probably ready with another comeback. I keep my face calm, this is serious. I want to know what she thinks without the bullshit jabs and jokes. I think over if I should reveal my interest in Angelina. My sister interrupts with a stern, "No! Don't even think that! I forbid you to go after her." She wags her finger as she sits up in her lounge chair and faces me.

"How do you know who I'm talking about?" I sit up straight, my body is tense with anticipation of an argument.

"I'm not stupid. There is only one girl here who is completely different from your whorish girlfriends. She's smart, she's a hard worker, she has opinions, she's a writer, she's strong, and she's giving and kind. No, I will not let you test your sudden desire to have a meaningful relationship with Angelina. Find someone else, leave my friend alone." When she is done, her breathing is fast, her nostrils flare.

"I don't want to test anything on Angelina. I don't want to hurt her."

"Well, find yourself another bimbo then." She gets up and walks to the pool and then back to her lounger sitting opposite of me.

"Kai, you are my brother and I love you, but Angelina, she is my friend." She puts her right hand over her heart. "How would you imagine your relationship with her? You've accepted a job here. She lives in New York. You will have a great few days, she'll fall for you. She's always liked you—since middle school—and then she would need to leave you here. What then?"

I take a long sip of my beer; my sister's logic is solid. I know long-distance relationships are doomed, but if I don't try to change Angelina's mind, I will forever regret it. "I don't know Jenna ... I can't explain it ... she's like no other girl … I wouldn't do anything to hurt her on purpose. I told her already I like her." I swallow hard and stare at my sister.

"You are so dumb. Why are you here then, telling me all of this?"

"Listen, I realize I should've talked to you first. Angelina wasn't excited about my revelation, but I think … I think if you approve … she, she might take a chance on me."

"What would you say to all of this, Brian?" She turns to her fiancé, who has propped his chin on his fists stacked on one another on the side of the pool, while his feet kick the water slowly so he can float. He shrugs his shoulders at first, looks at us and then says, "You're both making decisions for another person. I think she is an adult, and even though you have the best of intentions, you have to let her make the decision."

My sister and I both stay quiet. Brian is right. Why am I discussing Angelina and her decisions? I need to show her that my intentions are serious and let her decide how to proceed. She is not the kind of a girl who makes rush decisions. Yes, I could totally fail, but I'll regret it if I don't try to change Angelina's mind.

"That's why I fell in love with you, honey boo. You always say the right thing," my sister praises. He pulls himself out of the swimming pool, runs up to Jenna, picks her up and runs back to the swimming pool with my sister hollering, "Don't you dare. Ahhh! Don't you dare!" He doesn't listen and jumps into the water with my sister in his arms. They both reappear in the water, beaming, my sister splashing Brian's face.

"All right, guys! I'm gonna go." I wave and leave them be.

"Kai." I turn around when my sister calls my name. "I'll talk to Angelina. Just don't do anything stupid." She wags her finger and I nod in appreciation. I can still hear my sister's joyous laughter when I close the door of their villa behind me.

I have to speak to Angelina as well, just one more time.

# 10.

## GRETCHEN

I wake up early, as always. I don't have to check the clock. I know it is 6:15 a.m. My body has gotten into the habit of early rising since I've had Hailey. First, it was the morning feedings, then it was getting up and getting ready for my school and taking her to daycare. Then, it was getting up to start work and getting her ready for school. I lie quietly, trying not to disturb the pleasant silence of this vacation paradise. For the first time in a long while, I don't have to rush to take a shower, get breakfast ready, or pack a lunch. There are no dishes in the sink, no dirty laundry to wash, or clean ones to fold. There is no screaming about the homework to be done, and no thinking of what to make for dinner, or of what drama awaits with my ex. For the first time in a long while, there is a man who is giving me attention, and he isn't scared of me and Hailey.

Am I being selfish even thinking of Mitchel? I am first of all Hailey's mother, she is my number one priority. But she kind of likes Mitchel, and maybe if I've found a man who will treat me—us—right, it will give her a boost of confidence, a male role model for her future. Of course, she'd have to approve of the relationship ... I hope she would ... Mitchel is such a gentleman. I didn't even know such men exist. He stood up from the table when I left to go to the bathroom. He invited me for a dance and asked Hailey's permission first. He even chatted with her about video games and she conversed back, she didn't think he was some fake old man. Anyone over thirty for her is old.

I pick up my phone from the nightstand to check the time. It is 6:30 a.m. I want to let Hailey sleep a bit longer, so I open up my Instagram. My feed is filled with contradictory images of fitness models calling me to just start working out and pictures of decadent mousse cakes and beautifully plated restaurant dishes. I sigh. It's tough to be fit when all of your time is taken up by work, dealing with a preteen, and stress. I pause my scroll when the image of my ex-husband pops up on my screen. His eyes are glazed over, he looks sweaty with a shirt unbuttoned down to his belly. His hand is dangling over the shoulder of a blond girl, who stares into the camera puckering her lips. She is new. I haven't seen her before on his social media. She's skinny. Probably has no kids and is still in college. Her hand is squeezing his chin, nails long with rhinestones, the girl is definitely not working very hard with those hands.

The picture's tagline is 'Party Time in Las Vegas. Come get your freak on now! #partyanimals with @candy_girl.'

Did this schmuck ditch his own daughter so he could fly to Las Vegas to schmooze with his girlfriend? I scroll through more pictures which show the drunken couple taking shots, dancing, kissing … disgusting. I close Instagram and stare at the ceiling. I know Hailey is going to see this. She will be devastated. I rub my eyes, trying to come up with the pep talk that I have to force myself to give to make her father somehow seem like a decent human being. God! What am I going to say? Maybe I'll try to keep her busy so she will stay off social media. Is it even possible? That girl is glued to her phone. The gratification of instant replies is addicting. I wish she didn't have the phone at all, but it was the judge's order. She must have it to keep in touch with her father. Only, he never calls or replies to her texts. I have to nag him to send her a message.

She finally starts to stir and stretches her arms above her head. Her eyes are still closed, but there is a smile on her face. She looks so much like her father: the color of her hair is the same raven black, an identical hairline with a widow's peak, the shape of her lips has passed down to her from his side, even the shape of her fingernails and toenails are all his. But she is my child, my baby. I will forever love her and protect her.

"Good morning, sleepy head," I greet her, a child who is growing up too fast.

"Morning, Mommy." Her morning voice is cracking. She turns on her side and puts her hands under her cheek, staring directly at me. I do the same. Her eyes move over my face, examining it slowly as if seeing it for the first time.

"Mommy, you are so pretty," she whispers. The unexpected compliment shrinks my always-present mommy guilt and inflates my hope that everything might turn out to be all right for the two of us.

"Thank you, honey. That's very nice of you to say. I love you very much."

"Can I come to you?" she asks while still staring at me and smiling.

"Of course, munchkin. Come." I lift my blanket, and she springs from her bed and climbs into mine. She turns her back to me, I wrap my arm around her little body, and clasp her hand tight. I put my nose into her hair and take a deep breath. I think I can still smell her baby smell or maybe it's just the shampoo that she is using; nevertheless, it reminds me of her soft baby skin, her helplessness and total need for me to be near her.

"I love you, my beautiful girl," I say into her ear, and then place a kiss onto her head. This moment of closeness is so rare I hope she remembers it. I know I will treasure it, returning to it when she is screaming and yelling that I am a bad mother.

"I love you, too. Mommy? Why did Dad leave us?" she asks the question that freezes my breathing and sends my mind racing trying to come up with the right answer. I know she will listen to me now. She will analyze every word and intonation of what I am saying.

I breathe out slowly and then begin. "Your daddy and I, we were young when we met. Still in high school. But we loved each other very, very much … and then we had you. I was just sixteen, your dad seventeen. It was hard to be young parents, but we love you so incredibly much, and we couldn't imagine our lives without you." I pause to see if she will say anything back, but she stays still and silent, so I decide to go on. "Your dad had a lot of dreams, he wanted to be an architect or an engineer, but he had to start working so he could provide for our family, so he wasn't able to go to school that he wanted. And I think as he grew older, he just got frustrated that he wasn't as successful as some of his friends. He started to feel that maybe if he didn't have the family, his life would be different."

"So, he didn't want us anymore?"

"I think he's just very confused. I know he loves you very, very much, he just doesn't love me. Sometimes, adults, they fall out of love with each other. You know? And it's okay. That's life. It doesn't always go according to plan. We learn from it, and we become stronger."

"Do you still love Daddy?"

"I will always love him, because without him, I wouldn't have you." I squeeze her tighter.

"No, not like that … you know what I mean."

"I'm afraid not, Hailey, but he will always be in my life." I breathe slowly, as quietly as possible, afraid to miss any stirring, a sigh or a whimper that may give me an idea of what my little girl is thinking. "Does it make you sad, Hailey?"

She shakes her head no, and then says, "I was sad when you and Daddy were fighting, but I think you and Daddy are happier now, but I still wish I had a family." She sighs and presses her curled body closer to mine. I give her a tight squeeze of a hug.

"You do have a family. You just have parents who live in different houses. Think of it this way: you can celebrate all the holidays twice and your birthday twice and get twice the amount of presents." I have to find a positive for my baby in this unfortunate situation.

"But what happens when you find a boyfriend? Do I have to call him Dad?" she continues her inquiry.

"No, honey, no. Of course not. The only man you call Dad is your dad. And why are you asking about that? I am not planning on having a boyfriend."

"Mitchel is kind of nice. He might be a good boyfriend for you." Her tone goes up at the end of each sentence, she is revealing her observations to me and at the same time, questioning if they are correct.

"He is very nice. But I think we should just enjoy this vacation, celebrate Jenna's wedding, and not think about any boys."

Hailey turns toward me, her face so close I feel her breath on my face. She moves her eyes slowly over my face, her hands touch my hair, running her fingers through it. "Mommy, I think you should take Mitchel on a date. I think he likes you, and I think it's okay if you like him back."

"You are such a silly goose, Hailey." I try to make light of her serious proposition.

"No, Mommy, I think you need to give him a chance, really ... I like him."

"Okay, missy. How about we get up, brush our teeth, go get breakfast, and if Mitchel is there, we will invite him to have breakfast with us. Does that sound like a good idea?"

She nods her head vigorously, and I tickle her sides just as I used to when she was little. She bursts out laughing, throwing her head back in an act of pure joy.

"Mommy, Mommy stop. All right, all right, I am going to brush my teeeeeth."

"What, what is it that you say? I can't hear youuuuuu." I keep on tickling Hailey.

"I ... will ... goooo ... brush ... my teeeeth," she screeches, laughing and arching her back, trying to get away from me. I stop and pull her towards me, hugging her tight once more. I feel her heart racing, its drumming rhythmically, resonating against my chest. Her breathing is fast and she is warm from all the squirming. I hold her tight and place a long kiss on her forehead.

"I love you, Hailey. Always. Remember that," I whisper into her ear. I feel her nodding and she squeezes her arms tight around me.

"All right, now let's go and brush our teeth." I pat her bottom, and she jumps out of bed and races to the bathroom, skipping and hopping.

I swing my legs down to the floor and stretch my arms up. This is a good morning. I wish there were more mornings like this for me and her.

Once washed up and dressed, we head out for breakfast. The cozy restaurant by night is turned into the breakfast buffet. We are seated near the window by a pleasant, plump waiter who greets us smiling. I place an order for coffee and my daughter asks for orange juice, and we then go to the buffet to fill our plates. When we get to the room filled with the smells of maple syrup, bacon, and pancakes, we see Mitchel staring at the food while holding an empty plate. When he sees us, his brows go up and his eyes light up. He chuckles, showing off his empty plate.

"I'm not used to so many options. It seems I can't decide on what to eat."

I hear Hailey sigh loudly as she takes a few steps towards Mitchel and grabs his plate.

"Come, I'll help you chose." She walks slowly around the central counter that has cheese, fruit, and cold cuts, and then heads to the counters against the wall that have hot food: hard-boiled eggs, scrambled eggs, bacon, sausage links, hash browns, French toast, pancakes, oatmeal, and various juices. Once she's examined all the food, she turns to Mitchel, pops her hip, and puts her left arm on her waist, while effortlessly holding Mitchel's plate with the other.

"I can see how the food choices could overwhelm you," she says with a surprisingly authoritative tone of voice. "I suggest, to make food selection easier and more adventurous, you stick to two of your favorites, and also try two foods that you don't usually eat. Do you like your eggs scrambled, boiled, or sunny side up?"

"Hard-boiled," Mitchel answers promptly.

"Good. Bacon or sausage links?"

"Bacon."

"Good. For the two unusual picks, I suggest that you try muesli and passion fruit. Does that sound like a good idea?" The authoritative tone continues. My daughter unexpectedly takes charge of breakfast, and I silently observe her unusual behavior.

"That sounds great," Mitchel replies agreeably.

"Now, do you, like, want me to make you a plate, or you got it from here?" She moves her hair away with a flick of her wrist.

"I think I've got it now. Thank you, Hailey, you have been most helpful."

"Anytime, now let me make my own plate. I am, like, starving." She hands Mitchel his plate and walks off to grab oatmeal and a banana—her own breakfast rarely varies from these two food choices.

"Wow, Gretchen, Hailey is something else." Mitchel comes closer to me as we both stare at my daughter, taken aback by her authority.

"I'm sorry, she can be bossy at times. I hope she didn't offend you." I make sure to apologize.

"No, no, not at all. It was nice, actually. I always have trouble making decisions about my meals."

"Do you want to sit with us?" I decide to take advantage of Hailey's good mood and her positive disposition towards Mitchel. I really enjoy their interaction. He listens to her and takes her suggestions seriously. I like that, and I like him.

I get my eggs and bacon, then wait for Hailey and Mitchel before we walk together to our table where a coffee and orange juice are already waiting for us.

"Here, Mom, I grabbed some mango for you." Hailey passes me a small bowl of bright yellow diced fruit.

"Thank you, honey." Hailey hasn't been this sweet in months. I want to make sure I praise her for it. I want her to know that I am noticing.

Hailey and I start eating right away, but our forks stop midway to our mouths when we notice Mitchel bowing his head down, while his hands are folded in front of him, he mouths a quiet prayer and makes a cross over himself. When he opens his eyes, he looks at both of us and starts eating. Hailey and I look at each other and our forks finally make it to our mouths.

"I didn't know you were religious," I tell him.

"Ha-ha," he chuckles softly while chewing his food. "Believe me, I am far from religious. There are some customs I stick to, like taking a moment and saying a prayer before each meal, but I don't go to church on Sundays and I never keep Lent. Did I make you uncomfortable?"

"No, I—we—are just not accustomed to it. My parents are Christian and we did church on Sundays and said a prayer before each meal, they still do. I resented it when I was younger, but now looking back, I think it was kind of nice. It creates something that the family does together, it connects people."

"It's cool, whatever. Doesn't bother me." Hailey makes her opinion known.

"Was your wife religious? If you don't mind me asking?" I poke at slippery pieces of mango in the bowl.

"No, not at all." Mitchel hands me a spoon to help my struggle. "She was Jewish. We had a Christmas tree and we lit a menorah. I learned to bake challah and she made my favorite pork roast. Our religious backgrounds were never an obstacle that we needed to overcome."

"She sounds lovely."

"She was," he replies.

"Why didn't you have kids with her?" Hailey intrudes. This time, I nudge her and give her a stink eye. "What? I'm just asking a question," she snickers at me.

"It's fine, really." Mitchel motions with his hand and takes a sip of water, he then proceeds, speaking directly to Hailey as if she were another adult. "We wanted to have kids, but my wife was diagnosed with breast cancer, so she had to undergo chemotherapy and surgeries. We had to put all our effort into the treatment, and unfortunately, she didn't make it."

My daughter puts her fork down, leans back and sighs. "That sucks, I'm sorry."

I nudge Hailey's leg under the table, making my eyes bigger, trying to let her know that she is saying too much, but she just shrugs her shoulders and starts eating her banana.

"You're right, Hailey, it does suck," Mitchel says.

She turns and gives me a stretched out, fake smile. I frown slightly at her, letting her know that she can't gloat, and nod towards her plate so she finishes her breakfast.

"What are your plans for today, ladies?" Mitchel changes the topic of conversation.

My daughter's mouth is full of banana, so it gives me an opportunity to speak. "We are just going to lay on the beach, catch some rays, and swim. You are welcome to join us."

"I'd love to."

"Just bring the chess," Hailey requests with her mouth still full.

"I will make sure I do. Determined to learn, you are, young Jedi." Mitchel pronounces the last sentence in the voice of the creature from a galaxy far, far away. I am sure Hailey will think he is weird, and I will have to hear all about it later on.

"Underestimate me, don't you?" Hailey shocks me when she speaks in the same voice. I never knew she even saw the movies or knew the characters.

They stare at each other in silence, both squinting their eyes, the scene is quite funny and I can't help but burst out laughing. Hailey and Mitchel follow suit. I wonder if we look like a family to people who don't know us, because this small moment of joy is something I yearn to have.

# 11.

## ANGELINA

My head feels heavy, my body is slow, every move requires an effort. I decide to lie down and take a nap, hoping to recover from last night's drinking before I have to meet Gretchen and Jenna at the spa. I collapse onto the bed facedown and close my eyes, but my mind refuses my command to shut down for recovery and keeps posting images of Kai demanding my decision on what he means to me. I open my eyes and stare at the wall where the shadow of the palm tree's branches swing as if dancing to the melody of the wind. My skin erupts in goose bumps remembering the ride to the hospital, the feeling of Kai's breath on my shoulder as he leaned in to show me the ships in the bay. He was so close that the heat from his body warmed me in the air-conditioned car. I press my fists into my temples, trying to stop the thoughts about this man. What would Jenna think? She always complains about all of Kai's girlfriends—they are too self-absorbed, too dumb, too pretentious, too selfish. I wonder if she is just super protective of her big brother. What would she think if Kai and I ever got together? Would she find me fake? Would she resent me?

It would certainly be weird. What if Kai and I argue? I would not be able to go to my best friend and pour my heart out. What if we break up? I would not want my relationship with Kai to affect my friendship with Jenna.

My head squeezing doesn't produce the desired results, I turn on my back and sit up. I grab my laptop from my nightstand and put it over my lap. My fingers move on autopilot, they click the buttons of the keyboard and open up the file with my manuscript. I know every word by heart. Three years of work spilled onto the pages. I've edited it multiple times, correcting the corrections. I love the story, but self-doubt tells me it is stupid. It was good to hear from Kai that he loved it. I open the folder with my query letter and the list of agents who accept manuscripts for publication. I've sought out the names for months, I've rewritten the query letter so many times it doesn't resemble the original anymore. Today is the day I feel I should send it out. My work is as good as I can make it. I open the mail browser and proceed to copy and paste the names and my letter and hit send. When the last query letter is sent, I take a deep breath and slowly release the stream of air through my pursed lips. I feel light; I've unloaded the precious weight, the value of which will need to be determined by others. I lean my head back against the wall, close my eyes and collapse into deep sleep.

I am jolted from my slumber. I'm still sitting up in bed, propped up by the wall, my laptop has slid down beside me. The screen is dark, it too had taken a nap. My movement wakes it up and the screen lights up with a window requesting the password. Closing it, I set it back on the nightstand. The clock shows it is 4:00 p.m., at six, the girls and I are scheduled to have a massage.

I get up, wash my face with cold water, and brush my teeth. My hair is a tangled, disheveled mess. I brush it and put it in a high bun. I stare at myself in the mirror: a petite girl, with unremarkable features, blue eyes, hair that is not quite straight or curly, freckles on my nose. I don't consider myself beautiful, yet I am happy with the way I look. I have my mother's eyes and cheekbones, my father's chin and lips. My mother has frequently told me that I look just like my father, that I am beautiful. She loved him, she loved him even after he left her for another woman when I was just a few months old. He tortured her with multiple returns, promising her the family she wanted to have with him, yet leaving her when life required him to provide emotional support, strength, and hope to his wife and his child. He didn't do well with familial responsibilities, he ran away from them. I was twelve when my mother was cooking a dinner of Caesar salad, steak, and roasted potatoes and an apple pie for dessert. I knew the dinner was meant to be for someone else, we didn't eat steak, we didn't like Caesar salad. When I asked why she was making all of this, she turned to me with such a big smile, ran to me, hugged me tight and whispered, "Daddy is coming home today!" She looked straight into my eyes, kissed my nose, and headed back to the stove, humming an unfamiliar song. I wanted to be happy, but I was more worried that he would leave again, the pain of his abandonment overshadowed the joy of his return. But he never showed, we sat at the table with food getting cold, my mother quiet. I'd pretended to read a book. I just hadn't wanted to make her more upset than she already was. I'd been angry at him; how could he have chosen someone else? I was his only child and he'd left me; he didn't love me. Why? What was wrong with me that he couldn't love me? The ring of the phone startled both of us. My mother wiped away tears that she was hiding and picked up the phone, her high pitched "Hello?" sounded strange in the silence of our apartment. She'd said nothing else, she'd listened, her eyes darted to me, her brows arched up and then came together, collapsing over eyes that closed tight as she'd started to sob. She'd nodded while holding the phone, then slammed it down on the table. She'd gotten up slowly from the table, dragging her body towards me, supporting herself on the table. When she'd reached, me she'd collapsed over my knees and cried inconsolably.

"Mommy? Mommy?" I'd tried to lift her up, to see her face. I'd known something bad had happened. "Why are you crying? You are scaring me, what happened?" My voice shook and tears pooled in my eyes.

"Your daddy … he … he is … he died." She'd cried more than I had. My anger grew, turning into rage. I'd swung my arm, sending the plates of food onto the floor. My mother ceased sobbing and stared at me. "Angelina? Why did you do that?" Her body was shaking from crying.

"He did it on purpose!" I'd yelled, rage erupting into the verbal volcano, tears streaming down my cheeks, burning my skin. My mother's face had become still, she'd had no emotions. She took a deep breath, pursed her lips, and slapped me across my cheek. The burn of the slap sealed the memory of that evening forever.

I wasn't an easy teenager. My mother struggled to tame me. I'd challenged her every decision. I despised my dad for abandoning me and my mom, and I didn't understand how she could forgive him. The only explanation that my young, egotistical brain was able to produce was that my mother was stupid, hence her every decision was stupid. I would never let anyone treat me the way Dad treated her. I was smarter, I was stronger than her. But my mother *was* smart. She'd understood that she would not win me over by screaming and yelling. She'd stayed calm, she'd punished me by taking away the things I cared about, the things I took for granted.

When she'd caught me lying about hanging out with people I wasn't supposed to, she took my bedroom door off the hinges and didn't put it back until I'd changed my attitude.

She'd then decided to sign me up for Jiu Jitsu, a sport she'd heard taught self-control, self-defense, and perseverance. She'd bribed me to try it by promising to buy me a cell phone if I lasted a year.

At twenty-seven years of age, I'm still attending. I've earned a black belt. I've learned self-reliance, self-control, patience, and confidence. I love it. I love the feeling of finding a second wave of energy just on the edge of giving up. When my heart and breathing steadies, I close my eyes tight for a few seconds. My brain calms and I repeat my mantra: *don't give up, I can do it.* And when I open my eyes, I take a deep breath, and find the strength to push through, to fight my opponent until submission or a take down. When I am the one who is submitted, I take it as a humbling moment that shows me I have much to learn.

I leave my room to meet up with the girls. I know the three of us will have fun, just the way we always have since school.

I'm the first one to get to the spa. A smiling receptionist dressed in all white with a short pixie cut greets me and offers me a glass of champagne while I wait for Jenna and Gretchen. A few minutes later, panting, Gretchen comes in.

"Sorry, am I very late?" She reaches for a tissue and blots her forehead. She says hi to the receptionist, and nods to her offer of champagne.

"No, sweetie, you are not late at all. Jenna isn't here yet." I wait for her to get a glass of bubbly and cheers her before taking a sip.

"How is Hailey? What's going on with her?" I inquire.

"I think she is getting hormonal, plus her father hasn't been paying much attention to her. So, you know, I'm the only one who is her sounding board." She rolls her eyes and sighs loudly.

I rub her arm reassuringly. "I was a very angry teenager, let me talk to her."

"Thank you, but I don't want you to deal with something like this on your vacation." She waves me off and takes another sip.

"Are you kidding me? I don't know what to do with myself here, at least it will make me feel useful."

"Are you sure?"

"Yeah, we're friends, aren't we?" I nudge her and we clink our glasses again.

As we finish our champagne, in rushes Jenna—always a tornado of noise and excitement. "Hello, bitches! Are you ready to relax?" She hugs both of us and gives us loud air kisses.

"Yeah!"

"Woo-hoo," we reply.

"All right, what are we waiting for, then? Let's go!" She comes between Gretchen and I, wrapping her arms in each of ours.

136

The receptionist, seeing that all three of us are ready, ushers us in. Inside, there is a large central pool with hot tub, and all around are multiple doors. The receptionist leads us to one and when she opens it, there are three massage tables. At the head of each, we are greeted by three women who introduce themselves as our masseuses. They hand us robes, take us to the dressing rooms where we change, and then we head back and lie down on the tables. The pressure of the massage feels nice, my body relaxes instantly.

"Let me ask you guys," Gretchen begins, her voice sounds like she has a mouth full of food as her face is pressed into the hole of the massage table. "How old were you when your parents spoke about sex?"

"Hahaha, never." I let out a laugh as my own voice sounds funny. "I learned from Jenna … my mother would never talk about that …" My masseuse stretches and pulls my skin, relaxing the knots of tension in my back. "… she still changes channels when there are people kissing … and I'm in the room. I didn't even know what menstruation is, Jenna told me what tampons are for. Do you remember?"

"Did I?" Jenna mumbles with her face pressed into the table.

"Yes, it was a bunch of us girls circled around you. Someone brought in a tampon and we were talking about what it was for. And some girls were saying it was for cuts on your hands. You know, because in commercials they are holding it inside the fist and would pour water on it."

"Oh, yeah, I remember something like that. I think I was the one who brought it in, because my mom had just explained periods and hormones to me, so I was eager to show off my newfound knowledge," Jenna admits, giggling.

"I found out about periods when I got one. I think I was about twelve," Gretchen replies.

"Do you guys think I should speak to Hailey about sex?"

"What do you mean?" Jenna asks.

"I know, I know, I am a terrible mother … it's hard for me to talk to her about that stuff, you know."

"Gretchen, you were sixteen when you were pregnant, Hailey is just five years away from that age. I bet she knows a lot by now. It's better if she finds out things from you and knows that she can turn to you, rather than hear stuff from her probably very misinformed friends." I try to encourage my friend.

"Are you shy to talk about penises, Gretchen?" Jenna teases our friend. "Just repeat after me, p-e-n-i-s. C'mon … just say it."

"Sorry, but I caaaan't. You guys, I can't." Gretchen sounds muffled, her face pressed into the massage chair.

"How about if you say vagina?" Jenna keeps teasing.

Gretchen giggles without replying, but then says. "This is embarrassing, but I haven't even seen mine up close."

"How is that possible, Gretchen?" I interject, surprised by her revelation. "I think you were the first one to have sex and you have a kid, I would expect you to be well-versed in the anatomy."

I hear Gretchen sigh loudly. "I can't even look at myself naked in the mirror. Especially now that I look like a hippo."

"Stop it, sweetie. You are beautiful," I say.

"Don't be ridiculous," Jenna objects loudly to Gretchen.

"Thank you, guys, but look at me. I'm huge, I have rolls of fat everywhere, who would want to be with someone like me?"

"You mean someone who is kind and caring and loving and loyal like you? Anyone who has his head screwed on right," I tell her.

"Yeah those are nice things, but no man will be attracted to a woman who is kind. What is he going to say? 'Oh, my woman is so kind, I want to do her so much'?" She deepens her voice, imitating a man.

"I think Mitchel is attracted to you," I throw in my observation.

Gretchen giggles again. "He is very nice, and he is sweet with Hailey."

"Ew, isn't he old? You guys like old dudes, why?" Jenna mumbles.

"Sorry, but he is not old. He is probably in his early forties. Right, Angelina? That's not old?" Gretchen asks.

"I don't think he is old," I reply.

"Angelina is biased." I hear Jenna's muffled laughter. "She is dating an old dude herself."

"Correction. We are not dating."

"Shut up. When did this happen?" Jenna says loudly.

"Ah, officially … yesterday, unofficially … we haven't been together for a few months … we had a case of willfully ignoring each other … you know?" I try to explain my situation the best I can.

"Are you upset, Angelina?" Gretchen inquires in her soft, gentle voice.

"Hmm, no … I don't think so … at least not over the breakup … it's actually good to have the resolution … I am upset that he didn't have the balls to do it face-to-face."

"Maybe it is better that he did it this way, he showed his character," Gretchen replies.

"I guess."

"Well, now that you are single and ready to mingle, we need to find you a hot stud," Jenna chimes in.

"Ha-ha, no, thank you, Jenna."

"Why? You don't even know who I have in mind," Jenna continues.

"I'm afraid to even ask." I laugh off my friend's suggestion. All her guy friends are either gay or bad boys with commitment issues.

"I think you should give Kai a chance," Jenna blurts an unexpected suggestion. My mind starts to shuffle through the index cards of anxiety prompts, trying to figure out how to respond to my friend. But all I come up with are questions that I don't have answers to. Was I so obvious in ogling Kai? Did he say something to Jenna? Is she testing me, expecting me to say no?

I let out a nervous chuckle. "Jenna, you are crazy. Can you imagine Kai with me …? That would be so wrong."

"I actually can," she says with confidence. "I know you've always liked him."

"Yeah, when we were kids." My intonation betrays me when I say it. I know I sound fake.

"You guys looked very cute dancing yesterday … I could see the two of you together." Gretchen abandons her neutrality, taking Jenna's side. "Sorry, Angelina," she calls out.

"See. I'm not the only one who saw you guys have a thing for each other," Jenna mutters.

"Guys. You are crazy." I feel my body get hot and sweaty. I am embarrassed that my attraction to Kai has been on such a public display.

"We are not," Jenna gets louder. "Why? You don't like my brother?"

"Ugh, Jenna," I sigh when she corners me with her question. "He is your brother ... hello? ... and you are my friend ... I can't .... It would be too weird."

"*You* are weird, Angelina. He likes you. You like him. What could be the problem?"

"And what if we argue, what if it doesn't work out and we break up?"

"So? You move on, he moves on," Jenna shrugs off any hesitation.

"But how about you and I, our friendship," I press.

"Aw! You're very sweet, thinking of me before your own happiness .... We'll be fine. I promise."

"I don't know, Jenna ...," I mumble.

"I think you should go for it, Angelina," says Gretchen, who has been quiet for a while.

"Gretchen, I thought you would be on my side in this." I try to guilt my friend.

"Sorry, but I am on love's side," Gretchen replies.

"You are all nuts, just nuts. Can we talk about something else? I'm starting to feel self-conscious."

Our masseuses tell us to flip on our backs and start to work on our faces and necks, which keeps us silent for a while. When they move on to our chests, Jenna blurts, "I haven't had sex in months."

I look at Gretchen first, to see if I heard correctly. When she looks at me with the same puzzled face, I know my hearing is good.

"What?" I still say out loud.

"Brian and I decided not to have sex until we are married," she clarifies and turns to me with a beaming smile.

"Why?" Now Gretchen raises up on her elbows, but her masseuse gently taps her to lay back.

"It's not that unusual you guys, okay? Ciara just did it," Jenna says with conviction.

"But why are you doing it?" I ask.

"Because I want to separate him from all the others that I've had before. It'll be like a fresh start. Isn't it something to say that we had sex for the first time as man and wife, to have that connection?"

"I don't know, Jenna, and what if the connection doesn't work? What if you are not compatible in bed?" I carefully voice my questions.

"It's impossible. His thing is huge! Plus, the way he kisses me, I can orgasm just from that," she rebuts me.

"Ha-ha, well, if he has orgasmic kisses, then you'll be just fine." I decide to not press any further, and we all burst out laughing.

Once our massages are finished, we change back into our clothes and eat a light, early dinner on the balcony of the nearby restaurant, and when we are finished, we all go to our rooms.

In the enclosed space of my vacation retreat, I get the chance to process what Jenna has told me. She's given me her permission to date Kai, but can I give myself permission to like him and push aside my fears of 'what if we break up?' Jenna is always living in the moment, thinking of instant gratification rather than the potential consequences of her actions. It's possible she doesn't realize the affect me dating Kai could have on our friendship. Jenna must be completely consumed by her pre-wedding bliss and wants to sprinkle some of it on everyone surrounding her. It's tempting to let her happiness be contagious and allow myself to be spontaneous for a change. I wonder if Kai is even thinking about all of this? I pace the length of the room, pondering my emotional predicament. Not coming up with definitive answers, I decide to go see Gretchen. I'll take Hailey out for some ice cream, and see what's on her mind.

Their room is in a building five minutes away from mine up a picturesque trail that is adorned by banana trees and bright flowers—red, orange, and yellow, the names of which I don't know. Still, an iguana is enjoying the sunrays on the pavement, not paying attention to me. I run up to the second floor of the building and find their room to the right of the elevator. Hailey opens the door when I knock and greets me with a huge smile.

"Hi, pretty girl," I greet her.

"Hey," she replies.

"Who is it, Hailey?" Gretchen yells as I walk into the room.

"It's Angelina, Mom."

"Oh, hey, sorry. What's up?" Gretchen apologizes first as always.

"I wanted to see if I can take Hailey out?" I ask Gretchen, and give a wink to Hailey as if it's a spur of the moment decision.

"Hmm ... are you sure?" Gretchen asks.

"Please, Mommy," Hailey begs softly, her hands clasped as if praying.

I mimic her and clasp my hands as well. "Yes, please, Gretchen, I promise we'll behave and I'll keep my eye on her."

"Okay, okay, go. Hailey, make sure you listen to Angelina." She comes up to Hailey closer, frowns and wags her finger.

Hailey stretches her mouth in a wide smile and whispers, "Promise, Mommy." Only then does Gretchen's frown relax, and she places a kiss on her daughter's forehead.

"Have fun, girls." She sends us off, and we leave the room giggling as if plotting a secretive mission.

We walk to the Sweet Spot bakery, and I order a cup of cappuccino, a crepe with Nutella and banana and Hailey orders a strawberry milkshake and a brownie. We take a seat outside; the small table and metal chairs make me feel like we are sitting in a cozy cafe in Paris.

"So, what is happening with your life?" I lead with a generic question and it makes me feel like I am an adult, wise beyond my years. The tall plump waiter dressed in all white with a tall chef's hat brings out our treats. We follow the sweets with our hungry eyes from the tray until they're placed in front of us. Hailey's milkshake is a tower of chocolate-covered glass with a cloud of whipped cream, jammed with a chocolate waffle straw, and a fresh strawberry, drizzled in chocolate syrup.

"Wow! Are you sure you can finish all of that?" I ask Hailey who licks her lips and pulls the glass towards her.

"Watch me," she responds confidently to my challenge, and takes a long sip from the straw.

"Okay, okay," I nod and take a small bite of my crepe that melts in chocolate deliciousness in my mouth. "Have a piece." I offer it to Hailey, but she shakes her head no, firmly attached to the straw of her milkshake.

"You know, your mom and I met when we were your age," I start. Hailey nods her head yes, a loud slurp escapes from her glass as she blows a bubble.

"Did she tell you that she saved me from embarrassment when I got my period and I had no clue about it, and she gave me my first pad?" I keep talking, trying to throw pebbles of conversation topics, hoping that Hailey will pick them up and follow towards an open heart-to-heart. But she only raises her eyebrows in surprise, nods, and continues drinking her milkshake.

"She was also there when I needed a friend to lean on when my parents separated once again, and then my dad died."

Hailey stops drinking her milkshake, letting go of the straw. She looks up at me with big blue eyes. "Your parents got divorced?" she breathes out quietly.

"Mm-hmm, they did." I take another bite of my crepe, trying to appear calm and collected.

Hailey licks her lips, looking down at her fingers that she plays with. "Did you ... like ... did you feel like they didn't love you anymore? Like, it was all your fault ...?" She formulates the questions I clearly remember asking myself when I was in her shoes. I stay silent for a moment, processing every word that will come out of my mouth. I need to make sure what I say will feed the roots of positive thinking for her.

"I did. I thought that if I wasn't there, my parents would probably still be together. I blamed myself—my behavior, my appearance, my grades—for my father leaving and not loving me." I punctuate each word while Hailey is

145

staring directly at me without blinking, her mouth slightly open.

"I cried so much, I argued with my mother. I thought it was all her fault as well. I thought she couldn't possibly understand the way I was feeling. That she was a complete fool. I was trying to hurt her by yelling, staying up with friends, not helping out. I was trying to hurt her with my behavior, you know?" I stir my coffee, and look up at Hailey whose eyes gloss over with a wall of tears, her nose reddens.

"It's all my mother's fault that Dad is not with us. Like, all she used to do was yell and scream at him, that's why he left." She wipes her nose and the tears start a slow roll down her cheek. I move my chair over to hers and take her hands into mine.

"Look at me, Hailey. Your mom is amazing. I remember when she fell in love with your dad, as he did with her. But they were little kids. They just grew apart and want different things from life, but ... but it doesn't mean they don't love you. I know they do," I say softly, as Hailey's tears fall down over my hands that clasp hers.

"Yes, it does. My dad didn't even let me stay with him this week, like he promised. He, he wanted to be with his girlfriend instead." Hailey's voice trembles as she gasps for air while talking through the tears. Her father was immature and clearly didn't think of his daughter's well-being, but I had this girl in front of me, vulnerable and naive. I had to make sure I did not disparage her father.

"Hm, I know adults do things that don't always make sense, but you know what I remember?" I nudge her to look up at me. "I remember that your father was the first one to hold you when you were born, he wasn't scared at all, aaand … he even changed your first diaper. He didn't go away to college, like he'd planned, but instead went to a local community college, so all of you could be a family. You know what?"

"What?" Hailey says under her breath.

"I think he probably feels strange around you because you are becoming a teenager, and maybe he just needs a bit of time to adjust, you know?" I try to find something positive in her father, Hailey nods and forces a smile through her sniffling.

"I remember when he tried to make pancakes for me, and they all got burned and he burned his fingers, and he was shaking his hand so much that he spilled water and broke a glass on the counter. But, like, those were the best pancakes ever."

"See, just remember those good moments, and I know there will be more of them. Sometimes, we just have to wait. How about your mom? Do you have any good memories of her?"

"I know Mom loves me. I don't know why I give her so much of a hard time. I mean, I do, because I'm angry, but, like, at the same time, I love her, too," she tries to explain in her childish simple sentences, but I understand the deeper meaning behind her words.

"You know it will mean the world to her if she hears you say that." She listens to me, nods, and takes a sip of her milkshake.

"I thought your mom was crazy for getting pregnant at sixteen and deciding to keep you. But I can't imagine you not being here, and I know she tries very hard to be the best mom for you. Sometimes she learns as she goes, and she might not get it right all the time, but you are her precious little baby and you always will be, no matter how old you are. She'll do anything for you. And if you ever need to talk to somebody, you have my number, call me."

Hailey smiles at me, "Promise."

I take my coffee and cheers with her milkshake.

# 12.

## MITCHEL

A soft knock on my door distracts me from my thoughts about Gretchen. It was nice to sit together with her and her daughter, it almost felt like we were a little family. My sister would probably laugh at me for liking someone as young as Gretchen, I can just hear her calling me an old fart. She's turning into our mother who was always spreading misery. *You know she has a child?* she would probably state the obvious fact. *The girl is almost a teenager. You do realize that? Why? Why would you take on such a burden? Raising someone's child? I would never.* She would press her thin lips together and turn the corners of her mouth down, shaking her head as if she'd just smelled something unpleasant. I am glad that Brian didn't inherit her negativity, but I am sure he has to hear how unhappy she is about his sudden wedding.

I walk to the door wondering who it could be. The room has been cleaned, the fridge has been stocked. I open the door and find Gretchen smiling at me, nervously playing with her fingers at first, then running her hands over her dress to fix invisible wrinkles.

"Hi! Sorry to bother you," she says, her voice trembling. I feel the air enter my lungs, expanding them fully, I slowly breathe out, enjoying the curves of her face, the blushing of her cheeks, the nervous shuffling in front of me.

"Don't apologize, you are not bothering me at all. Come in. Is everything all right? Where's Hailey?" I ask as Gretchen hesitates to enter my room.

"Oh … Angelina took her out for some ice cream. Are you sure it's okay that I come in?" She lingers in the doorway.

"Yes. Come in, come in." I step to the side so she can pass by me into the room.

She laughs nervously. "I'm really sorry. I feel completely stupid." She looks down the hallway, biting her lip. "I shouldn't have come. This is so embarrassing." She shakes her head.

I stretch out my arm, I hope she takes it. "Gretchen, what's going on? You can tell me." She keeps her eyes down, then gazes at my hand and takes a step forward. Her proximity pulls me towards her. I know she is here to be with me, she must be feeling the same attraction that I am. I take a step towards her, our faces within inches of each other. I feel her breath on my lips. Her porcelain skin is flushed, she bats her eyes framed by long lashes, her nostrils flare. I take her chin and lift it up, forcing her to look into my eyes. My other arm wraps around her waist, pulling her closer. Her beautiful blue eyes call out to me. My heart beats faster. "I'm glad you came. May I?" I ask permission to kiss her, and she nods and leans in towards me. My mouth touches her soft lips, Gretchen's body presses against me. Her hot tongue greets mine. I close the door, take steps back, leading her into my room, still kissing. Her hands lift up my shirt and take it off. I find the zipper on the back of her dress and pull it down. I step back to see her. She is beautiful. I want to savor each moment with this woman. She looks at me, her chest rising fast, her warm fingers buried in the back of my hair. I hook my finger under the strap of her dress and slide it down her shoulder. She closes her eyes and tilts her head, revealing the long curve of her neck that calls out to be kissed. I trace a line of kisses from behind her ear to the place where her bra has left a pink mark. She smells sweet and feels warm, my other hand finds the opposite strap and slides it down as well. Her dress falls to the floor, revealing Gretchen's stunning, soft curves. She covers up. "Can we get under the covers? I'm not used to being like this."

"You are gorgeous ... I want to see you." I step back to take in the full view of her body that makes me burn with a desire that I haven't felt in years. I need to make her feel worthy, confident. I know I can, I hope she lets me. She lets out a soft giggle. She unhooks her bra, and when it follows the dress to the floor, it frees her full breasts. She hesitates for a moment, but then takes off her underwear. She is finally standing in front of me, vulnerable and trusting with the body of a Greek goddess. I follow her lead and take off the rest of my clothes. My aging body responds to her young one with fast hardness that I didn't think was possible. I reach for her hand, interlock my fingers with hers, and pull her closer to me. The heat of her body is intoxicating. She leans in for a kiss, and I dive in, my thirst for her to be mine is unquenchable. I lead her to my bed, and we fall into a white cloud of blankets and pillows.

The shadows of the palm trees swing slowly across the walls of my room, the tweeting of birds serenade our lovemaking. The release comes fast. Her fingers dig into the back of my neck, her legs wrap tight around my waist as she yells my name at the peak of ecstasy. I bury my face in her neck and breathe in her sweet scent.

"Thank you," I whisper into her ear. She covers up her face with her hands and shakes her head.

"I'm sorry. You must think that I am terrible … easy. I swear, I have never done anything like this before," she says, her voice is trembling. I pry her hands away from her face, but she looks away. I turn her face towards me and plant a soft kiss on her lips.

"You're not terrible. You're wonderful." Another kiss on her nose. "Beautiful." Then one more on her eyes. "Kind." And then her cheeks. "You make me feel young again."

"I like you, Mitchel." She raises her head and returns a kiss on my lips. "But I am … my life … it's complicated … I have Hailey … and an ex-husband … I could never ask you to deal with all that."

"You don't need to ask. Hailey is a great child."

"Ha, great? You haven't seen her in the morning or when she gets frustrated. She scares me."

"She's a child who's overwhelmed, like many of my students. Believe me, teenagers don't scare me. I enjoy talking to them, teaching them. They are still children that are suddenly bombarded by hormones that detonate lots of feelings. Inside, they are very, very shy and scared. And your ex-husband … hmm …. Do you still have feelings for him?"

"No, no," she says, shaking her head vigorously.

"Well, I'm not bothered by him at all then." I move my gaze from her lips, to her nose, to her eyes, taking in small details so I can remember them. I move a wisp of her blond hair, and she pulls my hand and kisses my palm.

"You look at me … hmm … like … I can't explain it … like I'm the only woman in the world … no one has ever looked at me like that …. I like it … a lot."

"You deserve to be admired." I slide down and pull her towards me, her back presses against my chest and abdomen, my left hand wraps around her soft belly and the other traces her fingers. We look at the aqua sky of Grenada through the window. I savor each move, scent, and touch.

Gretchen stirs, "I don't want Hailey to know anything yet."

"Of course, whatever you say, I'll respect your decision." I know children are quite protective of their divorced parents. I want to make Hailey feel comfortable and not be threatened that I will take the attention of her mother away from her.

She shifts closer to me. "This is so nice, but I have to go. Hailey will come back soon." I reluctantly release her from my embrace, she sits up and pulls the covers over her naked body. "Don't look at me, Mitchel. I'm not used to it," she says without looking at me.

"You need to get used to it, because I want to see you like this as much as possible," I reply. She laughs, throwing her head back, and this laugh is not shy, it's loud and confident, and I enjoy the sound of it. Gretchen then lifts up her arms like wings, the cover drops and she lets me look at her back, she giggles and looks back at me. I really don't want her to go, I sit up and perch myself behind her, my hand moves her hair to the side and I place a kiss at the spot where her neck meets her shoulder, she moans softly.

"Go," I give her a verbal nudge. "Let's all have dinner tonight. Does Hailey like sushi? I hear the Asian restaurant here is excellent."

"That girl is picky about food, but she loves sushi and she can eat a lot, it's good this place is all-inclusive." Gretchen stretches and walks over to her clothes. I prop my head up, still lying in bed watching her every move.

"Do you want me to meet you there or come to your room?" I ask.

"I'm sorry, but it's probably be better if we meet you there. I don't want Hailey to know about us just yet, she acts like a little adult, but she is very emotional. I need to give her time to come to terms with my dating someone."

"You have to stop being sorry, you make complete sense. I'll see you there. Is nine o'clock good for you?" I ask Gretchen, and then get out of bed myself and put on my shorts so I can say goodbye and walk her to the door. When she is done, I pull her towards me and pause, looking at her face, I stroke her cheek and she leans into my palm. She is so familiar and comforting, her presence fills me with a contentment I didn't know I was missing. She raises up on her tippy toes and kisses me. "Thank you," she whispers.

"It's my pleasure," I reply. I then wrap my arm around her waist and walk her to the door. I open it for her and my arm lingers on her body. I wish she didn't need to go.

"See you soon, Mitchel." Gretchen walks out into the warm evening of Grenada.

For the next hour, I keep busy reading proposals for improving my school based on the most recent budget. At quarter to nine, I pace my room, ready in my dress shirt and beige pants. My heart beats fast with anticipation of seeing Gretchen, but the clock on my phone decides to torture me by showing the same time as I glance at it over and over again. I flip through the channels, then the room catalogue. I open the mini fridge, but close it without taking anything out. I am afraid that soda will make me gassy, and alcohol before food will give me a buzz, and I need to act presentable in front of Gretchen and Hailey. Time finally takes pity on me when it's ten minutes to nine. I leave my room, and the humidity and my anxiety make me sweaty before I even get to the restaurant. I play out possible greetings in my head. Should I go in for a hug or a kiss on the cheek? I need to be friendly without giving away my attraction for Gretchen to Hailey. I check my pocket for the chess, I can play with Hailey, she seems to enjoy the game and I can talk about it for hours. I'm a few minutes early, Gretchen and Hailey aren't here yet. I decide to get a table and tell the hostess that I am expecting to be joined by two more people. She smiles and nods, leading me to a table with two chairs on one side and a couch that runs the length of the wall on the other side. The waiter pours me a glass of water with ice, and I check out the menu, so I don't stall from all the options later on. I manage to zero in on appetizers of steamed pork dumplings, rainbow roll, dragon roll, and Alaska roll, and even manage to decide that I will have green tea and nutmeg ice cream for dessert. I take out my phone and look at the clock. It is 9:10, and Gretchen isn't here yet. I hope she hasn't decided that sleeping with me was a mistake. Did I do something that turned her off? I replay our rendezvous in my head over and over again, but don't stumble on any underwater, creepy boulders. The waiter comes up to me a few minutes later and asks if my friends are going to join me. I look at the time, 9:17.

"Let me have an order of edamame and lychee sake please. I'll give my friends a few more minutes to get here." I place the order to stop him from hovering nearby. I get out my chess and set it up on the table so I don't keep checking my phone incessantly. I make the first move, black pawn one square forward, I then turn the magnetic board around and make the move with the white pawn one square forward. The edamame arrives, as well as my drink when I have already taken down two white pawns. I take a sip of warm, sweet sake and start to work on the edamame. The waiter arrives when four black pawns are down and my edamame is finished. "Sir, would you like to order your main course?" he asks, and pours me a refill of my water. I take a look at my phone, it is 9:45 p.m.

"I guess, I might as well." I try to avoid looking at him and I open the menu once again having forgotten what I'd decided to order. "Would you mind if I move to the bar? It seems like too much space just for me, since my friends aren't here." I would feel less insecure sitting at the bar.

"Of course, sir. Let me help you, sir." My waiter doesn't show any emotion, but takes my glass and brings it over to the bar and I follow him.

"Let me have salmon teriyaki." I give him my order, deciding to stick to something that I usually order every Friday night. It seems like it's safer to stick to something I know rather than try rolls I may not like. The waiter scribbles quickly on his pad and retreats into the kitchen. I get out my phone and scroll down the news feed. I press on the catchy headlines and even read the articles that I am not interested in just to pass the time and to look like I am a confident, single male, preoccupied with life while on vacation and not a lonely man, who eats the same breakfast, lunch, and dinner, and who hasn't shopped for new clothing in years.

I finish dinner and decide to go back to the room. The restaurant has gotten crowded with couples that hug and kiss each other, and the sight deepens my sense of longing for the touch of the woman who stood me up for a reason I can't seem to comprehend. Maybe my sister is right, I am getting old and I'm out of step with the younger generation that Gretchen belongs to.

I stroll through the open reception area. It's empty except for the one concierge who looks up and smiles at me, "Good evening, sir. Do you need help with anything?"

Yes, take my loneliness away, is what I want to say, but instead, "Have a good evening, thank you, I'm all right." Outside of reception, a running taxi is parked on the circular cobblestone driveway. I look around, curious who might be looking to leave the resort at this hour. I see a couple running from the opposite direction, then there is another who joins behind them. Crazy kids. Probably going to the city to party. When they get closer, I recognize Brian, Jenna, her brother Kai, and her friend Angelina. Their faces do not look relaxed and carefree, they are dressed too casually in tanks and shorts to be going out to a party.

"Hey, guys!" I yell and wave to them as they climb into the car. "Where are you going?"

"To the hospital," Brian replies. "Gretchen's daughter got hurt, we just found out."

"What happened?" No wonder she never showed, this is serious and here I was selfishly whining about being lonely. She must be terrified, her child is hurt, and she is there in the hospital all by herself.

"We're going to find out. She was taken there about an hour ago," Jenna tells me from the back seat of the car.

"I'll come with you," I take the front passenger seat while the others squeeze into the back.

"Why are you coming, Mitchel? You hardly know Gretchen," Jenna inquires as the taxi starts to drive.

"I spent some time with her and her daughter on the plane and we were sitting together at dinner last night and today at the beach I saw them again. I play chess with Hailey. I'm just concerned." I stay mum on my true feelings towards Gretchen at this time. I don't know how much she tells her girlfriends.

"It's just so strange. I took Hailey out for dessert, and we went swimming afterwards, and when I took her back to the room, she was fine. I'm racking my brain," Angelina speaks up.

"I feel bad I couldn't speak to her, she was able to reach reception from the hospital, but now her phone isn't working. The concierge just told me that Hailey was hurt," Jenna adds.

"Well, let's hope that she is in good hands." I try to stay positive.

"The ER at St. John's is great. I'm sure she is well taken care of," Kai supports me.

We stay quiet for the rest of the ride. When we finally reach the hospital, I open the door before the taxi has come to a complete stop, the rest of my ride fellows follow me, only Brian lingers behind, paying the driver.

"Follow me. I know where the ER is." Kai takes the lead and we follow him.

At the nurses' station, Kai inquires about the where-abouts of Gretchen and Hailey, and we're directed to a bed a few feet away, separated by a curtain. When we get there, I spot Gretchen; she is standing with her back to me, talking to a physician. When the doctor shifts his gaze at us, Gretchen turns around, her white dress has a large blood stain right in the middle of her chest. Her eyes are red and puffy. She forces a smile and waves, then turns around to finish the conversation with the physician; when done, she walks towards us. Angelina and Jenna push us men to the side and rush to hug their friend. I hear Gretchen say, "I'm sorry, guys. I'm sorry for bothering you. It's not that bad. I just wanted to let you know that we were here." She looks at me with her big blue eyes and I can tell that she is happy to see me. I give her a quick nod, but stay behind all her friends.

"What happened? You are covered in blood!" Jenna asks.

"Hailey tripped and fell and split her brow, it was terrible, there was so much blood. The plastic surgeon just finished suturing, she is bruised and has a headache. They'll keep her overnight, but the scan showed there is no bleeding in the brain and no broken bones." When I hear Gretchen's recap, I sigh with relief.

"I'm glad she is okay," I offer my words of support, grab her hand, and give it a quick squeeze. I feel Gretchen squeeze back, but then let go, so no one pays too much attention to us.

"Come everyone, I'm sure she will be happy to see you. She has been snapping selfies so she can show them to her friends later on." Gretchen pulls back the curtain, and Hailey is lying with a big white bandage covering most of her left eye. "Look who came to see you," Gretchen announces to Hailey, who stops looking at her phone, smiles at all of us, and waves. Gretchen takes the spot at the head of the bed with Jenna and Brian by her side, Angelina stays on the other side with Kai beside her, and I find a spot at the foot of the bed.

"You scared us, rookie," I tell this little girl.

"I'm sorry," she says softly, her gaze traveling from face to face and then landing on her mother, who pats her head gently with one hand and holds her hand with the other.

"Don't be sorry, we just care about you," I add.

"We do."

"We do."

"We are here for you." Everyone chimes in and her lips stretch into a wide toothy smile.

"Thank you, everyone," Hailey replies. We all stand in silence. "I can go for a round of chess right now, if you want," she directs her attention to me. "Is it okay, Mom?"

"I'm sure Mitchel just wants to go back to the hotel, we already took up so much of his time, honey." She gently prepares her daughter for my refusal.

"I really have nothing to do at the hotel, I'd love to stay and keep you girls company." All the eyes move from me to Gretchen. She blushes and her chest erupts in red hives, but she nods yes to me. Hailey claps her hands gently, and I get out my chess and start placing them on a small table that I'll be able to wheel right over to Hailey.

"Do you want me to bring you a change of clothing?" Angelina comes over to Gretchen and rubs her arm.

"No, no, not necessary. We'll be back at the hotel tomorrow, and I'll change then, but thank you. Go back to the hotel everyone, I'm sorry I made you all panic, but I really appreciate your coming."

"Let us know if anything changes, okay? Here, take my battery charger, it should give your phone enough charge until tomorrow," Jenna tells Gretchen coming up to her, then throwing her hands around her friend, and giving her a kiss on the cheek.

"Angelina, Kai, let's go and figure out how to get a taxi from here." Jenna rounds everyone up as I push the table towards Hailey.

"Bye, everyone."

"Bye."

"See you later."

"Goodnight." A chorus of voices exchange farewells, and then all goes quiet as the four young people leave the room.

"So, are you ready, rookie?" I sit down on the edge of the bed and ask Hailey. "Black or white?"

"Black. Why do you call me a rookie?" She takes a pawn and moves it two squares forward.

"Aha! History of chess you want to know." I master up my best Yoda voice.

"Mgh-hmm," she giggles.

"Well, all first-year chess players are called rookies," I take my white pawn and move it two squares forward so it faces Hailey's pawn now. "They are called after the rook, it's usually the last piece that is moved into action in chess, and so are the rookies." I gently flick Hailey's nose, and she tucks her neck in and giggles some more before moving her next pawn.

I turn around, sensing a gaze upon me. Gretchen is standing behind my back, peering through the curtain. A smile decorates her tired, but peaceful and beautiful face. She comes around and sits at the head of Hailey's bed on the opposite side of me, stroking her daughter's hair, observing our chess game. My eyes drift toward her once in a while, but swiftly move away, so as not to give away anything to Hailey before Gretchen is ready to do so herself. After about the tenth move, Hailey takes longer to

161

decide what piece to use, her yawns become frequent and she blinks often, but slowly.

"Why don't you go to sleep, honey. You need to rest," Gretchen suggests.

"Okay, Mommy. Love you," she agrees without any argument.

"Love you, too, baby," Gretchen replies.

"Good night, Mitchel," Hailey says to me.

"Good night, rookie," I tell her. She turns on her side, tucks her hands under her ear and her breathing soon becomes deep and slow. I try not to make much noise as I put away our game and move the table to the side. Gretchen places a soft kiss on her daughter's head, she then gets up, walks around the bed and when she gets close, she reaches out for my hand, grabs it tight and puts it to her lips. When I rise, she takes charge and leads me just outside the curtains that give Hailey some privacy.

"I'm so glad you are here." She wraps her arms around my shoulders and tucks her face into my chest. I place my hand on her back and pull her closer to me.

"I'm glad I am here, too." I kiss her hair. No one knows us in this place, and with Hailey asleep we don't need to hide our affection.

She nuzzles into my neck and then I hear a giggle escape her, it's brief and soon her body shakes with what I think is laughter, but when I pull her face from me, I can see it's drenched in tears.

"Why are you crying?" I ask, puzzled by the sudden tears.

"I'm sorry, I'm so sorry, but this is my life." She wipes her face, sniffling. "There is always a disaster, an emergency, a fight. Just when you think you are able to stay on the surface, another wave of whatever bullshit comes and smacks you, pulling you under. I'm always tired. I'm not sure if I'm doing any of this the right way. And you." She smacks my chest with barely any force. "You have your life, your work. You have no distractions. No one is yelling at you. You are so nice, so caring. Where did you come from? Why are you here? Why would you be interested in being with someone like me?"

I press her palm that just hit me into my chest, with my other hand holding her waist even tighter than before. I don't want her to have any doubt about me. My words have to be an anchor that will sink into her soul and hold her opinion of me tight, regardless of any storms that may rage.

"I welcome the emergencies and disasters. They don't scare me. What scares me is a life that has no purpose. I'm tired of my days. I know exactly how they will begin and how they will end. I have a heart that wants to care about someone. I want to have a home, a family. I can see myself coming home to you ... to Hailey. I'll face any disaster with you, we can overcome any obstacle together if you let me care for you," I say slowly, not taking my eyes off of her. Her tears still pooling in her blue eyes that are red from crying, the last tear rolls when she finally blinks.

"I'm afraid that this is all but a dream. How ... how is this possible that you exist?" She keeps staring at me, her hands run from my shoulders, squeezing lightly all the way to my fingers, I catch her hands with mine and put them up to my chest.

"I am here. I am not scared. We'll take each day as it comes. Okay? Please don't say you're sorry. You are not an inconvenience; you are a person, who is important ... to me," I tell her. She doesn't try to pull away anymore.

163

Gretchen nods her head yes and puts her head over our hands. I then wrap my arms around her and pull her closer. I'll show her what it's like to be taken care of.

# 13.

## KAI

On the way back to the resort, Angelina and I take the third row in the van and Brian and Jenna stay in the second. Angelina is looking out the window of the car, and only the occasional road light intrudes on the intimate darkness between us. She has her hair up in a bun revealing her tantalizing neck, it calls out for my fingers to caress it and bury my face in the curls of her hair. I stretch my arms up as though for a pretend yawn, but quickly capitulate the move realizing it's childish. My wrist accidentally touches her back before embarrassingly jerking away. She turns to me, and all I can manage is another fake yawn. She smiles and turns to the window again. Her outfit is simple, shorts and a tank with thin straps. The light glides over the back of her neck, shoulders and bare upper back, disappearing into the darkness until the next one takes over—teasing me by being able to caress Angelina where I wish I could touch her myself. In our proximity, I notice her skin erupt in goose bumps. She rubs her crossed arms. "Hey," I nudge her. "Are you cold?" I place my hand on her back, her skin is warm and soft under my palm. She turns her face to me again, keeping her eyes down, shaking her head slightly, no.

"Come closer," I whisper so only she can hear me. I reach out for her hand, my fingers glide over hers, clasping them and pulling them gently towards me. She doesn't resist, but stays perfectly still, her eyes flicker and she finally looks directly into mine. In the occasional light intrusion, I see her chest rising fast, she is peering into my eyes and I see the fear, anxiety, uncertainty, and desire in her face. I lean in and whisper into her ear, "Come closer to me. I just ..." I pause to prevent myself from repeating myself. "I want you ... to be closer." Her fingers gently squeeze mine, she scoots over, leans into me, and lays her head on my shoulder as my arm wraps around her, our hands holding onto each other. A sensation of calm relaxes my body. I have no doubts about this girl. She is unpretentious, she plays no games, there is nothing she needs from me, but I'm the one who needs her. We stay like this until we arrive at the resort. Jenna and Brian get out of the car, and we linger in the back, Angelina not stirring. Only when Jenna peers back into the car—shrieking excitedly, "We are back, you guys! Quit fooling around!"—does Angelina rise up, startled. Her face sleepy, she stretches her arms up smiling with the most satisfied smile I have seen yet on her. "You slept well?" I ask.

"Mm-hmm," she replies without revealing anything else. She then gets out of the car, wishes Jenna and Brian a good night, and starts walking towards the rooms, leaving me behind wondering what should be my next step. I decide to catch up to her.

"Hey," I start off vaguely.

"Hey," she gives me a short reply, continuing to walk.

"That was nice, you know, back in the van ...."

"Mm-hmm," she doesn't elaborate, strolling slowly down the path amongst the well-groomed grounds. The resort is quiet and empty. Most people are asleep or enjoying nighttime activities in their rooms.

"Listen," I run my hand through my hair trying to control my anxiety. "I want to tell you...I want to try...try to explain...I like you, Angelina." I chuckle nervously. "I'd like to get to know you. I mean, I know you, but I want to know you in a different way. Oh, God! Why do I sound so ridiculous?"

"You don't," she replies, which gives me a bit of encouragement. There is hope. After all, she doesn't flat-out reject me.

"Okay, er ... Let me try it again. Ahem," I clear my throat. "I'd like to date you, Angelina. I have to ask— again—for a chance." I am finally able to say a concise statement of my intentions. Angelina stops short and turns her whole body towards me.

"That isn't funny, Kai. I told you already it's just not the right timing, the right place, the right anything." She frowns.

"I'm not laughing. Seriously. Ah, Angelina, I know, I didn't expect it at all, but when I saw you on that plane, it's as if my heart had a hiccup and was reset. I finally have a clear vision of what I want, what I need, what feels right."

"What's that?" She cocks her head to the side, folding her arms across her chest.

"You."

She shakes her head and starts walking away slowly, leaving me standing.

"Angelina, wait." I catch up to her and pull her towards me. My force is stronger than I intend and her body slams into mine, her face just inches away, her hands on my chest. She looks up at me, her hands start gliding slowly up towards my neck, then my face, her fingers trace my lips and when she looks into my eyes again, I no longer see uncertainty, I know she wants me just as much as I want her.

I press one of my hands into the small of her back, the other cradles her head, our lips collide in a kiss that quenches our thirst for each other. It takes my breath away, as if I'm running a race. I feel blood rushing faster through my veins, my heart drumming away, calling me to go after a sweeping victory. My brain pulls back on the eager emotions, I know Angelina deserves bending of the knee and total surrender ... and I am willing to give her that. Her body is pressed against mine, taut, standing on her tippy toes, her arms wrapped around my neck. Her lips are soft, her tongue invades my mouth, eviscerating any previous doubt about us. But all is gone the minute she pulls away.

She shakes her head, "We shouldn't. I'm sorry."

Before I am able to persuade her otherwise, she runs away leaving me standing in the quiet darkness, the only witness to our kiss is an iguana who is crossing the pathway, a disappointed audience member who hasn't gotten the satisfaction of finishing the show.

I am confused and unsure of what to do next. Angelina's kiss is telling of her desire, running away shows her fears. I have no idea what will prevail. I go to sleep without having the answer. In the morning light, I have more hope. I will show her there is nothing to fear.

My alarm goes off, and at first, I jump, jolted by the habit that it's time to go to work. But then I remember I am in Grenada, and the alarm is set just in case I oversleep our scuba diving lesson. I get up, make myself a cup of black coffee, and head out to the dive shop for the scuba dive training that my sister wants to do before she gets married.

Brian and Jenna are already here, their cuddling against the banister gives away their still-newly-in-love status. I search for Angelina and find her standing with her back turned to me, chatting with one of the employees of the shop. Let me see you. I send her a mental message. Her face will tell me how she is feeling today, in the sunlight of this Caribbean island. She turns to face me, responding to my silent message as if I called her name out loud. When our eyes meet, she casts her gaze down, blushing. She turns away, but I spot a barely-there smile. I have a chance after all.

There are only four of us who are taking the lesson today: my sister, Brian, Angelina, and I. Gretchen and Mitchel are still stuck in the hospital and I assume will be skipping the underwater activities to tend to Hailey. A skinny man dressed in a rash guard and shorts comes out of the diving shop and waves to all of us to come closer. I can't tell his age, maybe late twenties, or maybe late thirties, his dark brown skin doesn't reveal any age-telling wrinkles.

"Hi." He raises his hand, speaking rather low. Intuitively, we come closer to him. "My name is Prince …," he says with a Creole accent. He looks up at us, his dark brown eyes move slowly across our faces, his own face is rather emotionless, and I can't read if he's being funny or serious. "… Charming. I'll be your instructor today." Angelina and Jenna giggle at his introduction. "Did I say anything funny?" He stares at the girls. He is neither smiling or frowning. The girls shake their heads and he proceeds. "You will listen and learn, and today you will dive. But first," he pauses and raises his pointer finger up in the air, "there is a test. Here." He passes out pieces of paper titled *Pre-Test*. "Don't cheat."

We take the paper, and he disappears into the shop. Brian and Jenna sit side by side on the picnic-style table near the shop. I glance at Angelina who seems hesitant to sit opposite my sister and her soon to be husband.

"Sit with me. I don't bite." I nudge her towards the steps that lead up to the shop.

"How do you know that I don't?" she says, and I sense a lighthearted teasing.

"I don't think I'd mind that," I whisper into her ear, sitting down on the steps. She turns on her heel and decides to sit next to the lovebirds after all. I chuckle at my own wittiness. I know she is just avoiding me because she doesn't want to admit to herself that she likes me. But she does, and I will just give her time until she tells me that herself.

When we are all done with our tests, Prince collects our paperwork, introduces us to the gear, and explains in his emotionless tone all the parts and how to operate them. Once we master the pre-check of the air tanks, we pick flippers and masks, and head to the pool. The gear is heavy. Angelina lags behind, she looks small in the vest with the attached tank, carrying flippers in her hands.

"Let me give you a hand," I offer.

"I'm okay," she replies, looking at the ground. I nod and keep walking, but slow my pace so I can help her in case she changes her mind. But she never does. Sometimes she stops to hoist the sliding gear back up. I stop and wait for her but stay quiet. Then when she takes her step, I keep moving ahead, looking back occasionally.

When we get to the pool and enter the water, she sighs loudly, "This is so much better now." The buoyancy of the water relieves the weight of the air tank and cools our heated bodies.

"Let me put some whale sperm on the masks." Prince pours blue liquid inside his diving mask and rinses it in the pool, he then collects our masks and does the same. We all look at each other, I still can't figure the man out; his intonation doesn't betray the true meaning of his intentions.

"Relax people, this is just so the glass doesn't fog up." He finally smiles and the row of white teeth gleams against his dark lips. We all release a short chuckle and wait for his next instruction. He goes over secondary air supply in case of emergency, he also teaches us underwater sign language. I have to commit to memory that a thumbs-up underwater means 'going up' not 'all is well.' Prince pairs us up, and by default, I end up with Angelina, which I am very happy about. Her skin has gotten a shade darker from the sun, small freckles adorn the bridge of her nose. Small beads of pool water lay still on her face, as if enjoying Angelina's beautiful features as much as I do. We work together to learn how to save one another and float in case we are left behind by the ship. Finally, we have gone over all the rescue skills for our level and understand how to behave on the surface of the water. The time has come to do the underwater lesson. I put the breathing mouthpiece into my mouth, cover my eyes and my nose with the diving mask, and take a deep breath, expanding my lungs to their full capacity. My chest has to labor hard, the compressed air isn't easy to inhale, my body reacts with a faster heartbeat and anxiety to the decrease of oxygen. I look at Brian and Jenna who have already submerged their faces under water, but Angelina is still standing up. She glances at me, and I see the fear in her large eyes. I take my mouth piece out and lift my mask, she follows suit gasping for air.

"Hey, hey! Don't panic. This is just your body reacting to the lack of oxygen. It takes a few minutes, but you'll adjust, just keep pulling in the air steadily." I try to calm her. "Like this. Do this with me." I pull the air through my mouth and motion her to do the same, she follows suit and closes her eyes. "That's right, now let it out, slowly." I breathe out, and Angelina does the same. We repeat the exercise a few more times.

"Are we all right here?" Prince raises his head out of the water to check on us.

I nod to the inquiry and glance at Angelina. "We're fine," she confirms. Prince dives down, and Angelina puts on her mask. Before she puts her air supply tube in her mouth, she grabs my hand in the water, gives it a squeeze, and whispers thank you.

I nod in acknowledgement, put my mask on, take a deep breath, and put my mouthpiece in. I submerge my head underwater, where Prince shows me an okay sign and I reply the same. I inhale slow and deep and exhale a steady stream of bubbles. The sunrays play on the walls of the swimming pool, the sound of the outside is muffled, water is pressing against my eardrums. We take a swim around the pool adjusting our buoyancy, making sure to keep our bodies horizontal. I've never imagined it is so hard to float under water. I appreciate the difficulty of the newly acquired skills. My heart finally steadies and the anxiety disappears.

"Now, the final test," Prince announces. "You will learn what to do if water floods your mask while you're underwater. Watch and learn." We all dive and observe Prince purposefully flood his mask. He tilts his head up, opens the bottom of his mask up at the same time he blows forcefully through his nose, creating an eruption of air bubbles. He then presses the bottom of the mask to his face, and now it has no water in it. The motion to free the mask of water is swift, but the mind hesitates to blow air out of the nose while in the water. I know I just have to do it quickly before my brain starts to escalate the anxiety into full panic. I dive down and follow the exact steps that Prince has just shown, the trick works and my mask is free of water immediately. Brian is the next one who passes the test, and he helps Jenna out when she can't do it at first. Angelina dives down but quickly resurfaces, coughing. She takes off the mask and drops her air supply into the water.

"Hey, are you okay?" I resurface to check on her.

"Just breathe through your nose."

"Lift your arms up." All of us voice our concern or useless advice. She finally clears her lungs and takes a deep breath, her eyes are closed as she puts her face to the sun.

"I'm fine," she says quietly and wipes away water running down her face.

"You do it again, right away," Prince barks an order without any concern for her experience.

"Don't be scared Angelina. I just did it, and you know me, I'm the biggest wuss." Jenna tries to encourage her friend.

Angelina nods, forces a smile, and puts the mask over her face. She puts the air supply into her mouth, she looks around and then into the clear water of the pool. I see that she hesitates.

"Go on, miss," the diving instructor pushes her.

I see her chest rise and she submerges under the water as does our instructor. I put on my own mask and a snorkel and submerge my head. I stay just behind Angelina so she cannot see me observing her. Prince fills up his mask with water, swiftly turns his head up and blows forcefully with his nose, liberating himself of the water so he can see clearly. Angelina shows him the okay sign. She fills up her mask with water, and she starts to tilt her head back, but then quickly ascends to the surface before finishing the skill. I lift my head out of the water and see that Brian and Jenna are sitting on the edge of the pool, ordering a drink from the waitress passing by.

"Do it again, miss," Prince repeats monotonously.

Angelina looks at the water, her head hanging low, she puts the mask on her forehead and rubs her arms that are covered in goose bumps. I sense she needs reassurance to power through this challenge. I tread through the chest-high water to face her, her lips have turned light purple, she starts to shake, her eyes are red from the water, and she is avoiding looking at me.

"Hey, hey ... you don't look like you are having fun," I whisper only for her to hear. "You don't have to do this. We can just go and bum around on the beach instead of this stupid activity. What do you say? Let's go do paddle boarding. I promise I will look like a complete clown on it, and I will even let you record me so you can use it for future blackmail ... huh? ... what do you say?"

She slowly raises her eyes and stares into mine for a few moments without saying anything, and then her lips stretch into a smile. "I'd like that, but I want to finish this or I'll regret it." She lets out a sigh.

"I don't want you to regret this, come, we'll do it together, you just look at me under the water, okay?" I tell her and she nods her head and puts back on the mask. I follow suit, and we both dive in the shallow pool. Prince does the same, and he goes through the now familiar steps again, and when he has finished, he motions for Angelina to repeat the same. She shows him the okay sign. I swim up to face her and give her an okay sign myself. Her eyes are wide. I know she is panicking. I grab her hand and put it over my heart, with the other, I motion her to take a deep breath and then slowly release it as a steady stream of bubbles. She blinks quickly and follows my instructions. I feel pulsation in my ears, and I know her heart is pounding even faster. I wish I could block all the muffled noise and distractions so she can just concentrate on believing in herself. I know she can overcome this, she just needs a bit more time to steady her emotions. After a few deep breaths, she lets go of me, lifts up her mask to flood it, all while breathing steadily. She looks directly into my eyes, and I know she is ready and will succeed this time. Angelina tilts her head back and blows air hard through her nose, the bubbles push out the water, and when she faces me again, I see her eyes squinting delightfully and her hands throwing the okay sign. When we resurface, she takes her mask off, her mouth is free from the breathing tube that is now making bubbling eruptions in the water, and she squeals in excitement. I can't help but enjoy being the witness of her personal success.

"I did it. I so did it!" she yells. "Thank you, thank you so much for helping me." She treads through the water towards me, and throws her arms around me, squeezing me tight. "It really helped me," she says into my ear. She tries to pull away, but I hold her by the waist to prolong this moment of closeness.

"I knew you could do it," I whisper back and release her. She goes to Jenna and Brian who high five her, congratulating her for passing the challenge.

"Everyone," Prince calls out to us to pay attention to him. "Congratulations on finishing your training ... in this pool," he says without much enthusiasm in his voice while moving his gaze across each of our faces. I feel embarrassed for feeling happy about learning scuba in his presence, this man has probably been diving for years, and our baby steps are no big win in his life.

"Why are you all so sad all of a sudden?" He questions our solemn demeanor. "You are in Grenada, you just learned to scuba. Life is good." His tone finally changes to cheerful, and a wide smile comes across his face. We all smile as if his change in intonation has given us permission to do so.

"Man, I thought you didn't like us or something," I say out loud what has been on my mind.

"Nah. I was just tough with you guys. I like everyone. I'm a happy guy. Everyone is happy in Grenada," Prince replies. "Okay, now, you look like you might be getting a bit cold from being in the water so long. Go have lunch, I will meet you by the dive shop in one hour, and we will do our first dive in the ocean."

"Okay."

"Thanks."

"See you, thank you."

"Great, thank you," we all reply in unison. We get out of the pool, take off the flippers, and carry the heavy vests back to the shop where they will be cleaned and the air tanks refilled for the dive. Brian and Jenna tell us that they will order room service and almost skip to their private oasis. When Angelina takes off her vest, the T-shirt she has on over her bathing suit is still wet and clings to her body, tightly accentuating every curve of her fit figure. She shivers, and her body erupts in goose bumps in the shade of the store with the breeze of the ocean blowing lightly, she rubs her arms and smiles at me, then looks away, but I cannot keep my eyes off her.

"Come into the sun, you look like you're freezing," I urge her. She takes a step forward into the small area illuminated by the sun. It feels as if we are under a spotlight that shines just for the two of us, or is she the spotlight that shines so bright that I am drawn to its warmth and comfort?

"That was so difficult, but I feel like I just won the hardest fight," Angelina reveals. Smiling, her full lips have changed from purple to lush pink, she is warming up, and I myself feel elated with her achievement. She picks up the bag with her clothing and puts on the shorts she'd taken off before the class.

"I don't feel like eating by myself. Care to join me?" I try to keep her near me for as long as possible.

"Sure," she agrees without any hesitation.

We stroll through the shaded path, then across the large, open space occupied by the pool where we have just taken our scuba class. I grab one of the fresh towels and throw it over Angelina's shoulders to keep her warm, and then we enter the cafe that has a view of the pool. We take the seat closest to the beach, a waiter comes by and gives us the menu. Angelina quickly looks over the menu, and before the waiter can step away orders blackened cod with a side of sweet potato fries. It sounds delicious, so I decide to go with the same choice.

"Oh, and can I have a Russian Mule," Angelina calls out to the waiter.

"Make it two," I add.

"I sent out my book to the agents." Angelina looks at me from under her eyelashes then takes a sip of her icy water through a straw.

"That's great. I have a friend in publishing, I can give him a call," I say.

"I appreciate it, but don't," she unexpectedly declines.

"Why? You don't want any help from me?" I am surprised to hear her say that. Usually people jump at opportunities of connecting with the right person.

"No, it's not that." She lowers her gaze, looking away and blushing. "You must think it's silly, but I don't want favors. I want to go through this process myself. Don't get me wrong, I don't expect agents to fight for my manuscript, it's not like it's the next best seller, but I think it's important to go through rejection, it keeps you grounded."

"Does it?" I question her, and she bobs her head lightly.

"I think so. I know, it absolutely sucks, but many authors get numerous rejections before they're discovered. I'm prepared for that."

"If there's an opportunity to get to know someone in the industry, you should take it. It's not a favor, it's not cheating, it's just luck." I try to explain my point of view.

"I like negative reinforcement, when someone tells me that what I do is not worthy or not good enough, that drives me even more to be better at whatever it is I'm doing. I don't mind it, but if I get tired of it, I'll come to you, I promise," she says teasingly. The waiter brings us our drinks in copper mugs, and I decide to make a toast to cheer Angelina up.

"Congratulations on persevering and making it through the flooded mask test. I'm proud of you that you didn't give up. Cheers!" I tap her glass lightly and take a sip of the pleasantly sweet and spicy drink that runs down my throat, warming up my insides.

"Thank you for helping me through it. I really struggled, it was so scary to breathe out of my nose in the water, so unnatural. You really helped me steady my anxiety and push through. Cheers," she reciprocates.

"We made a good team. I enjoyed it …." I take another sip of the drink, before I proceed again. "I enjoyed our kiss last night as well …."

She takes a long sip of her drink, and she is about to say something, but is interrupted by the food being delivered to us by the waiter. We wait in awkward silence for him to finish and leave before anything more is said between us.

"Listen … listen, Angelina. I'm being very honest with you. I like you. I like the way you make me feel. There is no fluff, there is no pretense, no fake, no made-up appearances. I see you, and I know this is you and I want to get to know you beyond you being my little sister's friend. I will keep asking because I know you like me, and my calculations tell me that my attempts have a high probability of achieving a positive result."

She takes another sip of her drink and chokes before she is able to say anything. When she is finally able to speak clearly, she laughs. "God! Liquid and I are not friends today." She then takes a deep breath, straightens her back, puts loose strands of hair behind her ears and looks straight into my eyes. She doesn't blink, it seems she is not breathing for a moment before she says anything to me.

"It seems everyone around me is aware of how much of a crush I had on you since middle school. It's funny … gosh … I always imagined the moment … when you tell me you like me and I had these perfect responses …," she rubs her temples and shakes her head. "But I don't have any perfect responses."

"I just need one imperfect yes from you," I beg. She stares at me, she wants to say something but stops. She twists her fingers and then bites her lips. I know she wants to say yes, but she still hesitates. I get up from my seat and walk over to her. I ask her to give me her hand and then pull her up to stand. "Hi! My name is Kai. I have a really annoying sister that I love. I recently realized I like a girl. She's smart, she's tenacious, she's brave, she's everything I want in my life. I'm just asking her to give me a chance, so I can show her that I'm more than a boy she used to like in school." I look into her eyes that are the color of translucent blue, they pull me into their depths. I break the gaze by touching her cheek and then slide a strand of her hair behind her ear. She leans into the palm of my hand and closes her eyes, the corners of her mouth go up and her beautiful lips form the most satisfied smile.

"I would like for you to show me more of you then," she murmurs.

The words wash over me as if like a hot shower after a dreary day. I know now that the cold and the gray of my existence are over, and I can enjoy the calm and be content with this girl by my side.

# 14.

## ANGELINA

It's funny how life can change in just a few short days. Here I am in Grenada, waiting for my best friend to get married. My long-dead relationship with Jack received verbal confirmation of its demise just a few days ago, but I am not sad or devastated by that. Deep down, I've been prepared to hear that for quite a few months now; I just thought he would do it in a less cowardly way.

I've been going over the years spent with Jack, and my fresh unemotional perspective makes me realize that I'd been a convenient maid for him. I'd responded to and anticipated all his needs so he could craft his stories—he is the artist, he has the needs, he can't be disturbed—all the while, I'd forgotten about my own desires, my wants, and my aspirations. I am a writer. I have stories to tell, and the only person who has finished reading them is Kai.

Kai is the one who encouraged me to seek an agent because, according to him, my writing is amazing. He is the one who held my hand when I was freaking out underwater. Kai is the one whose kiss raised such a strong wave of desire that I ran away because I was afraid I wouldn't be able to control myself. Here he is, standing in front of me, asking me to be his girlfriend. I've tried hard to resist, but I could no longer withstand his persistence. And the way he spoke—such honesty and vulnerability. After hearing my affirmative answer, he picks me up and spins me. I squeal in delight from him being so excited and from feeling elated that this man likes me.

We finish lunch, our hunger satisfied, and our bodies are finally warm when we return to the dive shop. Brian and Jenna join us a few minutes later. Jenna skips down the path holding on tight to Brian who is beaming with glee. Prince comes out of the store, and this time his demeanor is completely different, he greets us smiling.

"Hiiiii!" he stretches. "Is everyone ready to dive in Grenada today? Is everyone happy?" He points to each of us, and when we nod or grunt in affirmation, he does a little dance and a quick spin that ends with his back turned to us. Then he starts walking away with a little hop and a skip. We remain standing, not sure if we should follow him or wait here. "C'mon, happy people, you need to follow me. I'm not gonna carry your scuba gear for you. You're going to work today," he yells over his shoulder, and we all scramble to follow him.

We gear up, go through the safety checks of the air tanks and our vests that we learned earlier, we then walk down the steps and through the beach to the motorboat. Prince and another scuba instructor take us out into the open water.

"There is a current here that will help lead us right to the beach at the resort," he explains, pointing in the opposite direction, away from the resort, as the boat carries us away from the shore. The weather is perfect, and the ocean is calm. The water is so clear that the ocean floor appears deceptively close. When we arrive at the diving spot, Prince drops the guiding line with an orange flag that will point to our location on the surface of the water. We put on our flippers and masks, the air supply goes into my mouth. The moment I take in the compressed air, my heart begins to race, the anxiety resurfaces, and I feel a tightness in my throat.

Before he covers his face with the mask and his mouth with the breathing tube, Kai leans in and tells me, "Remember, the anxiety is normal. It'll pass once your body adjusts to the breathing. You just look at me. I promise I'll be next to you. Okay?"

I nod and give him the okay sign. His reassurance is slightly calming, and I feel safer knowing he is nearby. Prince instructs us to sit on the edge of the boat and fall into the water back first. He is the first one in, Brian and Jenna are next, Kai follows. I take a deep breath and throw myself backward. The fall is not pleasant, it is disorienting until I am able to resurface. The water seeps into my ears, and I feel the strong pull of the current that I need to tread against to stay next to everyone. My heart is still racing, and I am contemplating if learning scuba is such a great idea; it's a dangerous activity full of potential risks from sharks to drowning. Jenna was so excited about doing it that she easily persuaded me that it would be amazing, life changing, and memorable. I will for sure remember this as the most nerve-racking activity. I wish it were over already. Prince motions for everyone to dive down, and I press the button that releases air out of my vest allowing me to sink. Water fills my ear canal, pressing against my tympanic membrane. I look down and see the floor of the ocean, the water is crystal clear and I can spot shells and corals on the sandy bottom. The current is the wind of the ocean, carrying small particles of ocean life past me. I keep releasing air out of the vest to continue the dive. Prince shows me the okay sign, and I show him one in return. Kai is right across from me, descending at the same rate, he sends me the okay sign as well, and I reply back with one. The water starts to forcefully press on my inner ear, I stop my descent and swallow hard to equalize the pressure. It works and then I proceed to go lower. Kai checks on me every few feet with the okay sign. Prince swims down ahead carrying the guiding line to the bottom. Brian and Jenna stick together, having no trouble with the descent. I am able to hold my body horizontally, my breath steadies, and I realize that my heartbeat is not a gallop, but a calmer trot. The engine of my body is working efficiently without the emergency lights blinking, signaling the danger zone.

I take in my surroundings, the clarity of water allows me to see much of the underwater world, Kai swims closely by my side throwing an occasional okay sign. I appreciate his sweet care of me. Small parts of the underwater plants drift in the current, little fish dart back and forth, and as we near the bottom of the sandy floor, I discover it's covered by a forest of corals; they are stiff, yet alive in this underwater oasis. Some close up and hide their tentacles as we approach, some are overgrown by shells and house little critters. A large starfish nestles in the sand, Prince picks it up and brings it to us for a closer look and then gently puts it back where it belongs. He swims without any devices, easily orienting himself and leading us along the current that he's taken countless times, but which is invisible to us novice divers. We dive deeper, large seashells decorate the bottom of the ocean. Orange and blue fish move along, not paying any attention to us large, dark intruders in their weightless world. Prince shows us an eel that swims out of a small cave. It is black, thin, and doesn't look happy—he hides as soon as we get closer. I keep checking my oxygen supply, and I am nearing halfway; we must come up soon. Prince keeps on swimming, looking around as if searching for something. Finally, he swims to the very bottom, and reaching the sandy surface, motions for us to get closer. At first, I don't see anything except for the sand, but then a large sea turtle surfaces from underneath and slowly swims away. The creature is magnificent, it glides with such ease and grace, it would not be able to do that on the surface. Prince moves his hand across its shell and invites us to do the same. The turtle doesn't mind, swimming slowly as we pet it, but soon it has had enough and decides to leave our presence to go somewhere less crowded, I bet.

I check my air supply, and it's almost time to go up. Kai swims over to check on me, I'm about to give him the okay sign when I notice that my mask is filling up with water. My brain turns on all the emergency lights, letting my body know that it's in danger. I have to get back to the surface. Right now. I start my ascent. I see the sun right above me, the roof of the surface is right on top. I just have to swim faster before the water covers my eyes completely, before I have to perform the dreaded trick of blowing air out of my mask. My heart is racing, pumping my blood throughout my body, propelled by the primal instinct of survival. My ascent is interrupted suddenly by a firm grasp of my leg, and when I look down, I see Prince vigorously motioning me to stop, to free my mask of air. He is showing danger. Danger is right here; the water is in my mask I want to yell to him.

Kai swims to me, the water is almost halfway up the mask. I see his eyes, they are so dark, they pull me in, calling me to pay attention to them. He motions me to steady my breath, he grabs my hand, and puts it over his chest. He is here, he is with me, I will be okay. I finally can think clearly. I can't ascend quickly, there is a danger of decompression, I could hurt myself. I pull air deep into my lungs, overtaking the emergency response of my body to the water in my mask. I know what to do. I've just learned. I take another deep breath. I look into Kai's eyes and give him an okay. He returns the same reply and lets go of my hand. I tilt my head back and forcefully blow bubbles into the lifted mask, freeing myself of the water in it. The trick works, just as it did during the training. I look around and all the concerned faces are staring back at me. I feel terrible, they must think I am such a coward.

Prince takes the lead, and we slowly start our ascent along the rising walls of the underwater sand dune. I feel as if we are emerging from a deep cave as the water becomes warmer. My body doesn't have to fight the current, my fins touch the bottom of the ocean floor, and I am able to stand up with my head above water. Prince has led us to the beach right in front of the dive shop. I look in the direction of where we dove from the boat and I'm amazed by his navigation under the water. There are no roads, no lights, no buildings, and yet he seemed to know exactly where he was and where the most interesting ocean creatures reside. I swim on my back towards the shore, and as soon as it gets very shallow, I take off the flippers and walk, my feet sinking into the fine-as-powder, soft sand. Once we get on shore, I take off my mask. It's liberating to feel the breeze of the warm wind on my face, I have missed the air—every inch of my body has missed it.

"I'm sorry ... Um ... I panicked there," I tell Prince who stands waiting for us to gather around.

"Don't worry, miss, you had me there. Nothing would happen when Prince is around." He smiles with water droplets covering his head and beading on his curly black hair.

"Thank you ... I really appreciate it," I tell him. He nods at my gratitude and starts walking up the steps.

"Bring up the scuba gear, and drop it off over there. Prince is done for today," he says over his shoulder.

"Hey. Are you all right?" Kai comes up to me and helps me remove the heavy air cylinder. "Your eyes ... you looked so terrified. I was worried you would come up too fast," he says softly and grabs my hands. His long, wet eyelashes frame his beautiful eyes that stare at me with concern.

"I didn't like that at all. I don't think I'll ever scuba again. I did it once, and I think I've had enough for the rest of my life .... I feel like such a scaredy cat," I explain.

"Are you kidding me? You did great. You got scared, but you were able to concentrate and overcome your fear, not a lot of people can do that. I'm proud of you, even if you never scuba again," he reassures me, and I feel better about my panic.

"Wasn't it amazing!" Jenna yelps as she takes off her scuba gear. "I absolutely loved it. I want to do it again. Right, Brian?"

"Yes, honey boo, anything you want." He smiles at her lovingly and pulls her in for a kiss. The kiss is long and they both seem to forget that Kai and I are right next to them, but I don't hold any grudges, they are about to get married. Once they both have had enough of each other, Brian wraps his arms around his soon-to-be wife and lifts her off the ground. She throws her head back and laughs loudly. I can't help but smile, witnessing my friend in a pure state of happiness.

Jenna then leans in and whispers something into his ear, he nods and she giggles in response. "You guys, we are going to catch some z's before dinner. We want to scuba dive again, so we're going to take the test tomorrow. After a dive to forty feet, we will be officially certified scuba divers. Yay!" Jenna raises both hands in the air in celebration.

"Yeah, right. Go ahead and catch those z's, or whatever you call it these days." I smack my friend's arm lightly. "I'll study a bit as well. I think I should just push through and complete the certification, otherwise I'll regret it, but I'm terrible at test taking."

"Kai is a great test taker." Jenna winks at me. "He was always an A student. I'm sure he will be a great study partner." My friend teases me and my cheeks start to burn. Kai unexpectedly comes close to me and wraps his arm around my waist, pulling me closer to his side. The touch is electric, making my skin erupt in a pleasant shiver. He is so much taller than me, I barely reach his shoulder, but his height is not intimidating it's the opposite, I feel protected in his presence. I press my hip against his leg and put my hand over his hand, pulling it deeper around me.

"I'm quite smart. I'll make sure you pass your test," he replies with all seriousness in his voice. "I bet we'll do better on it than you guys," he challenges his sister.

"Oh, the challenge is on. Baby boo, we need to win." She turns her back to Brian who unzips the wet suit and helps her get out of it.

"Come. I'll help you." Kai pulls me aside and turns me so he can undo the zipper of my suit as well.

"Thank you." I don't resist even though the zipper has a long strap that I can pull down myself. Kai stands close to me and puts one hand on my shoulder, and slowly pulls down the zipper.

"You have the most beautiful back," he leans in and whispers into my ear. His voice charges my desire in the pit of my belly and the heat of the sensation spreads pleasantly over me.

"Bye, guys!"

"See you." Brian and Jenna run off laughing before we are able to respond.

I watch them disappear behind the tropical blinds and then turn to Kai. My hands glide up over the wetsuit covering his body, I feel the firmness of his chest as it rises and falls slowly. I reach his neck and stare into his eyes, they are as dark as a stormy ocean, magnetic, pulling me closer to him. I wrap my hands around his neck. Standing on my tippy-toes I kiss his lips softly, tasting the salt water of the ocean. He lets me control the kiss, giving me time to enjoy the taste of his soft lips. I feel his one arm slide into the opening of my wetsuit, the warmth of his touch on my cool, wet skin relaxes me, and I press my body against him, every inch of me wanting to melt into his embrace. I wrap my arms tight around his neck, pulling him to me. My lips are no longer patient, they are yearning and searching for the satisfaction of my desire.

"Please, let's go to the room," he grunts, pulling away from me.

"Let me help you with your suit," I reply, smiling coyly. He obliges and turns his back to me. I reach up to his neck and undo the zipper, his back is a wide triangle of defined shoulders that come down to his narrow waist; those defined muscles flex under tanned skin. He turns around and takes off the top of the wetsuit. I swallow hard at the site of his bare chest rippling with muscles. He takes it off completely, putting it into the water bath with the others and I do the same. His skin is overtaken by goose bumps. I reach out and put my hand over his heart, he lets me linger on his warm skin for a few moments, before taking it into his hand and kissing it.

"Angelina, let's get out of here," he groans, growing impatient.

"I'm just enjoying the view," I tease, but then take his hand and lead him towards the rooms. The resort seems empty, most people are tired of the glaring heat and direct sun, hiding in their air-conditioned rooms. The morning birds are quiet, even the wind has decided to be still, letting humidity set in. We walk briskly, driven by the desire that is heating us inside.

"My room?" I ask and don't wait for him to reply. I get out the key card and tap it on the electronic lock, the light goes green and I no longer care that our timing might be wrong or that we would live far away from each other, in this moment he's never felt more right. He sweeps me up, and I wrap my legs around his waist. Our lips collide as if two seas have come together once the dam between them is taken down. Kai carries me into the room, collapsing on the bed. What little clothes we wear, come off quickly. I am breathless, and my heart is drumming away even faster now that I have all of Kai naked in front of me. The man is beautiful—tall and lean, his defined abs flat and hard, disappear into the narrow point of his groin pressing firmly into my thigh.

"I'm so stupid," he utters suddenly. "Why haven't I seen you before?" He places a kiss on my lips, his tongue reaching, caressing mine. "You're the one I've always needed." He pulls away and moves to my breast, tugging on the hard nipple with his teeth.

"I'm here, I'm right here," I moan from his touch.

"I'll never let you out of my sight. I want you to be mine." He speaks the words like a vow as he enters the warmness of my body. He rocks like the waves of the Caribbean ocean against the sandy beaches of Grenada, flooding me with intense pleasure that spreads from the pit of my belly. I close my eyes, my hands glide over his smooth, hard back; his lips trace my neck with kisses, biting the skin gently. Pleasure twists and spins, tightening inside of me as his body crushes faster against mine until everything stills for a moment and then comes down with the power of a waterfall. My body arches from the force of intense orgasm, and I let out a loud scream, sharing with the universe my voice, when Kai takes me to the peak of ecstasy. He collapses on top of me. His body is hot and sweaty, his heart galloping fast. I feel its pulsation against my chest, and my own heart answers back, keeping the pace from our lovemaking.

"That was amazing," he murmurs, nuzzling into my neck, his warm breath reflecting off of my skin.

"Ahh … It was," I respond slowly.

# 15.

## GRETCHEN

The morning air is refreshing when we leave the hospital. The sun has already come up, its light a perfect golden glow that feels good after the night spent in the hospital. Hailey slept well and woke up without any nausea or vomiting. Only a slight headache persists, but she says it doesn't bother her much. I feel tired and achy, sweaty and sticky. My dress is a wrinkled mess, and I avoid any reflective surfaces so I don't catch a glimpse of my most likely puffy face and stringy, oily hair. The amount of blood that came out of a half an inch cut was shocking. I panicked more than Hailey, who merely tugged on my dress, blotting the blood with it, saying calmly, "Mom, I'm okay, it's just a little bit of blood. Mom, stop yelling," as I continued to call for help.

I feel bad that everyone made the trip to the hospital. My phone died, and I just wanted to let them know not to worry, but I guess my message was exaggerated when it was received by my friends.

"Hey, girls. Over here," Mitchel calls for Hailey and I, waving his arm while standing next to a car that I guess is a taxi. I'm happy he came. I still don't know why he would choose someone like me with the life I have. I tried to conceal my emotions for him by ignoring him when everyone arrived. I am not yet ready to answer all the questions and objections the girls might have. The hospital would be a test for him, of what my life is like, and I will see what kind of a person he is. Would he run away? Would my daughter and I be too much for him? But he stayed; he stayed all night sleeping on an uncomfortable chair and bringing me coffee before I woke up. He looks at me so ... as if I matter, as if I'm beautiful. Yesterday I was drawn to his room, my legs carried me to him, and my mind wasn't willing to fight against it. I didn't know what I would say of my presence there, my voice trembled as I spoke, my heart raced, but I still knew what I wanted: I wanted Mitchel. I decided to take a chance for once, and I am glad I did. I didn't know what lovemaking could be, that it could be about satisfying my desire as well. Mitchel took his time, he knew the final destination where our bodies would take us, he was purposefully stretching the trip, enjoying all the stops, kissing me where no man ever had, showing me that getting to the pleasure peak is just part of the fun.

"Moooom." Hailey tugs my hand. "C'mon. Why are you smiling like that? You look like a crazy lady. Mitchel found us a taxi. Let's go."

"Yes, I'm sorry, of course, let's go," I apologize for my daydreaming. I have to be more aware of my facial expressions, I don't want to give away how I'm feeling.

"Are you ready to get back to the vacation, without any more hospital visits, rookie?" Mitchel teases Hailey, she sighs loudly and rolls her eyes at him. He chuckles, waits for us to get in the back seat, closes the door behind us and then takes a seat in the front passenger seat. He converses with the driver, Hailey lays over my lap, and I take in the sights of the island through the half rolled-down window of the old Jetta. My gaze moves towards the side mirror. Mitchel has his arm out the window, laughing at something the driver is telling him. He is handsome in a way that isn't pompous or arrogant. The lines on his forehead and between his brows tell of his deep intelligence. I wonder what he is thinking about right this very moment. Is he contemplating his purpose in this universe, is he thinking about what he is going to have for lunch, or what mess he has gotten himself into by getting involved with me? As if sensing me staring at him, he glances in the same mirror, and when his eyes meet mine, he smiles and winks at me. A hot wave washes over me, I smile and look away. There is something exciting in us stealing moments, in these intimate, silent gestures. This is just ours, for us and nobody else. Hailey stirs, "Mom, did you tell Dad about what happened to me?"

"I will once we get to the resort, honey," I reply. A conversation that certainly will not be pleasant. I know that he will yell, probably call me a terrible mother. I sigh, pushing down the thought of the conversation I need to have. Will he really care that his daughter was hurt? I think he mostly cares that he looks like a good father and that I look like a bad mother who can't handle parenthood. When Hailey would get cuts and scrapes from normal childhood behaviors, he would not miss the opportunity to establish his superiority over me. If he would've been there she wouldn't have fallen, if he were near, she wouldn't have gotten that cut. The problem is that he was never there. Not when she was hurt and not when she was happy, dressed up in her pretty clothes, her hair made up in perfect pigtails.

"I miss Daddy. I wish he liked spending time with us." Hailey reveals the feelings of her child's soul. A revelation that is so rare for her to make vocal, it's painful for me to hear. My heart aches for her. What will my relationship with her father mean for her future relationships with men? Did I damage my girl's perception of men and how she will be affected by them? I have to make sure she feels loved, that she never lacks affection, so it will be just my motherly adoration, that is all I can ever promise her to be constant. I will always be there. I will always protect her. I will forever feel guilty for causing her any pain. I hope when she grows up, she can understand my choices.

"I know, honey. Why don't you call him when we get to the resort?"

"Mm-hmm," she replies. I know she is excited to tell him about her gruesome injury. I can already hear her speeding through words in one breath so she can quickly get to the ending where she got three stitches, and she wasn't scared a bit. I sigh heavily, trying to lift the weight of unpleasant anticipation of what I will hear from my ex, but it doesn't help. The warmth of the air and the steady movement of the car rock me to sleep, and I wake up to Mitchel opening the car door for us.

"Ladies," he gives me his hand for support so I can get out of the taxi and does the same for Hailey.

"Thank you, Mitchel."

"You're welcome, Gretchen," he replies as our eyes meet, he gives my hand a squeeze that transfers energy to my tired body. He charges me with hope for happiness, and I am looking forward to when we can be alone again.

"Thanks, Mitch." I hear Hailey's familiarity. I want to correct her, but Mitchel shakes his head and smiles, giving me a sign that it's not necessary.

"Let me take you to your room. I want to make sure you don't fall again, rookie," Mitchel insists.

We meet occasional early risers on our way to the room, some are ready for the beach with towels thrown over their shoulders, some determined couples are in their workout gear heading to the gym. I wonder what they think of us looking disheveled, wrinkled, and with a bandaged child in tow, we must appear an odd couple.

We are soon standing in front of our door, I open it, and we are greeted by bopping balloons that overtake the whole hallway. *Get Well* is the message on some of them. Hailey pushes us aside, "Are these for me?" she exclaims.

"I think so," I tell her, uncertain of who is responsible for this gesture. "Mommy, there is an envelope, too." Hailey picks up a white envelope at the bottom of the weight that is holding the balloons down, her name is written in a pretty cursive. She tears it open impatiently.

"Mommy, it says it's a spa treatment for both you and I. We can have a free manicure and pedicure." Hailey reads out loud the message. She passes it to me to read, and heads towards the bed where she turns on her phone. I know she will be disconnected from reality for quite a bit, catching up with all her friends and taking lots of selfies. I run through the offer that is written on a stationary with the resort insignia underneath it.

"I guess it's from the hotel. It's kind of nice, right?" I turn to Mitchel who is standing in the doorway, leaning against it, staring at me with a hungry look in his eyes.

"It's nice. Can I just show you something out here?" he motions me to come just outside the door.

"Honey, I'm just outside. Call me if you need anything," I yell out to Hailey, but she doesn't respond in her preoccupied state with her phone. Mitchel stretches his hand and I give him mine. He pulls me towards him and I walk out, closing the door behind me gently.

"What do you want to show me?" I whisper back. He puts his finger to his lips and points to the bush right outside of the building. When I look, I see a bird that looks like a dove, but its wings are dark brown with a white stripe in the front, on the chest and over its head, the belly of the bird is a beige color. It doesn't look impressive or unusual, and I wouldn't even notice it passing by. Mitchel hugs my waist standing behind me, his chin resting on my shoulder. "This is a Grenada dove. It's an endangered species. We are lucky to spot it here."

"This plain looking bird is rare?" I ask, surprised. "Why?"

"No one is really sure, but it probably has to do with the change of their habitat. No one has seen one flying beyond the forest. This is a once-in-a-lifetime treat. Isn't it amazing?"

It's amazing how much this man knows, and he is taking his time to teach me. "How do you know about this bird?" I lean into him, enjoying his closeness while no one can see us.

He chuckles. "Ah, my life is very boring …. I have lots of free time … so I took up bird watching."

"Bird watching? So, you just sit and watch?"

"Mm-hmm, I just sit and watch. It's very calming, you learn patience, and you learn to appreciate little intricacies even in the most usual things." His voice resonates throughout my body, raising my desire as he nuzzles into my neck. He turns me around and his lips graze mine, the touch is tantalizing. I grow impatient, we don't yet have the luxury of time, my lips want to taste his. I lean in, but he pulls away, smiling, "You are full of intricacies, I like learning about them."

"Moooom," Hailey yells impatiently.

I can only laugh at this interruption of our secret embrace. Mitchel places a kiss on my forehead. "Go. I'll see you later."

"I'll see you later." I linger against his lips for a few seconds before leaving him to see what Hailey wants.

"Heeey, what happened, Hailey? Are you okay?" I try to sound natural, so she doesn't suspect anything.

"What's wrong with you?" She stares at me, squinting her eyes.

"Nothing, nothing is wrong with me. Why? Do I look like something is wrong?" I turn away so my face doesn't betray me.

"You look … weird." I feel Hailey's stare drilling into my back.

I pour myself a glass of water before I speak. "Are you hungry? I'm starving. You want to order room service?" I try to change the topic of conversation.

"Yeah, I guess." She returns to her phone.

"I'll order you some pancakes."

"Mm," I get a short grunt of a reply from Hailey. "Mom, your phone is ringing, it says it's Miramar Dermatology."

"That's okay, let it go to my voicemail." I'd visited the dermatologist two weeks before the trip and they biopsied a growth, they were probably calling to give me the results.

I will call them later. I dial the hotel phone number and place an order for our breakfast.

Hailey stays on the phone and I walk out to the balcony to ponder my feelings for Mitchel. Am I being too selfish? Is it fair for me to have a relationship with him? I am forever Hailey's mother; he will one day realize that he can find a girl without kids who will make him a priority. He might just decide that I am fat and my daughter doesn't treat him with the respect that he deserves. The warm breeze of Grenada whispers to leave the worry behind. The sun warms my hopes for a future where I might have a chance at love. Should I wait for that time, or should I not even allow for the countdown to start? My search for the answer is interrupted by a knock on the door. The waiter brings in the tray of food and leaves it on the table. The smell of pancakes draws Hailey out from the depths of social media. She skips towards the table, grabs one, shoves it into her mouth, and then returns to bed where she types something frantically on the screen of her cell.

I take a bite of my pancakes and ask her, "Hailey?"

"Mm," she grunts, acknowledging that she is listening without taking her eyes off from the screen.

"You know that I love you … very much … more than anything in the world," I continue.

"Mm," she mumbles with her mouth full.

"You know that one day your dad and I, we might start dating other people …." I clear my throat before proceeding. "And I wanted to ask your opinion about that."

"Mom, you are so weird. Dad's had, like, five girl-friends already." She rolls her eyes, chewing and posing for selfies.

"And you would be okay if I dated someone?"

"Mom ... don't be so dramatic, I told you, Mitchel is cool. Like, go on a date with him already." She puffs up her cheeks and then releases the air through her pursed lips, giving me yet another roll of the eyes. Clearly, she is onto my main reason for this conversation. Is she really so relaxed about me seeing Mitchel? Maybe I should take a cue from her and not overanalyze this situation. Her dad clearly doesn't. Five girlfriends! He is keeping himself busy.

I put a piece of pancake on the fork and dip it into the jelly. I stare at the white of the plate and then draw a heart with the jellied pancake piece on the plate. It looks messy and sticky, I put it in my mouth, and it tastes perfect, sweet, soft and satisfying.

"You have cancer!" Hailey's scream pierces me. The pancake gets stuck in my throat, and I have to cough before I am able to speak.

"What?"

"The voicemail, it says you have cancer." Her chin shakes and her eyes swell with tears. She is holding up my phone screen facing me, but the text is too small for me to see. I rush towards her bed and tear the phone from her hands. She is starting to sob.

"Hailey, wait, stop crying, let me see what it says." My eyes run through the voicemail that was converted into text by my phone.

"No, I can't wait," my daughter yells through the tears that pour down her cheeks. "It says you have cancer. You didn't even tell me you went to the doctor."

*Your biopsy ... basal cell cancer ... not dangerous ... surgery ... call us.* My eyes scan the text, trying to pull out the most important words.

"I didn't tell you because it was just a regular visit. Please stop crying." I try to pull her towards me to give her a hug.

"No. This is not fair. I hate you for having cancer." She jumps up from the bed, wiping her cheek with the back of her hand, and before I am able to say that this is not a terrible diagnosis, that I just need surgery for the condition which is not life threatening, she storms out of the room, leaving me sitting on the bed trying to grapple with the hormonal changes of my girl that rock her emotions from highs to lows. How will I be able to survive the actual teenage years? When I look up, I see Mitchel standing in front of me with bewilderment in his eyes.

"I just ran into Hailey, she is hysterical. All I got was that you have cancer? Is it true?" he asks, and comes up closer, sitting across from me on the other bed.

"It's just a little growth, a skin cancer, but not a bad one, it's not life threatening at all," I reassure him.

"I panicked there a little bit. I was running through what I would say to you and if I had any friend doctors to call to get you a second opinion." Mitchel takes my hand into his and kisses it.

"Mitchel, please leave. I can't … I can't allow you to be like this with me." My throat tightens, my nose gets stuffy, and tears swell in my eyes.

"Why? I don't understand."

"My life … it's a mess. Look, you want excitement. There is damn excitement every day. I will not let you shackle yourself to me. This is not fun, this is not interesting or enjoyable. You will be unhappy with me. I am saving you from misery, please leave." I pull my hand away from his, and he sits frozen, not uttering a word, just staring at me.

"Look. I know you have it tough with Hailey and all—"

"No, you don't know, you cannot possibly know," I interrupt him. I feel my skin flush red. I am angry at him for being so perfect, so understanding and for my life being such an out-of-control mess. "Leave, Mitchel. I can't look at you. Pleeeaaase," I beg him, my body shaking from sobbing. I cannot see his face through my tear-flooded eyes. He gets up and walks away, leaving me alone, just the way I asked, but not how I want to be. My life is truly a misery. I push this wonderful, kind, interesting man away because I like him. I collapse onto the bed, with the blanket stifling my crying, I punch the pillow until my tears dry up and my sobs quiet down. I sit up with my head throbbing, this trip can't get much worse. Jenna and Brian are crazy to get married. I hope they realize that love is not all that pink fluffy stuff you see in rom-coms.

I slowly walk out of the room and peek down the long hallway. I expect to find Hailey sitting by the door, crying, but the hallway is breezy and empty. Where can this girl be? I walk towards the reception that is full of new arrivals and their baggage, I force a smile passing strangers by. My worry stirs as my eyes start to dash across the property, trying to figure out where my little girl could have gone. I walk across the large square with four fire pits that were lit up last night. The midday sun feels scorching in this shade-free area. I rush towards the next covered pavilion with games and TV on one side and the bar on the other.

"Hailey!" I raise my voice hoping she will peek at me from behind tall curved couches that are facing the pool.

But only the barman raises his head up in this place that is completely empty.

"Can I help you, ma'am?"

"I'm looking for my daughter. She's eleven, dark hair. She has a large dressing over her left eye," I tell him.

"I think I saw her about twenty minutes ago, she went towards the beach." He points me in the direction of the water.

"Thanks," I tell him over my shoulder as I walk briskly towards the beach. I pass by the sunbathers on their loungers by the pool, they are red and motionless, taking in as much sun as they can before they to return to their cold reality.

My heart is racing from my fast-paced walk, from my anxiety of not finding Hailey yet.

I step on the beach, the hot sand burns the sides of my feet as I walk to the water, sinking into the softness of the surface. My head moves left and right, I turn around trying to see if Hailey is on one of the loungers, but all the little kids are crowding near their parents and I don't see my daughter anywhere.

"Hailey!" I call out, my voice trembles from the fear of losing her or something happening to her. Why did I let her run out? This is all my fault, the tears pull in my eyes, my nose starts to run. "Hailey!"

A couple of the resort staff come up to me. "Can we help you, ma'am?" the woman asks. They are both dressed in white. The woman's braided hair is wrapped into a large bun. Her name tag says she's Gloria. Her coworker is Jonathan, he stays behind her, seemingly waiting for instructions on what to do.

"My daughter. She's eleven," I start to explain, showing with my hand her approximate height next to me. "She's upset and she ran out of the room about twenty minutes ago … she has a dressing over her eye … I have looked for her everywhere …."

Gloria gets a radio from her belt, turns it on, and spreads the message about the lost girl to someone on the other end. The radio crackles, and I hear the voices responding that they have received her call for help. I count at least fifteen replies before she puts the radio away. "Jonathan, please go to security and stay there, make sure every car is checked before it leaves the property, report directly to me," Gloria orders to her subordinate who dashes away from the beach. "Don't worry ma'am, she's here, we'll find her."

I nod to her, my tears rolling down, I clasp my hands, twisting my fingers. This woman must think that I am a terrible mother.

"Mothering is hard." She squeezes my arm lightly. "I know you are doing the best you can. We all do. Why don't you go back to the room so your girl will find you there when she returns."

I shake my head in objection at first, but she nudges me gently and I oblige. I walk back to the room, this time slower, paying attention to all the chairs, benches and couches, looking into all the restaurants, hoping that Hailey will run up to me, and I will scoop her into a hug from which I will not let go soon.

"Gretchen," a familiar voice calls out from the table by the pastry shop. "What happened?" Mitchel gets up, rushing towards me. "Why are you crying? What's wrong?"

My whimpering erupts into breathless sobbing. I gasp for air trying to get the words out. "Hailey … she … she … ran off … I … it's my fauuult … I can't find her."

"Calm down." He pulls me towards him, pressing me into his chest, his lips kissing my head softly. "Calm down. We'll find her. Shhhhh." I believe him, I know everything will be okay. I am happy that he is here with me. "Let's go. I'll take you to your room, and I'll head out to search for her, okay?" he continues. I pull away and nod.

As we walk towards the room, we both call out Hailey's name. Mitchel goes up to every guest and staff member, giving them the description of my daughter and asking them to keep a lookout for her and to let her know that her mother is looking for her. He then returns to me and takes my hand, giving it a firm squeeze.

We soon reach the room, he puts both of his arms on mine, the warmth of his skin is reassuring. "Look at me," he says softly. "I'll go out to look for her. Stay here in case she decides to return on her own." I look up into his eyes that reveal no grudge for the way I kicked him out before.

"Thank you. I'm so glad you're here." I try to smile, expressing my appreciation. Mitchel departs the room, leaving me to wallow in my parental guilt. I pace the room countless times, walk out to the balcony trying to search for any signs that Hailey has been found. I scroll through my phone and count the minutes before the hour since she ran out is up. This is the time I tell myself I will call the police. The minutes crawl purposefully, torturing my tormented mind and heart. Fifty minutes have passed, and my phone hasn't rung, and Mitchel, or anyone else, hasn't shown up with Hailey. I rub my temples, trying to erase all the terrible scenarios that are playing out in my head. Fifty-five minutes and still, no one is back. My heart swells, pushing against my lungs, making it hard to breathe. Fifty-six minutes. I go to the nightstand with the hotel phone, I put my hand over it, preparing myself to dial reception to request police to come and assist in the search. I gasp for air and breathe out slowly so I can control my voice and not break down when I speak to the person on the other end of the line. Fifty-nine minutes. I pick up the phone, the dial tone greets me emotionlessly, my hand reaches for the button indicating reception.

"Mommy!" a sweet voice rushes into the room before my little girl appears from the hallway.

"Hailey?" I sob, covering my mouth. Tears run freely down my face, and I turn towards my daughter, collapsing to my knees, squeezing her tight, and feeling her tight hug in return.

"I'm sorry, Mommy. I'm really sorry I scared you," she whimpers into my ear.

"I'm sorry that you got scared. I will not leave you. I love you soooo much. That cancer is really not a dangerous one, okay? Do you understand me?" I speak firmly, trying to persuade her to abandon her worry.

"I know already. Mitchel, he explained it." She wipes the tears from her eyes, nodding her head which has been preoccupied with too much for her age. I glide my hand over her long hair, pulling her head towards me and kissing it, kissing it countless times, all the times that I might miss her.

When I look behind her, Mitchel is standing quietly leaning against the wall, I think I catch him wiping his eye. Is he crying? But he sends me a big smile.

"You two girls are crazy. Hailey didn't expect she would have the whole resort looking for her. On the way to the room, she was stopped by so many staff members and guests telling her that her mom was searching for her."

"Where were you?" I ask Hailey. "Where did you find her?" I say to Mitchel.

Hailey mumbles something indistinguishable, but Mitchel steps in. "Behind the bar, the one that's by the beach, there are steps leading to a private house right on top of the rock, she was sitting on the small platform right between the flights of stairs."

"You were there the whole time?" I ask. She nods yes, and I pull her in for another hug. "Don't ever do that again? Do you understand me?" I change my tone to that of a stern parent.

"I won't. I promise," she mumbles with her gaze down.

"Go watch some TV, let me speak to Mitchel. I'll be right outside, got it?" I get up.

"Got it." She walks off with her head hanging low, plopping herself on the bed before I step out.

I grab Mitchel by the arm and pull him outside, closing the door so Hailey doesn't hear our conversation.

Once in the hallway, I put my arms under his and press my body against him, my head on his chest. He wraps his arms around me tight.

"I know you are scared," his voice is soft, his hands holding steady against my back. He is firm support that I know will provide the softest of comforts in times of need.

"I can't promise I will always do things right. But ..." He puts a finger under my chin so I am forced to look directly into his eyes. "I promise I will always try my best."

I don't need anything more from him, my lips press against his, sealing what he's just told me.

# 16.

## ANGELINA

I open my eyes, processing everything that happened last night. Kai's body presses against my back, his arm wraps under my breasts, his warm breath is steady, reflecting against my shoulder. The room is silent, no outside noise disturbs our slumber. My fingertips trace Kai's arm, strength is felt in the firm muscles that are hidden beneath the skin, rough palms are ticklish against my bare body. I shift to pull my arm from under the pillow, he stirs and mumbles something indistinguishable, his arm tightens, holding me ever so close to him. I smile, the man who always had so many girls pursuing him wants me by his side, and it feels good.

Once his breathing becomes long and shallow, I slide from his embrace and get my laptop. I have an idea for a book and want to put it down before it escapes into the depths of my mind. I check my emails first, a new message titled 'Your manuscript' from an unfamiliar sender is up at the top. It reads:

Dear Ms. Shaw,

My name is Peter Lang. I am an agent for Richmond Publishing House. I recently received your manuscript, and I must say I am truly enchanted by what I have read and would love to arrange a meeting with you to discuss your future with my publishing house. You may reply directly using this email address. I wish you a wonderful vacation, Kai mentioned that Grenada is beautiful. I hope to hear from you soon.

Best regards,

Peter Lang
Richmond Publishing House

My heart jumps up and down with joy that one of the biggest publishing houses has contacted me, but my brain chills it with the realization that it has been done with help from Kai. Why hadn't he respected my wishes, have I not been clear with how I want this process to go? I want it to be on my terms—without anyone's help. He must think that I am not good enough, that I am not capable, that I am some weak girl that needs his protection and help. No. I will not allow it. I've already lived with a man who thought little of me. I don't need Kai to doubt my capabilities, I will not tolerate it. I pick up a pillow from the chair and throw it at him with all the strength of anger that is boiling inside of me. It hits him over the head, he jumps up, lost and disoriented from being rudely awakened.

"What? What just happened?" he says in a raspy, sleepy voice, rubbing his eyes.

"Why did you do this?" I demand, pointing at my laptop.

"Do what? What are you talking about?" he squints, trying to make out the text on the screen of my computer.

"I told you that I don't want any help with the book, and here you are asking one of your buddies to take a look at it."

"Did Peter get back to you? That's awesome," he replies with satisfaction in his voice that I do not appreciate.

"Leave me, Kai," I ask. He doesn't see anything wrong with what he has done and I have no desire to explain what I've made clear before.

"Wait. What do you mean leave? Your book is great. Peter can help you."

"I don't want him to help me because he knows you or because you think that my book is great, why don't you understand?" I try to explain through my clenched teeth. "Just because you're rich and you know people, it doesn't mean that you need to go saving everyone around you. I don't need your help. I am very capable of doing everything on my own."

"Hold on, Angelina. I think you are overreacting here." He sits up and scratches his head.

"Don't tell me I am overreacting." I get up and throw his clothing to him. "This was a big mistake. Huge. We should never have gotten together. I see it now. You need to have girls who act helpless, so you can come in and sweep them up and act a hero. So you can feel better about yourself. Well, let me tell you, I am no helpless girl. Get out. I do not need your help." My voice fills up the small room.

"Angelina, I'm, I'm sorry. I didn't mean anything bad by it. Let's just talk," he stutters while putting on his clothes.

"If you don't leave, then I will."

"All right, all right. Jeez. I'll leave," he sighs and finishes getting dressed. I walk towards the other end of the room and turn away. My emotions are overwhelming, it hurts that he doesn't see my point of view. I bared all of myself to Kai, he doesn't understand me. I hear the sliding door open, I hold my breath waiting for the crushing goodbye.

"Really, Angelina? Why are you doing this?" he asks, his voice is full of sadness.

"Just leave," I force a cold request. There is a moment of silence before I hear the sliding door close, then I collapse to my knees. The weight of the silence that presses down on me crushes my hope of having a relationship with Kai, it grinds any stirring of reassurance to dust, and instead envelops my heart in a hard cast that will ensure its protection. I don't know how long I spend on the cold floor. I move when I can no longer feel my feet. I stretch them out, allowing blood to reach my toes, punishing me with an unpleasant tingling sensation. Once the numbness disappears, I get up and go outside to walk around and clear my mind.

The sun is annoyingly bright, the birds sing cheerfully, but I'd rather they be quiet. Couples stroll hand in hand to the beach or breakfast, and their embrace makes me march past them faster, so I don't have to witness their happiness. My stomach rumbles, and I decide to head to the buffet to tame my hunger. I pass the tall fence that separates the private villas from the rest of the resort, and I spot Kai's mother pacing next to it. She's on the phone, gesturing and yelling in Portuguese at someone on the other line. She speaks fast, and I can't make out what she is saying. When she spots me, she throws her hands in the air, yells goodbye to the person on the phone, and rushes towards me.

"My God, Angelina! My daughter is mad!" She grabs me tight by my arms, her eyes are large, her nose is flaring. I don't yet understand if she is angry or scared.

"What happened?"

"She is calling off the wedding. This girl ... I swear she will be the death of me ... It's true, she wants me to have a heart attack." She puts a clenched fist over her heart, looking up at the sky.

"What do you mean, calling off the wedding? Why?" I can't comprehend how this could be.

"Go, go," she pushes me towards the villas. "Maybe you'll make sense of what is wrong with her. Because I don't understand what she wants, I don't think *she* knows what she wants."

I try to come up with reasons for why Jenna wouldn't want to get married. The news is sudden and doesn't make sense. She probably just has cold feet, that's all. Nina wraps her arm around mine, leading me towards Jenna's villa. Once we get there, she stays outside and makes a phone call, leaving me without any further explanation to face her daughter.

"Sweetie?" I call out for my friend. "What's going on? Your mom is telling me something about the wedding .... Can we talk?" I walk through the living room that is overtaken by luggage that is sprawled open with clothes thrown into it in a hurry. My friend doesn't respond. "Jenna? It's Angelina ... let's just talk, okay?" I stay still, listening for any stirring that will point me in the direction of Jenna's location, she still doesn't respond, but I hear low whimpering coming from the bedroom, and I head there.

More of Jenna's clothes are strewn around the room, her wedding dress lays on a chair out of its clear, protective bag. The big bed looks like a huge fluffy cloud with large pillows and blankets piled on top of each other, but I still don't see Jenna. I am about to turn around and try outside when I hear sniffling coming somewhere from the depths of the bed.

"Sweetie?" I climb on top of the bed, digging through the bedding as if it's the rubble of a collapsed building, and I am trying to find a person who is buried underneath it all. The sound of my friend gets a bit louder as I pick up and move the enormous pillows, one by one, until I find her squinting at me, her eyes and nose swollen, eyelashes stuck together, wet from tears. Her body shakes, and she turns away sobbing into the pillow.

"Hey, hey …" I say softly. "What happened?" I rub her arm, but she shakes her head no. "Tell me, I promise I'll just listen … Jenna, c'mon. You can tell me."

She turns her head to the side, her hair stuck over her face. "I don't want to get married," she breathes out. The corners of her mouth turn down, she squeezes her eyes shut, but the tears roll down, dripping on the pillow from her nose.

"Okay, okay." I reach over and move her hair, so she can breathe better and I can see her face. "Just tell me why … Let's just talk, okay?"

"Brian … he … he," her body shakes. "He told me, that … that he doesn't like any of the things I do."

"What do you mean? I know he loves you." I voice my confusion. Jenna takes a deep breath and sits up. Her cheeks are blotchy, she grabs a tissue box, but it's already empty, and she wipes her nose with the back of her hand. I run to the bathroom and grab a roll of toilet paper.

"He said ... he said that he did all the things, not because he liked doing them, but because *I* liked doing them." She tears off the toilet paper and blows her nose loudly.

I sit silent, trying to process what Jenna is telling me and how to respond so she doesn't think I'm betraying her by defending Brian, but at the same time help her get over her most-definite cold feet before the wedding.

"What kinds of things doesn't he enjoy?" I start with a relatively neutral question.

"Everything. Mountain climbing, diving, we went to a rave, and it turns out he hated it. How am I supposed to marry someone who doesn't enjoy all the things I love?" She looks up at me, questioning her relationship that she has just recently been calling true love.

"But that's normal, sweetie. He loves you, and that's why he does all those things. I think that it's really sweet of him," I say.

"It's sweet now. But how about five years, ten years down the line? I don't think he will be so sweet. Then what?" She frowns, her face hardens.

"Then you figure it out. You love him, Jenna. I know you do." I reach for her hand, but she pulls away.

"I don't know if I do." She looks away. "I'm confused ... I need time."

"I think you are just having cold feet. Have you told him how you feel?"

She nods, takes a deep breath of air and shocks me with, "He left. I told him the wedding is off."

"Jenna! Why? This is crazy," I say in a low voice to minimize my complete disbelief of what is happening. "I think you've made a huge mistake."

"Don't tell me about my mistakes. It's not like you are so perfect," she snickers back at me.

"Wow. Where did this come from?" I pull away from my friend, sensing an attack is about to follow.

"You're so terrified of admitting that you like my brother that you started dating some old man who treated you like you were his maid. You're the one who has some issues you need to deal with before you start doling out advice to others." Her words feel like a carpet bombing of our friendship. The devastation is crushing and survival is unlikely. I decide on complete retreat.

"Jenna … I think you need some time to think things over." I get off the bed and head for the door. "I know you love him, you just sabotaged your relationship because you're scared," I say over my shoulder. Jenna avoids looking at me and covers herself with a blanket, sending me off in complete silence.

I step outside where the sun feels scorching. There is no shade to hide from the damaging rays. Jenna's mother is still pacing, screaming at someone on the phone. When she sees me, she covers the phone with her hand, "Did you talk some sense into my crazy daughter?"

I shake my head no, which makes her throw her hands into the air while screaming, "My God, she wants to kill me, I will have a heart attack!" and then goes back to the conversation on her phone where she yells something to the person in Portuguese. I wave goodbye to her, she mouths "thank you," and I head to the beach. I sit on the sand close to the water, digging my fingers into the hot granules and squeeze them in my fist. Each sand particle is so miniscule that it's easily carried off by the slightest wind, but together they make up the soft surface that surrounds this whole island. This trip was supposed to be a celebration of love and commitment, but instead it has turned into heartache and disappointment. Life is like this ocean. It crushes us with the waves of reality, carrying us off into different directions, and I feel all but powerless to struggle against the current. Just recently, I've believed that our friendship was strong and reliable, but now I am not sure if Jenna even considers me a friend anymore.

I lie back on the sand and close my eyes, cutting off visual stimulation to my brain, which is on the verge of overload given all the recent events. The vibration of my phone in my pocket wakes me up from my daze. The phone number has a New York area code.

"Hello?"

"Hi! Angelina?" a male voice responds.

"Yes, who is this?"

"This is Peter. I'm, I'm the agent ... from Richmond Publishing House."

"Oh. Hi. How are you?" I reply, surprised by this phone call.

"I sent you an email earlier on, but decided to save time and talk to you over the phone. Do you have a minute to chat?" he continues, and I wonder how I should cut him off because I am not interested in any help from Kai's friend.

"Yeah, sure."

"Not to waste your time, I really loved your manuscript. I wanted to schedule you to come in and discuss your future with us, and also to see if you have any other work that I could take a look at?"

"You're kidding me, right?" I reply, Kai must have set this up. "Did Kai ask you to call me?"

"Kai? Hm … I'm not sure what you are asking," Peter replies.

I hesitate for a moment, but decide to continue being direct. "I really appreciate the phone call, but I don't want you to do Kai any favors by accepting my manuscript, I'll make it easy for you and decline your offer."

"Wa—wai—wait, Angelina." I hear his stuttering as I pull the phone away from my ear, it stops as I press the red button and hang up the phone. I put the phone into my pocket, but it vibrates impatiently again. The same phone number lights up on the screen. Why would he call back, wasn't I clear? I slide the green round button up on the screen.

"Angelina, don't hang up. Hi, again. I don't know what Kai has told you, but he didn't ask me to do him a favor. The only reason I mentioned him is because I did a google search on you when I read your manuscript, and it showed that you were from the same school as him."

"Ooo-kaaay," I stretch awkwardly, biting my lip from embarrassment of my rushed assumption. "So, how exactly do you know Kai then?"

"Kai and I were co-editors on our college newspaper," Peter explains.

"So, he didn't ask you to accept my manuscript because, well, I don't know, because he is your friend?" My voice goes up in a high pitch and I bury my feet deep into the sand, wishing I could bury my head as well.

"That's not how it works." I hear him chuckle into the phone. "I worked very hard for my reputation. If I listened to my friends and family about publications, I'm afraid my career would be nonexistent. The decision about your manuscript was made well before I called Kai."

"Oh, I see, huh, I'm sorry then, for my, my attack on you." I laugh nervously.

"I'll be more careful next time mentioning any names." His laughter is stronger and more relaxed now. "So, can we schedule for you to come in and chat?"

"Sure, sure, I'll be happy to," I reply excitedly.

"This is my personal phone number, please reach out once you are back in New York. I'll be looking forward to our meeting. Bye, Angelina."

"You'll be the first person I call in New York, bye!" I reply and hang up, still cringing at the awkward beginning of this conversation. I pull my knees to my chin and wrap my arms around my legs. I feel my cheeks burning up, embarrassed over my outrage at Kai. Am I sabotaging the relationship because I am scared just like Jenna? I need to get back and speak to Kai, but before I am able to get up, Gretchen hugs me from behind, startling me.

"Sorry, Angelina." Her breathing is heavy and fast, she looks sweaty, she sits down next to me pausing to catch her breath. "What's happening? Mitchel told me the wedding is off, Brian already left with his mom, and Jenna is not making any sense. She's packing up."

I nod while drawing squiggles in the sand. "The wedding is off." I draw an exclamation on the surface, sticking my finger firmly down. "I was surprised when I heard that Jenna decided to get married. I was ... happy for her. But I always thought she would be the last to get married out of the three of us, you know? She was just always so indecisive. But, Brian, he is so perfect for her. I think he is what she needs, but ...."

"She's scared?" Gretchen finishes.

"I think so, because it just doesn't make sense." I shrug my shoulders in bewilderment.

"This whole vacation has been crazy. I came here for a wedding, looks like the wedding is not happening, but I am leaving with ..." she stops, looking away smiling coyly.

"What?" I ask her.

"Mitchel. We like each other," she giggles, her cheeks turn pink. She is glowing with a quiet happiness that I have never seen on her.

"That's wonderful, sweetie. I'm happy for you. I think we need to give Jenna time to think things over. I'm sure she'll see that Brian is perfect for her. Come, let's have one of those nutmeg ice creams." I get up and offer a hand to Gretchen, pulling her up from the sand.

"It's such a strange taste, but I kind of like it, too." We brush ourselves off and stroll up the beach to the tiny cafe that smells of nutmeg and cinnamon, the spices of Grenada.

"Hey, fatty," a tall, unfamiliar man yells. I turn to give him a dirty look, feeling Gretchen tense and come closer to me.

"That guy, he was on the airplane. He was rude, got into argument with Mitchel," she whispers, increasing her pace.

"Yeah, you. What, you don't have your boyfriend around defending you?" he slurs, visibly drunk.

"Why don't you shut your pie hole," I throw over my shoulder, wrapping my arm around Gretchen as we continue walking. People are starting to stare, but it doesn't stop the guy from continuing his harassment.

"Aw, look at you, you fat ass, your little skinny friend is barking." He gets up with a bottle of beer in his hand, walking fast to catch up to us. There is no one around to stop him. He is tall, at least six feet, his shadow is already catching up to ours, his breathing is getting louder, I smell alcohol that is emanating from him.

"Just walk faster, Angelina," Gretchen begs, squeezing my hand, pulling me ahead.

"Look at you, you fat, ugly bitch," he growls. Gretchen releases me, I hear her starting to sob, she dashes towards the safety of the cafe. I turn around sharply to face the mean drunk.

"Back off, before I hurt you, asshole," I shout a warning, taming the rage that is fighting to be released. He throws his head back, laughing loudly. Guests are now staring at both of us. I see some resort employees dashing across the large patio, talking into the radios, but no one is coming close.

"I'm so scared." He shakes his hands in pretend fear, the beer spilling out of the bottle. His eyes are red and puffy, he hasn't shaved in a few days. His arms and shoulders are red from sun burn with white tan lines covering his hairy chest and prominent belly. He leans forward and whispers, "What are you going to do, you little midget?" He puts his finger to my chest.

"I'll make you beg for forgiveness," I promise. He leans back slightly, the corner of his mouth is slowly starting to go up, his finger is still on my chest, the pressure releases my calculated purpose to teach him a lesson with the skills I have polished over the years. My right hand covers his hand, so he can't pull it away from my chest, my left hand grabs his elbow, locking it, preventing any movement. I curl my back and shoulders, his wrist in my control, I press it back, his eyes grow big, the beer falls out of his hand and he arches back.

"Beg," I order.

"Shit," he spits angrily, his knees buckle, sending him to the floor, now I tower over him, his eyes dart from my face to the hand that I am controlling. He swings his free arm, but I am too quick for his sloppy drunk movements. I duck twisting his arm behind his back.

"Beg," I whisper with menace.

"Fuuuuck." His body lunges forward, his forehead on the ground now. I take his back, my legs hook around his waist, my arm curls around his neck, locking in the hold I know he won't be able to break.

"Beg," I breathe into his ear as his head is turning red and veins on his neck are starting to protrude. His arms flail. I see security rushing towards us, and Gretchen runs back with Kai and Mitchel right next to her.

"Beg." I tighten my choke.

"I am sorry," he manages to wheeze with saliva dripping down his chin.

"Beg louder." I need Gretchen to hear him.

"I am sorry," he manages to say, and I know Gretchen has heard him. My muscles flex and I feel his body go limp. Hands pull me off the man to my feet, I feel supportive pats on my shoulder and voices telling me, "Good job", "He deserved it", "You did good."

Gretchen rushes in, scooping me into a tight hug. "Why did you do that? You are completely nuts. You scared the bejesus out of me." She releases me, shaking me by my shoulders.

"He was insufferable. I couldn't let him speak to you that way, clearly he was a prick." I just shrug my shoulders.

My friend stares at me without blinking and then pulls me in for another hug. "You are okay, right?"

"I'm okay," I reply.

"Thank you," she whispers into my ear, as other people start to crowd me, and security helps the drunk get up, pulling him away to a nearby bench. A tall man comes up to me dressed in all white, the name tag bears the name Garry, manager.

"Miss, I am sorry this has happened. The police have been called and they will contact you to make a report. Is there anything I can assist you with, or compensate you somehow for this terrible inconvenience?"

"You actually may." I pull him aside to explain my idea for the evening. He nods agreeably and assures me that everything will be done just as I desire. He walks off speaking into his walkie-talkie, sending orders to the gate security to alert him of the arrival of the police. The crowd disperses. And the drunk disappears. Gretchen and Mitchel chat with each other. There is one person who hasn't come close to me yet. Kai.

He is sitting on a bench in the shadow of the palm trees looking directly at me, his face doesn't reveal any emotions. I take a deep breath and walk towards him. He gets up, and takes slow steps towards me. I am sure he is cautious, not knowing what to expect from me. I don't want to push him away, I don't want to fear my own feelings, suppress them, or run away. Instead, my legs pick up the pace, my heart bounces joyfully, no longer restricted by illogical fear. My lips stretch into a big smile that I send to Kai; his face lights up, he smiles. He opens his arms up as I jump into his embrace, my legs wrap around his waist, his hands wrap tight around me. My lips cover his, my tongue invades his mouth, and he welcomes my kiss by pulling me closer, his tongue responding with a passion that leaves me breathless. I bite his lower lip gently before I pull away, leaning my forehead onto his, my hands are pressed against his stubbly cheeks. "I'm sorry about this morning." I stare into his eyes.

"I know you don't need to be saved. Quite the opposite, I think you saved me." He releases a chuckle.

"So, am I forgiven then?" I rub my nose against his.

"I'll be forgiving you over and over again today if you let me." The corners of his eyes squint mischievously. He lets me come down to the ground, and I place a soft kiss on his lips.

"Jenna, she called off the wedding." I break the news to him.

Kai sighs heavily and rubs his forehead. "I know, I was just there, my mother and I were trying to talk to her, but she's not listening .... I don't know what's come over her. Mitchel just came back from the airport, Brian's plane already left. We were just talking over this whole wedding debacle and how Brian looked crushed." He pulls me in for a hug. "My sister is stupid for rushing into marriage and then breaking it off with Brian like that. The guy was the best thing that's happened to her."

I wrap my hands around his face, nodding my head pressed tight against his firm chest. When Mitchel and Gretchen walk over, we stand awkwardly staring at each other. This trip is supposed to be a celebration of love, but the two people who we are supposed to celebrate are no longer interested in proclaiming love for each other.

"What are we going to do, guys?" Gretchen asks.

"This is quite a predicament, I must say," Mitchel replies, shaking his head. "Brian didn't say much to me, but I could see he was completely devastated. I know he loves

Jenna. I'm sure he's confused, he just needs time to recover."

"I think Jenna needs time as well. She loves him, more than she's willing to admit, that's what freaked her out—the enormity of her own feelings. I think they are meant for each other."

"My mother is trying to cancel what can be canceled. I'm planning to stay here as planned for the next few days. Jenna is leaving tomorrow morning," Kai adds, holding tight onto my waist.

"I'll talk to both of them again," I tell everybody.

"I'll come with you," Gretchen adds. We say goodbye to our men and head back to the villa, our arms wrapped tight around each other's arms. We stroll slowly, this time not rushed by anyone.

"I don't know how you were not scared of that guy," Gretchen says.

"Are you kidding? I was terrified," I answer sincerely.

"But how did you find it, to … to stand up to him? All I could do was just run. I don't even know where I was running to. If I hadn't stumbled into Mitchel and Kai, I would probably still be running," she laughs nervously.

"I don't know. I just felt like I had to stand my ground, like he was every man who has ever been mean or rude, who didn't believe in me—like my father who kept leaving me over and over again." I laugh loudly at my own sudden realization of what made me persevere. "I felt that if I didn't do anything about this guy, that he would win …." Or was I standing up to my own frustrations and fears? "Plus, I couldn't let him get away with how he was behaving. You know?"

"Thank you … really … I mean it," Gretchen says, giving my arm the lightest of squeezes. We reach the villa quickly, Jenna's mother is no longer pacing outside but is the one who opens the door to us. She motions for us to come in and puts a finger to her lips so we'll be quiet.

"She is finally asleep. I had to give her some pills, she was being too hysterical." She rolls her eyes and releases a long sigh. She walks over by the table and picks up a glass of wine. "I need to keep drinking to deal with all this mess. Girls, anything for you? Please, the bar is stocked." She motions in the direction of the minibar across the room.

"Yeah. I guess I'll have a beer." I walk to the fridge and grab a light beer for myself. "Gretchen, you want one?"

"Sure, the same one you're having."

I pop the bottles open releasing the pressurized air as small bubbles rush to the top, but I stop the foam from spilling by taking a gulp and pouring the beer into a glass for Gretchen.

"I still can't wrap my brain around it, girls. I thought this was it … a happy ending for my girl … you know?" Nina takes a long sip of the wine, pacing the room. "Brian was the only boy who let her be her. All her other boyfriends were just terrible, and she took on whatever their interests were, totally abandoning her own needs. I was afraid she would be just like bland white rice, taking on a flavor of whatever was next to her. Agrh." She rubs her forehead and takes the last sip of wine before she walks over and pours more into her glass. My eyes dart to Gretchen, she stares back at me with a look of concern and helplessness.

"How can we help, Nina?" It's the only thing I manage to come up with.

"Yes, Mrs. Gable, we are here for Jenna and for you," Gretchen adds.

"Thank you, girls, but I believe the only thing that can help is time … and wine." She collapses onto the couch and closes her eyes.

I take a gulp of beer and walk over to Gretchen, but before I'm able to sit down, a scream startles me. A scream that is full of the distress and hopelessness of a lonely person. We rush into the bedroom where Jenna is curled up in the fetal position amongst the pillows and blankets, her body shuddering from her monstrous moan.

Her mother, with surprising agility, climbs right next to her, scoops her up, and places Jenna's head against her chest. "Shhhh, baby, shhhh." She tries to console her, placing soft kisses on her head.

"Mommyyyyy, what have I done? Please tell me, tell me it's a bad dream," her voice breaks as she gasps for air.

"Shhhh, shhhh. It's going to be okay." Her mother intuitively rocks back and forth.

I turn around and start to make my way out of the bedroom with Gretchen.

"Don't leave me," our friend cries out. "Don't leave, please." She raises her red, puffy face from her mother's chest and stretches her arm towards us.

Gretchen and I climb hastily into bed, wrapping our arms around our friend and each other. I have no tears, but my chest tightens with sadness for Jenna, and I hear Gretchen sniffling, suppressing the tears. I don't know why I'm not crying. I close my eyes tightly, trying to squeeze a salty drop of liquid, my lungs begin to quiver, but my eyes refuse to produce any tears for my friend's heartache. Nina continues to offer her "shhhhh" which doesn't seem to help any of the crying coming from my friends.

"Waaaaa-haaaaa," a loud cry erupts from Gretchen that stifles the noise of Jenna's crying. The sound startles both of us enough that we sit up to give attention to Gretchen.

"Why," Jenna gasps for air, "… are you," her body is still convulsing from sobbing, "… crying?"

"I don't know whyyyyyy." Gretchen covers her face. Her own body starts to shake as Jenna and I try to pull her hands away from her face. And Jenna's mother continues the mantra somewhere in the background, "Shhhhhh, shhhhhh, it's going to be okay."

"I am so fat, whaaaaa, my daughter hates meeeee."

"You are not fat. Stop it," I say sternly. "And she doesn't hate you." I try to console Gretchen.

"Hailey loves you … and you are beautiful," Jenna replies, now hugging Gretchen as I wrap my arms around both of them.

"She does hate me, like almost every day, whaaaaa. I am such a bad mom." Her soft body gets hot, tears run down her cheeks as I wipe them with the back of my hand.

"No, don't say that, you're the best mom. She's just being stupid," Jenna says, grabbing Gretchen's face. Our friend pauses her crying and frowns, but Jenna quickly pivots. "Not like stupid, you know what I mean, she just doesn't realize how great you are." Gretchen nods in agreement.

"Mitchel and I, we, we … we did it … and I like him, but he's just so nice. I'm terrified, that he just is too niiiiiceeee." Gretchen collapses into our embrace with another round of crying.

"Oh, that's great." I offer my support. "He's very nice and you totally deserve it, sweetie." I now smile.

"You *so* deserve it," Jenna adds, still clinging tight to Gretchen's chest. "Your boobs, they're so soft," she offers a sudden realization and her body starts to shake again, but this time a laughter escapes her chest. Loud and contagious, it passes on to the rest of us, making us erupt in the same relaxing, uniting, happy laughter.

"You girls are crazy," Jenna's mother concludes and gets off the bed. "You all need therapy. What's wrong with all of you? Why are you making up issues where there are none?"

We stay quiet, our heads hang low, and I shrug my shoulders.

"It's good you have each other. You should cherish this friendship," Nina continues. "I am going to get another drink. Just please, enough crying, I can't handle it anymore. Okay?"

We all nod our heads vigorously as she marches out of the room.

"I need to speak to Brian." Jenna starts to rummage through the blankets and the pillows. "My phone, I need my phone," she mumbles. Gretchen and I join in the search, lifting pillows and ourselves to see where the phone could be.

"I just had it here somewhere," Jenna says, still twisting and turning on the bed. When she turns around, I spot the phone.

"Jenna," I giggle, reaching out to her breasts. "It's right here." I grab the phone sticking out of her bra.

"You're lucky you have small boobs. That phone would've never been found if it were me," Gretchen laughs.

230

Jenna smacks herself on the forehead and her fingers press a button before she puts the phone to her ear. Her smile gets smaller with every long beep and no Brian's voice on the other end. She looks at the screen of the phone and frowns, and tears start rolling down her cheeks again. "It went to voicemail."

"He is still in the air," Gretchen comes up with a quick excuse.

"That's right. I'm sure he will pick up once he lands." I rub Jenna's arm.

She shakes her head slightly. "I've made the dumbest mistake. He won't pick up. He won't speak to me. I told him some mean stuff. I am so stupid."

"You were just scared. If he doesn't pick up, then you just have to find a way. You let us know if you need help, okay?" Gretchen consoles.

"Yes, we are here for you," I add.

"I think I'm going to write to him, I need to get it out right now while my thoughts are fresh. Do you mind leaving me alone, so I can do it?"

"Sure."

"Of course."

We give her hugs and say goodbye to her mother before stepping outside.

"I need to go check on Hailey, we'll probably go to the beach. What are you going to do?" Gretchen asks when we are outside.

"I'll go to my room and change and probably lay by the pool, read a book, I guess," I reply, shrugging my shoulders.

Gretchen gives me a hug. "Don't make stupid mistakes, okay?"

I laugh hugging her back. "I'll try not to."

# 17.

## KAI

I pin Angelina against the wall. "I've missed you."
She tries to kiss me, but I raise her arms above her head and lean back, teasing her.

"I was at your sister's," she breathes out heavily and licks her lips.

"And?"

"And she was trying to reach Brian ..." I shrug my shoulders.

"And now, you're here," I whisper into her ear and kiss the spot at the bottom of her neck. She moans and leans her head away from me. I trace a path of kisses all the way back to her ear, biting gently on her earlobe. She presses her hips against mine and turns her face to me. Her eyes stare into mine, the color blue I want to bathe in as much as possible.

"You are so beautiful," I tell her, releasing her arms, which she wraps around my neck. I lift her up as her legs tighten around my waist, and my mouth feverishly kisses her lips. I feel her fingers in my hair, pressing me closer to her. Her tongue enters my mouth, searching for mine; she is not shy, she is confident, she knows what she wants. She pulls my head back, slowly releasing my lower lip from her gentle hold between her teeth.

"Take me to that table," she commands.

I grin and follow her demand. I sit her on the edge of the table, and she pulls off my T-shirt, her fingers trace my chest then brush down my abdomen before sneaking into my pants to find my erection. "Angelina," a pleasurable groan escapes my lips.

"Yessss, Kai," she replies, her eyes sparkle with mischief.

"I want you." I lean in and kiss her again. My hands find the buttons on the front of her dress. I manage to undo them, revealing her breasts. They are small, fitting perfectly under my hands. My lips trace down to her erect nipple. I blow on it softly, watching it perk up even more before I lick it. She arches her back and brings me in closer with her legs towards her hot center. I undo my pants and let them fall to the ground with my boxers, then I take her panties and slide them off her slowly, prolonging this moment of anticipation that I know will heighten our lovemaking. I wrap my arms under her thighs and pull her towards me, her wetness greets my heated body, and I lean in to meet her soft, yearning mouth as I enter Angelina. A long moan escapes her lips as she stills underneath me, her fingers digging into my back. It no longer matters what's happening to other people. This woman makes me happy, she is exciting, I want to be with her always.

"Don't stop," she begs as my thrusts become faster. I can't last any longer, when her body tenses and she achieves her release, I let myself finish and collapse on top her.

"That was amazing," she breathes out. I scoop her up and carry her to bed. She takes off her dress and nuzzles close to me with her head resting on my chest. My fingers run through her curls, the strands slipping and flowing like a spring of water. There is nothing simple about her. Not her creative mind, not her tight muscles earned through years of training, not even the way she makes love.

"I'm starting my job next week," I probe the subject carefully.

"Yeah," she purrs, her finger tracing something on my stomach.

"I want you to come here and live with me," I say.

Her finger stops the movement and it seems as if she stills her breathing before she says, "That would be crazy. What would I do here?"

"Write more books...be with me," I suggest.

She stirs, folds her hands under her chin on my chest and stares, without saying anything, for what seems like minutes.

"I don't know. It's too risky. We are just starting something here. And I can't imagine just picking up everything and moving."

"How are we going to do it then? I want to be with you."

"We can do long distance ... it doesn't scare me ... maybe if everything, I mean, us, goes well, maybe then I'd consider moving here," she replies.

"Let's give it six months, and then I want to make a decision. I don't want to go on longer than that without waking up next to you every morning," I suggest.

"Okay. It's a deal then, six months," she agrees quite easily. "I have to go back and check on your sister, she realized she made a huge mistake by calling off the wedding."

"Jenna is being Jenna. She always makes rash decisions that she regrets."

"I'm glad she decided to get married here, we wouldn't have happened without that decision," Angelina reminds me.

"True." I trace her lips with my finger as she kisses it and licks it with the tip of her tongue.

"That is a dangerous move that might keep you in bed much longer," I warn her, feeling my heart start to beat faster.

She smiles and places a quick kiss on my chest as I put my arms behind my head, watching her climb out of bed and button up her dress.

"Come back soon. I need to spend as much time as possible with you before you leave me," I call out to her. She sends me a smile and walks out, leaving me to ponder my feelings for this girl. I've just asked her to move in with me. It's strange I did that; before, all my girlfriends begged me to live together, accused me of being distant and unable to commit to a serious relationship. It took me almost a year before I gave Candice the key to my place. I enjoy my space. I don't want any intrusions on my way of doing things. I am against conforming to someone else's way of living. But with Angelina, I crave her presence, and I want to share with her what I have seen and what I have experienced. I need her to know my plans and build a future with her. I am excited about us. I get out of the bed that still has the smell of her in it and take a long shower. Once out, I throw on a T-shirt and shorts and crack a cold beer. Stepping outside on the shaded patio, I sit back and kick my feet up. An iguana slowly moves across the short-trimmed grass, blending into the surrounding green. The air is heavy with the humidity pushing down on me. I take a sip of the cold beer that cools me off, but the liquid chokes me when I hear a familiar voice say, "Hi!"

"What the f—" I manage to say once I'm able to clear my throat and breathe. Candice, with her bleached blond, waist-long hair that I know is mostly extensions, stands in front of me in the most ridiculous pink tutu with matching platforms. A plunging piece of pink fabric covers her large, water-balloon breasts.

"Hi!" she squeaks again, giving me a wave as a bellboy arrives with three large, pink leopard colored suitcases.

"What the hell are you doing here?" I say calmly while I rage inside. I can't let my anger spill out, that would be too much gratification for her. I can't let her get a rise out of me.

"I have some neeeews," she sings, as if I haven't broken up with her over her cheating.

"I really don't care." I lean back, pull my baseball cap lower over my eyes, and fold my arms over my chest.

"You can put my bags over here," she directs the bellboy, pointing to the sliding door of my room.

"What do you think you are doing?" I manage to force calmly through my teeth.

"Oh, baby," she giggles.

"Don't call me that."

"Okay, as you wish." She comes over and sits on the edge of the chair opposite of me with her back perfectly straight while her luggage is unloaded. I decide not to argue in front of the stranger and sit silently until he finishes. When he leaves, Candice puts one of her hands on the table where her nails slowly drum annoyingly on the surface. They are freakishly long, covered with bright pink nail polish and shining with … rhinestones. This woman is a show I once enjoyed, but now I want to take another shower just from being in her presence. She looks down and giggles again.

"Well?" I demand an explanation of her presence.

"I came to tell you that you are going to be a father," she blurts out and claps her hands cheerfully.

Her words are a forceful kick that takes my breath away. My mind races through time, trying to pull up the memory of when we'd last had sex. It's been weeks, maybe even a few months.

"You're kidding me?" I force a nervous chuckle. "It's not possible, we haven't had sex since ..."

"About three months ago, I'm ten weeks pregnant," she interrupts. "Isn't it wonderful? This baby can give us a chance for a new beginning." She rubs her flat stomach.

"No ... no. If you think your pregnancy will change anything between us, you are very, very much mistaken."

"But, baby," she leans and puts her hand over my knee. Her touch disgusts me, I jump up and walk to the other side of the patio away from her. Candice gets up and follows me. "I know this is big news, but this baby will need a father, you can't abandon this helpless, little person." She puckers her lips and looks at me from underneath her false eyelashes.

"Oh, for God's sake, Candice, don't you dare give me a guilt trip." I turn away from her. Shit, this is the worst possible turn of events. I am going to be a father. I want kids, but not with her, not now. I can't trust her word, I need proof.

"I'm not, I know you will be a great father." Candice's voice is nasally and annoying.

"I am not anyone's father until I see a DNA test. I need to take a walk. I need … I need to talk to …" I have to speak to Angelina. I have to tell my mother. Shit, this is a mess—a complete clusterfuck.

"But what about me? I don't have a place to stay," Candice asks.

"You can stay in my room for now until I get you another. Leave the bags, I'll get them later," I throw over my shoulder, walking away. What am I going to say to Angelina? I'll just have to be honest with her, I'll just need to explain so she understands. I run to Jenna's villa, I pound on the door, but there is no answer. I have to speak to her before anyone else. I run to the beach. My eyes scan the bodies in the water and on the loungers trying to find Angelina, my sister, or my mother. When I don't find them, I sit down, trying to catch my breath. It feels as if my lungs are being squeezed by the enormity of the news, and I have no control of how it will influence my life. It's just a panic attack, I tell myself, trying to take deep breaths of the hot and humid air. Once my heartbeat slows down a bit, I get up and walk back, looking into every restaurant, hoping to find the girl that I want to build a future with before it's destroyed into dust.

I return to the room, covered in sticky sweat, without finding Angelina. I leave the bags outside because they need to be moved to the room I arranged for Candice. When I walk into my room, the cold air-conditioning feels good, but the presence of this woman irks me. She has changed into a short, skimpy, tight dress and is lying on my bed flipping the channels on the TV.

"Hi, baby. You're back," Candice greets me without sitting up or looking away from the TV.

"I told you, don't call me that," I bark.

"Oops," she covers her mouth and giggles. "Must be my pregnancy brain, I've been so forgetful. Do you want to rub my belly and talk to the baby? They say they can hear and recognize the voice of their mom and dad." She looks down at her belly, rubbing it.

"I've arranged a room for you. I'll help you with anything you need during the pregnancy, once the baby is born we can come to an arrangement for visitation and child support, if ... if this baby is mine. But now, I need you to go to your room." I throw her the card key to her room and dial for the bellboy to come transfer her luggage. She sits up on the bed with her skinny, spray-tanned legs dangling.

"Fine," she snickers. "I'll leave, for now. I'll have my lawyer contact you to arrange for everything. This baby will need to have the best of everything, be ready to pay up." She gets up, slides on her high heels, flips her blond hair, and walks towards the door. "By the way, while you were taking your walk, some girl came looking for you. I told her you were running around to spread the news of becoming a father. I hope you don't mind. Ta-ta!" She slams the door behind her, the last words squeeze the air out of my lungs and the blood from my heart.

I grab a pillow from the bed and throw it in her direction, it hits the glass door and falls on the floor, the white fabric now marred by the gray streaks of dirt. I leave the room and head to Jenna's villa again, I bang on the door with force, this time I hear steps rushing to the door. It opens up just a bit, and I see my sister peeking through the door, frowning, her nostrils flaring.

"Is it true?" she demands, her voice is low.

"Let me talk to her," I try to push the door open and come in, but Jenna leans her body against the door preventing my entry. "Jenna, please, I have to, I have to speak to her."

"I'm sorry, she doesn't want to see you." Jenna shakes her head, avoiding direct eye contact. "You need to give her time." She closes the door, shutting me out of the opportunity to explain, to have a chance to speak to Angelina before she makes up her mind about this whole situation, before she decides that this is all too much for her. I slam my fist on the door, but this time it doesn't open, and I feel my heart aching as if it has been pummeled by an opponent much too strong. I don't yet know if it will recover.

I walk slowly back to my room. The sun is burning my skin, blinding me with its bright light. When I am finally inside, I close the blackout curtains and then the thin drapes as well, submerging the whole room in complete darkness. I want to hide. I need time to think. I turn on the nightstand light and open the small fridge. The bottle of vodka catches my eye, a thought crosses my mind: this would be a good way of erasing the pain of this day. I unscrew the cap and take a sip. The liquid burns my throat, and I know it will take too long for me to get drunk enough to fall into a thoughtless black hole of unconsciousness. I pour myself orange juice and add vodka to that, the mixture goes down much smoother. I pour myself another glass, drinking it in big gulps. A few minutes later I feel the warmth spreading from my stomach, crawling to my head, slowing down the thoughts of the day. I pour another glass of orange juice and vodka, grab a bag of M&M'S from the fridge, and climb into bed. I shove fistfuls of sweet candy into my mouth, sipping my alcohol, and scrolling through the channels, not interested in the content, just trying to tune out. But the persistent thought of me being a father keeps smoldering. I am going to be a father. Shit. I know nothing about parenthood, how can I be responsible for taking care of another human being? What if I screw up? How will I know if I am doing a good job raising a person? Finally, I stare into the TV, my head is empty and quiet. I take another sip and put the glass back on the nightstand before my brain shuts down from being overloaded.

I wake up with the throbbing hammering of a headache, the bright light of the TV is blinding, and I have to squint to control the light's painful glare. My stomach rumbles and I feel nausea coming up my throat, then a flood of memories and thoughts burst through the alcoholic dam, intensifying the pain and realization that my life has changed. I get up with the pressure squeezing my brain and stumble to the door, sliding it open. The sun has set, cicadas fill the humid, hot air with their singing, I step out and plop in the chair. I shut my eyes and rub my temples, hoping to relieve the pain of this headache that I have caused myself. Just then I hear the door in Angelina's room slide open. She walks out with the one bag she arrived with and, without looking in my direction, starts walking away.

"Angelina!" I call out and cringe as the noise of my own voice sends piercing shocks inside my skull. "Is that it? You're going to just run away now?"

She stands still, not turning to face me. I get up and walk slowly, trying not to sway too much in order to hide my drunkenness. "Turn to me. I've done nothing for you to not look at me." I touch her arm, pulling it lightly, forcing her to face me. When she does, she keeps her head low, the curls of her hair falling and obscuring her face. I put my hand under her chin and lift her face so I can look into her eyes. She looks away, her face illuminated by the moon and outside lights. She frowns, clenches her teeth, and pulls her chin away from me. "It doesn't mean …" I clear my throat because my voice trembles from the overwhelming fear of losing this girl. "She doesn't mean anything to me."

She speaks with her eyes closed tight. "She is the mother of your child. She means a lot. She will forever be in your life."

"Yes, but it doesn't mean we are going to be together. We are done, we have been done for quite a while now. I don't want to lose you over this," I plead.

"We shouldn't have gotten together. It was a terrible decision. A vacation delusion. I can see clearly now, I've made a mistake."

"Is that why you are running away in the night, so you can avoid facing me? This is the mistake, don't make it … please." I try to pull her closer, but she takes a step back.

"I don't want to be the woman who you go home to when you have a child. This baby will crave your love and your attention and you cannot afford to have your energy elsewhere. You need to spend every free minute taking care of that baby's needs."

"What are you saying? That I'm not allowed to have a life of my own—to want a home, a family, a wife—just because my ex has my baby? Believe me, I won't abandon my child, but I also won't abandon my own desire to be happy, and I want to be happy with you." I take her hand and kiss her cold fingers. But she shakes her head and pulls away.

er

"You don't understand yet what will be required of you as a father. I can't be in the way. I will not be … just … please … let me go … I can't bear to be here any longer," she struggles to say, her voice trembling.

I can't look at her, knowing that I am causing her pain. I step away, she looks up at me, and I see profound sorrow in her blue eyes. She has made up her mind, I know that I can't change it; there are no words that will persuade her to believe everything could be the same for us. Maybe she is right, maybe she realizes that fatherhood will have an overwhelming effect on my life, an effect I'm yet to understand.

Angelina, not saying anything else, comes closer, raises up on her tippy-toes and places a kiss on my cheek. "I know you will be a great father," she whispers before turning around and walking away into the darkness, the sound of her suitcase wheels rumbling against the pavement linger after.

I stand alone, swaying, staring at the ground when someone taps me on the shoulder. I turn around to find a staff member of the resort looking at me, smiling.

"Yes."

"Mr. Gable?"

"Yeah," I nod.

"My name is Eugene. Please follow me. Ms. Shaw has arranged a surprise for you." He turns around and starts walking away from me.

"Hey man, wait up. There must be a mistake," I shout.

"No, sir, no mistake. This is completely complementary. The resort wants to bring apologies to Ms. Shaw for the unpleasant event that happened with another visitor today.

She was gracious to accept it and wanted to invite you to share the evening with her," Eugene explains.

"But ... but, I don't think she is coming," I tell him.

"I'm sure she will not miss this kind of dinner, sir, please, follow me," Eugene insists. I follow behind him until we get to the beach, holding on to hope that maybe she will be there after all. A candlelit table is set for two right on the sand, it is covered in rose petals. Eugene pulls out a chair and I sit, he then walks away leaving me by myself. There is a note on my plate. I open it and it reads, *Life is complicated, but I like having you by my side. I know everything will be okay. I will listen to the beat of your heart. Angelina.* I fold the note back carefully and put it in my pocket. I put my elbows on the table and lean my head into my hands, my fingers digging into my scalp, squeezing the headache. I have to make sure she is okay, life is complicated indeed. She needs time, time will fix everything.

"Sir, I am afraid Ms. Shaw will not be joining you," Eugene comes back to inform me.

"Yeah ... I know. It looks like it's just going to be me ... for a while." An ocean breeze blows gently, picking up the rose petals from the table and taking them with it, leaving behind a white tablecloth.

# 18.

## GRETCHEN

### Seven months later

"Mommy, Mommy!" Hailey screams, running downstairs as Mitchel and I are having our evening tea, a nice daily catching-up routine that we've settled into since he moved in two months ago.

"What's up, kiddo?" I answer.

"Look, look!" She shoves her phone in my face so I see text message bubbles from her father, but Hailey shakes her hand too much from excitement that I can't make out the content of the conversation.

"I can't see anything. What is it?" I try to take the phone out of her hand so I can read what she is so excited about, but she pulls it away and stares at the screen giggling.

"Oops, Dad said it's a secret, and I shouldn't tell you," her face grows serious.

I glance at Mitchel, who keeps reading a newspaper, seemingly not paying any attention to us. I kick his leg under the table, he looks up at me from under his eyebrows and nods in the direction of Hailey, but I shrug my shoulders signaling I don't know what to do.

"Then keep it a secret, rookie," he suggests. Hailey darts her gaze over to Mitchel, then back to me, biting her fingernails and shifting her weight from one foot to the other.

"I can't keep it a secret, please, please, I have to tell you, or I will, like, burst or something," she rapid fires.

"I don't think your dad would like it if you discuss this conversation with us," I caution her.

"I'm going to be a big sister," she blurts, ignoring my suggestion.

"What?"

"His girlfriend, Candice, is going to have a baby," Hailey continues excitingly.

"Who? I didn't know Dad had a new girlfriend." I try to say it without much emotion while vigorously kicking Mitchel under the table, but the man knows when to stay out of certain mother-daughter interactions, so he pretends to be busy with reading. "Have you met her?" I inquire.

"Yeah, like, a bunch of times. But, like, a while, a while back. She is a bit too much—like, glitter and a pink unicorn threw up on her. She's not, like, a new girlfriend, I just haven't seen her in a while." She shoves the phone in my face again, now showing a bunch of pictures of an extremely blond-haired, skinny girl with orange skin and large, pink lips. "But she's nice, she took me for a mani-pedi once and shopping at Sephora," my daughter chirps, clicking away on the phone screen.

"Did she now? I thought we agreed no makeup until you turn at least fifteen," I say and take the phone out of her hands and then scroll through the pictures where my ex-husband's apparent girlfriend has the same duck face in all of them, showing off her growing belly. I show the picture to Mitchel who puts on his glasses, stares at the image for a few seconds, grunts, but doesn't say anything, before Hailey gets the phone back. I recognize now that this is the same girl from the Vegas pictures my ex posted on social media while we were away in Grenada, the same girl who came to Grenada and said that she was pregnant with Kai's baby. This is so confusing, what is this girl doing? And whose baby is she really having?

"You both are weird," she snickers at us for our lack of excitement, and walks back up the stairs, face buried in her device.

"That's …"

"I know," Mitchel replies, completing the thought I haven't voiced. "What are you going to do?"

"I, I don't know yet. What can I do? Do I go tell Angelina, do I go and tell Kai that the baby he thinks is his, is really not, or is it? This is such a mess. What do I do?" I put my elbows on the table, digging my fingers into my scalp.

Mitchel gets up, walks over from his seat and starts massaging my shoulders. "Don't stress, sleep on it, I'm sure you'll come up with something." He kisses my head, wraps his arms around me, making me feel instantly calm and reassured. I could have never imagined this level of happiness exists. This man came into my messy life and he didn't get scared, I always have his shoulder for support and occasional tears. Every morning before work, he makes me coffee and calls me to tell me he loves me throughout the day. My daughter adores him, their games of chess have given her confidence to join the school chess club, she now looks forward to competitions and rushes home to finish yet another game. She still has dramatic tantrums, but they pass swiftly, not leaving any deep wounds on my motherly heart. My parental guilt has shrunk to a miniature size, and I am able to keep it tucked far, far away.

As Mitchel massages my shoulders, I come up with a plan for how to unfold this complicated origami and smooth out the page. I send a text inviting my ex and his apparently not-so-new girlfriend to lunch. I tell him since Hailey really likes her, I would love to get to know her. He takes time to respond, I fire off a few more messages before turning in for the night. Dave finally sends a confirmation for our meeting in a couple of days.

Two days later, while Hailey is busy preparing for yet another chess competition with Mitchel, I leave our house and drive to the city. It's the first warm and sunny day of May; the spring is evident in lush new green leaves. Freshly trimmed lawns release the grassy smell I enjoy driving through with my windows rolled down. Traffic moves well through the Verrazano Bridge and Brooklyn-Queens Expressway. The usual multitude of aggressive New York drivers is missing, or maybe they're enchanted by nature's awakening and not rushing to hit the road. The restaurant is just a few blocks away from the tunnel, and the spring fairies gift me a parking spot across the street.

I spot the ruffles of pink tulle at the outside table of the restaurant as soon as I get out of the car. I put my head high, fix my sunglasses, and brush out the wrinkles from a dress that took me two days to decide on, and confidently stroll to meet the new woman in my ex-husband's life. As I approach their table, I see they've already started eating. Candice's long, bright red fingernails dip a chip deep into the guacamole, when it gets close to her mouth, she opens it wide managing to shove the whole piece in at once. Her long, bleached hair looks blinding, but she is an unattractive site that I just can't look away from. Her large swollen breasts are bulging out of a low-cut top, almost as deep as her big belly.

"Hi!" she squawks in the most high-pitched voice. Dave turns around towards me, he looks … nervous? Well, that would be a new emotion for him. He raises his hand and gives a short wave.

"Oh my God! Oh my God!" Candice bops on the chair clapping her hands as I sit down. "This is so exciting to finally meet you!" She offers her perfectly manicured, thin hand and barely squeezes just my fingers before letting go. She smiles, "I'm Candice!"

"Yes, indeed. Gretchen," I reply back.

"Would you like some guac? We've already ordered, this baby makes me so hungry." She moves the plate of half eaten guacamole towards me.

"No, thank you. I'll order something." I motion for the waiter and choose a duck salad when he gives me the specials. "Hailey has told me you've been spending some quality time with her. That's very nice of you."

"She's such a lovely girl. And it's nice to do all the girly stuff with her. I've always wanted a girl myself, you know," she looks at her belly, rubbing it, "but I'm having a boy. Dave is so excited about that. He tells me he will finally be able to be a proper father. You know, he will connect better because he is a boy himself," Candice continues to babble. I look at Dave and raise my eyebrow, trying to imagine him taking on all the fatherly duties, but he avoids looking at me, sipping his beer.

"I'm happy for both of you. I wish I found out sooner about such great news, Dave." I stare at my ex who avoids my gaze.

Candice giggles. "Dave and I, we ... we reconnected in the last few months. He has really been working on himself, proving he is the man for me." She pats his head.

"I see. I'm glad you've worked things out. What do you do Candice? Hailey was trying to explain, but I don't think she knows herself," I ask.

"Well," she laughs. "I work, kind of. My daddy has a real estate firm, like a big one, so I am a realtor, but I really don't need to work, because I have a trust fund set up by my grandparents, so ... I do a lot of things. I shop, I travel and look for properties, and I like to design things, like interior design, you know." She sips water through a straw that is somehow pink as well.

"Well, that's nice ... not to have to work. Isn't it, Dave?" I look directly at my ex, who has been unusually quiet. The waiter brings me my water with a clear plastic straw and a salad.

"Oh, Davey's now a real estate agent as well, the tech world wasn't the right fit for him." She reaches her hand across the table, he takes it into his, giving it a kiss. "My daddy has big plans, right Davey?"

"Yes, baby," he replies.

"So, tell me, Candice, have you seen Kai lately?" I decide to ask her head-on and see her reaction. She chokes on the water she has been slowly sipping when she hears my question.

"Why?" My ex asks as he leans over to Candice to pat her back until she stops choking.

"Oh, she didn't tell you? She told Kai—you know, the one who used to be your best friend since middle school— that he was the father of this baby. She was sending him ultrasound pictures just a few months ago." I take a sip of my water through my plain, clear straw, observing as the eyes of the pink Barbie doll grow large.

"What? What are you saying? Candice, what is she saying?" My ex stands up straight, towering over his girlfriend who sits with her mouth open, but not saying anything.

"You might not have recognized me," I continue, enjoying the effect my question produced. "I've lost quite a bit of weight. But I was in Grenada last October when you flew in and claimed your baby's daddy to be Kai. You see, he is my best friend's brother. He also likes my other best friend, and your news threw a wrench into their relationship. And here you are, with my ex now, claiming it's his baby. And you take my daughter shopping, and I don't like it. I don't like *you*."

"Wait, wait. What? You told me you wanted to be alone, you wanted to think things over," my ex demands, leaning over Candice.

"She wanted to play both of you, this one … so disgusting."

Candice slowly moves her eyes to him as his face is getting red, and I see a large vein pulsing on his neck.

"I … I …" she stutters. "I was confused."

"About who the father is?" he snarls at her, and I am starting to feel bad for her.

"I am hormonal, you prick. Don't you hang over me like that, you're suffocating me," she snaps at him and my empathy disappears for this woman. My ex stands back, now he is the one speechless. "I love you, but you lost half of the company that Kai left you, and until my daddy decided to help you, you were a loser without any prospects and I couldn't, I couldn't have you as my baby's father," she calmly explains and then loudly sips the last bit of water from the bottom of her glass.

"What the fuck are you saying?" He slams his fist against the table, sending the glassware into a nervous jitter.

"Stop acting like a baboon, you're embarrassing me. Sit down. I was going to tell Kai …."

"When?"

"Exactly." We both reply at the same time.

"Oh, I don't know, whenever it pleases me. And be quiet, you pathetic moron." She directs her venom at me. "Why don't you worry about your bratty daughter instead of me."

"Oh, this woman is a piece of work, exactly what you deserve, and don't you dare bring her around my daughter." I throw my napkin on the table and push my chair back, but before I am able to get up, Candice's face contorts in pain and she screeches.

"What was that?" She grabs her stomach with one hand and with the other my ex's hand. "Oh my God, oh my God, you idiot, you made my water break, you have to take me to the hospital right now, get a taxi," her voice escalates into a high pitch. My ex gives me a quick glance, his eyes are full of fear.

"Go ahead, you are about to become a father … again," I offer my words of support.

"Okay, baby, okay, just hold on, I'm calling your doctor right now." He fumbles with his phone, but it slips and falls to the floor. Dave picks it up as the wannabe Barbie then slams her hand bag on his head.

"I said the taxi, you stupid baboon. I hate you. I hate you for doing this to me." Her skinny hands keep beating my ex, who covers his face defensively with his arm.

"Baby, baby, calm down, this is not good for you to be angry, the baby, think about the baby," he begs loudly as he becomes smaller and smaller in my eyes. I can't believe I loved this man once. I skipped on spending time with friends and school activities, just to be with him. I craved his attention and my value was determined by him, and now here he is, diminished into a pathetic punching bag for a Barbie doll. I throw money down for my uneaten salad on the table, get up and walk off, leaving him to tend to his pregnant baby mama. The visitors of the restaurant and passersby stop to look, smiles growing on their faces watching this dramedy play out in front of them.

I cross the street and get into my car. In the silence of my small vehicle, with the muffled sounds of New York City, I lean my head back on the head rest and take a deep breath before erupting into laughter. I laugh at my ex and his baby mama, at my sleepless nights when Hailey was a colicky baby, at my parents who preferred going to parties and traveling over being responsible parents. I feel light and free, I no longer need to apologize for being me. I don't need to stuff my own pain with food. I am enough for me and Hailey. I am the one who deserves love just because, without any conditions and demands. Mitchel is waiting for me at home with a cup of tea, he is the man who has shown me what love is.

I make a quick phone call before taking off to visit Angelina. "Hi! Kai? It's Gretchen. I need to talk to you ..." With my voice trembling from nervous excitement, I fill him in on the recent development and we decide it would be best for him to fly in and get an immediate paternity test, then speak to Angelina. Meanwhile, I will see how I can bring the two of them together.

# 19.

## ANGELINA

"Hi, I have to come all the way to Brooklyn to see if you're okay! Why have you been ignoring me?" Gretchen waltzes into my apartment.

"Hey! Agh ... sorry. I've been busy ... you know ... writing and stuff. What's going on?" I reply. Gretchen has changed over the past few months. I've never seen her so confident; she walks taller, she's slimmed down, I haven't heard her apologize like she used to do.

"I just stopped by to see if I can drag you out to celebrate my birthday tomorrow, since you didn't RSVP to my invitation." She comes up and gives me a kiss on the cheek. "You know I won't take no for an answer. How is the little munchkin today?" She rubs my belly and I feel the baby gently roll under her touch. I smile and rub the hard protrusion that might be his foot or his butt.

"I really don't feel like going anywhere," I moan and shake my head. I've come to love spending time at home and going to bed by nine o'clock. The thought of getting dressed and going somewhere tires me out. We walk towards the table to sit, Gretchen first puts one chair under my feet and then pulls another out for herself. "You've never celebrated your birthday before."

"Mitchel insists." She rolls her eyes and smiles. "He is thinking of getting Brian and Jenna together, but don't tell her anything just yet, okay?"

"I won't, promise. Brian came around?"

"It's Jenna who came around. She's a business woman now. Kai made her his partner in his new tech company. Her first serious job that she hasn't hated. I think I remember her saying she actually loves it. She's talking numbers and goals and attracting new clients. She's doing well, really well. She's in a good place ... to appreciate ... to be in a relationship with Brian. She complained that you haven't returned any of her phone calls. What's up with that? You've decided to ignore all of us?"

"No, no. It's not that. Gosh ... I don't know how I'll face Jenna. I'm not ready to tell her about my situation." I point to my round belly.

"Angelina, you've been friends with Jenna for so long. She loves you. She will love this baby. Believe me, it'll be nice for you to have help when this little one arrives. And ... you'll have to tell Kai." Gretchen leans in and rubs my knee. But I shake my head vehemently at her suggestion, folding my arms across my chest.

"Please explain to me, why? Again." She stares deep into my eyes without blinking.

"I've told you why so many times." I rub my forehead. "He is having a baby with *her*. That baby needs him."

"And this one doesn't?" She reaches out and rubs my pregnant belly again.

"That baby shouldn't feel that Kai chose someone else instead of him. It's a terrible feeling, I know it too well. This little guy ..." My hand gently glides over small peaks that appear and then flatten as the baby moves inside of me.

"He will be loved, I'll make sure he never questions if his father loves him, because … because … I don't know … I haven't come up with a reason, maybe I'll tell him he doesn't have one."

"What?" Gretchen asks.

"I don't know, Gretchen, I'm still thinking," I sigh.

"You have to tell Kai."

"I don't want the baby to feel loneliness waiting for Kai, knowing that there's another family he spends his time with instead of him, feeling abandoned and questioning what's wrong with him that his father would choose another over him."

"I know your own father was like that, but I'm sure Kai will be an amazing dad. He keeps trying to reach you. He calls me once a week to check if you'll see him and just to find out how you are."

"You didn't tell him, did you?" My heart beats faster.

"No … I didn't. It's not for me to tell." Gretchen shakes her head and grabs my hand. "Come tomorrow … pleeeease … It would really mean so much to me, and Hailey would be so excited to see you." Gretchen leans forward and rubs my belly. "Mitchel says hi, by the way." Gretchen gets up but motions for me to stay seated. "See you tomorrow, okay?" She kisses me on the cheek and leaves me sitting on the chair with my feet up. The door slams behind her, and I force myself to get up to lock it.

The baby kicks, and I put my hand on the spot where I can still feel the firmness of a knee or maybe a heel. Everyone keeps asking if I'm okay, if I feel lonely since the father of this little one is not in my life, but this life inside my belly makes me feel as if I'm never alone. I am filled with hope for the future and wonder.

"We're going to be okay, little one. I love you so much already. I promise, you'll never feel alone," I say out loud, looking down at my stomach, but the baby replies with a painful kick to my bladder. I get distracted from my thoughts by my cell ringing. A familiar phone number pops up on the screen.

"Hi! How are you?" I pick up and greet my agent.

"Hi, Angelina! Good news. Your book is getting massive interest. I'm scheduling a meeting with a producer who is interested in putting it on the big screen."

"Wow. Really? This is amazing. A movie. I'm … I'm a bit terrified, I think." I try to collect my thoughts into intelligible sentences.

"You'd better keep on writing. *New York Times* Best Seller list comes out tomorrow, I'll keep you posted as soon as I have it, but be prepared to sit down. I am sure, I am sure you will be in the top ten."

"Thank you, that would be a dream. I'll have someone pinch me to make sure I'm awake. Thank you. Really. Thank you for all you've done." Peter has been the biggest cheerleader for my book, and his excitement was so contagious, I harnessed its power and charged my writing with it, increasing my daily word count to five thousand a day. My fourth book in the series is finished, and I just need to edit it before I send it off for his approval.

"I'm waiting on the next manuscript, Angelina, don't keep me waiting too long—we need to keep your name hot."

"All right, all right. I know. It's almost finished. You'll have it in a week or so. Okay?" I try to reassure him.

"Have your phone on you tomorrow. Have a good night."

"Yes, yes. I will. You too." I press the red button and the phone call ends. I lift my feet off the chair, take a bowl of pasta from the fridge, warm it up, and head to bed. Carbs have become my best friend through this very hungry pregnancy. I place the bowl on top of my stomach while reclining in bed and staring at the TV. I finish my pasta before the episode of *Friends* ends. I still feel like I could eat more, but I'm too tired to walk back to the fridge. I put the bowl on the nightstand and perch my laptop on my round belly. I scroll through the pages by tapping lightly on the screen, my eyes gloss over the words, knowing them by heart, and soon put the laptop on the floor so it doesn't slide down my stomach when I fall asleep.

I wake up with my bladder on the verge of rupture. I dash to the bathroom holding the bottom of my belly to alleviate the pressure. Once my morning urge is relieved, I brush my teeth and try to tame my hair that has become thicker and curlier since I got pregnant. Everything has grown with the new life inside of me: my nails grow rapidly, my lips have engorged, as well as my breasts. I have become clumsier, too, dropping utensils and hair brushes constantly. My memory fails me occasionally, I have to think for a few moments before certain words come to me. Gretchen says it's 'pregnancy brain' and it's normal. But it feels strange—very strange—to not have full control of my own body.

The alarm clock shows 7:30 a.m., I turn on the TV while making a breakfast of peach oatmeal, the only breakfast food that doesn't make me nauseous. I eat it while watching a show about women who don't know they're pregnant until they're in labor at the hospital. The stories are unbelievable, my own pregnancy had become evident around eight weeks with daily morning sickness and fatigue that made me go to bed at eight o'clock every evening. I keep checking my phone to make sure I have reception and that I haven't missed any calls from my agent, but the screen only displays the time and date on the pretty wallpaper of raindrops.

By eleven o'clock, I get up and get ready for Gretchen's birthday. Jenna doesn't know I'm pregnant, and I'd rather delay her from finding out longer. Hopefully, she will be preoccupied with seeing Brian and won't notice my bun in the oven. I put on a blush dress with an empire waist that hides my stomach. A touch of mascara and lip gloss complete my look, and I walk out of my apartment into the pleasant, sunny May afternoon in perpetually-loud New York City.

Gretchen picked a hibachi place just a few stops on the subway. When I get there, she is standing by herself.

"Hey, sweetie! Happy Birthday!" I hug her and give her a kiss on the cheek. I give her a gift bag containing a gift card for a spa treatment. "Where is everyone?"

"Hey! Thank you, Hailey will be here any minute, Mitchel took her to a chess competition, I am waiting for a few more people, and then we'll go to the table. Okay?"

"Sure. Who else is coming?" I ask.

Gretchen avoids my eye contact, looking away, ignoring my question.

"Gretchen?" I tug her arm. Her eyes move slowly and look directly at me. She doesn't need to say the name of who else is going to be at the table. "I can't stay." I turn around and head towards the exit.

"Angelina, stay. Please!" Gretchen begs me. I feel trapped, I run through the possibilities of what will happen if I see him now. If he sees me pregnant. I'm not ready. This is not the right time and not the right place. I need to run away, my heart drums a fast pace that my legs are itching to pick up. I swing the door open and as I do, arms wrap tight around me as Hailey greets me, happily rubbing my belly and Mitchel walks in behind her. My escape is foiled.

"Hi, Hailey!" I hug her, trying to hide any panic in my voice.

"You're staying, right? You're not leaving?" she frowns and looks at her mother, then back at me. Her smile disappears, and her eyes grow large waiting for my reply.

"I'm not leaving, I'm not. How can I? I just thought I dropped something outside. But I didn't." It works because Hailey smiles and claps. Mitchel greets me and kisses me on the cheek and then walks towards Gretchen. He takes her face into his hands, stares into her eyes for a moment, and then kisses her lips. "I missed you. Are you ready?" I overhear him ask her. She nods and leans into his palms and then takes his hand and walks towards Hailey and I.

"So. How was the competition?" she asks Hailey, who cheerfully raises her index finger up indicating first place. We clap and cheer as Hailey performs an awkward happy dance.

"Nice job! So proud of you." She hugs her daughter. "Oh, here are the rest of my guests." She looks up at the door, and then her gaze dashes to me.

I know who is behind me. My skin erupts in goose bumps, like a magnet drawn to his presence. I put my oversized bag in front of my belly and slowly turn around, hiding part of my body behind Hailey. He looks just as handsome as I remember him, but is now more tanned.

His stare burns into me and I feel the heat as my cheeks get flushed. He shakes hands with Mitchel and kisses Gretchen on the cheek, gifting her a small bag. He comes up to Hailey and gets down to her level.

"Hey! Your mom mentioned you enjoy chess, so I brought you this chess set from Grenada, I hope you like it." His eyes look up at me while Hailey is busy feverishly opening up the box. I cannot hold his gaze and look away. Gretchen calls for Hailey and when I am about to lose her as my cover, an excited yelp bursts into the restaurant, and we all look at the door where our friend Jenna has just entered. I haven't seen her in a while. She looks different, a stylish gray business suit sits well on her body, her hair is slicked back into a low ponytail. She's different. She definitely looks the part of a business woman. My friend has become a grown-up, and I don't think she minds it. Brian just had one reply to her phone calls and text messages, a short, 'Let me know when you figure your life out,' that he sent a week after the wedding debacle. Since then, Jenna has quit all social media, she has read my book, and by the looks of it, she has figured her life out.

"All right, everybody's here! Let's go to our table, everything is set up," Gretchen calls out after Jenna made the rounds hugging and kissing everyone and gifting Gretchen a small box with a pretty bow.

She comes to me and we both say simultaneously, "You look different," and burst out laughing. I guard my belly with my bag as Jenna throws her arms around me. All this time, Kai watches me, his eyes follow my every move. I know he will want to talk to me, I have to find a way to leave before he corners me and finds out I'm with child.

"Come, everyone this way!" Gretchen insists and takes me by the hand, leading everyone into the depths of the restaurant until we reach our hibachi table at the end of the hallway in a private room. When we get there, a tall man has his back to us, and when he hears us enter, he turns around, and I recognize Brian. His height allows him to look above our heads, and I know Jenna sees him when I hear her loud gasp.

We all crowd at the entrance, waiting for these two to have their first meeting since their wedding fell apart. I feel Jenna nudge me and Gretchen aside, slowly, as she comes from the back. Brian's face lights up on seeing her, he takes off his glasses and rubs his eyes. She runs to his open embrace, jumps, wraps her legs around him, and starts to cover his face in kisses. I hear Gretchen whimper as she brushes tears from her face. Hailey lets out an, "Aw!"

Jenna suddenly stops her embrace and when her feet touch the floor, she takes a step back. We collectively gasp as she bends a knee and takes Brian's hand. He tries to pull away and pick her up, but she raises her left hand, calling for silence.

"I'm sorry," she begins, as her voice trembles. Mitchel passes a napkin to Gretchen, my own eyes stay dry, refusing to spill any tears in this sweet moment that demands it. "I'm sorry I wasn't brave. I'm sorry I doubted. I didn't doubt your love for me, but I doubted if I deserved to be loved that much. I was scared, I was selfish. I thought what I was, what I had, was the life. But when I suddenly didn't have you, I realized that was all fake, made up, pretend. The life that was real is the one I had with you. I want to ask you to forgive me. I want to ask you to be my boyfriend ... again. I want to ask you for a chance to show you that I no longer fear. I want to ask you to give me an opportunity to love you without any doubt." Jenna goes silent, we hold our breath waiting for Brian's reply.

He quietly meets Jenna on his knees, his eyes move across her face, he kisses her hand. "Yes, my honey boo. Yes, to all of it," he replies. The room cheers, Jenna throws her arms around his neck, covering his face with more kisses. They both stand up facing us, their smiles are big, and their eyes are wet from tears. We crowd them with hugs and congratulations.

"Okay, enough, enough. Thanks, you guys, thank you, but I think we've taken enough of the spotlight from Gretchen," Jenna addresses all of us.

"That's right," Hailey confirms with sass, and we all chuckle. Taking our seats, I settle to the left of Hailey with Brian and Jenna next to me. Mitchel and Gretchen sit to the right and Kai next to them at the end. The waiter pours us water and takes our orders, then Mitchel taps on his glass with a fork.

"Hello, everyone!" he announces in a very official tone, standing up. "As you know, today we are celebrating this lovely lady's birthday!" He claps and we all cheer as Gretchen blushes. "I first have to say thank you to Gretchen, for being the way you are. You are sweet, beautiful, smart, kind and you're raising such a wonderful young woman. Darling, you are an amazing mom. Thank you for loving and taking care of me, for making my life exciting. I look forward to every morning, because it will bring me another day with you. Happy birthday, my love." He leans in and kisses Gretchen. "Hailey, I also have a wish for you, which is to not fear the struggle. The struggle is what builds character. Character is what makes a person.

I know you will achieve much in your life, cheers to you, we all love you, and here is a small gift from your mom and I." He takes a silver box out of his pocket and puts it in Hailey's hand. She opens it promptly, her eyes light up, and her smile lets everyone know that she loves it. She proudly shows the contents of the box, a thin gold chain with a queen chess figurine pendant.

"I love it!" Hailey beams and puts it on her neck.

"Yay!" I clap and give her a hug. The chef comes in wheeling a small cart with bottles of sauces and oil and plates of food for the hibachi. He presents two metal spatulas, taps them on the hot grill in front of him making them jump and flip in the air as he masterfully catches them and juggles them, as if in the circus. The hibachi show has begun. I feel my phone buzz in my bag and when I look at the screen, I know I have to pick it up. I motion to Gretchen that I will step just a few feet away to answer the phone call. Brian and Jenna are submerged in the world of rekindled romance, Hailey is not taking her eyes from the hibachi chef's tricks, only Kai follows my every move. I take my bag, holding it strategically in front of me and step to the far corner of the room where I pick up the call from my editor.

"Hey!" I say quietly into the phone.

"Hello, hello! I have some news!"

"Yes?" I feel my belly tighten and I rub it with my free hand, putting my bag on my shoulder.

"Angelina, you are number … one. You … are … number … one!" he drums out excitingly.

"Oh my God!" I whisper into the phone, not to take attention away from Gretchen's birthday party. "This is crazy!" My stomach muscle relaxes, and my hand stops moving as my mind tries to comprehend this enormous achievement. "Thank you, thank you so much!"

"Don't thank me, you wrote the book. This is ninety-nine percent your achievement, I'll take credit for just one percent. Listen, I hope you are celebrating tonight and can come by tomorrow. Everyone wants to personally congratulate you here."

"I will come by around noon, then. Bye! Thank you, again."

"Keep writing, Angelina. See you tomorrow."

I stare at the screen of my phone for a second, still shocked by becoming a *New York Times* best seller. The baby kicks, and I rub the spot where his tiny body part pushes hard against the wall of my stomach. A loud gasp makes me turn around, my smile collapses against all the eyes that are staring at me. The chef throws an egg into the air, which lands on the side of the spatula, cracking and pouring its insides on the hot grill.

"My book just hit number one on the *New York Times* Best Seller list." I wave to everyone, but everyone stays silent.

"You're pregnant!" Jenna screams out, and I realize that I have exposed my secret by rubbing my belly while talking on the phone. My friend gets up and runs towards me, hugging me tight. "Why didn't you tell me? How far along are you? Your belly is so cute."

I look around hoping to find help, an escape, but all I find are eyes questioning my decision, my pregnancy, asking me so many questions that I no longer have answers to. My dress starts to feel tight, constricting my chest, I can't inhale, and I pull on my collar against its constriction.

My neck itches as the room pushes down on me. Just then, Kai's face appears right in front of me.

"Breathe, Angelina. Look at me. Steady your breathing." His eyes lock mine in, drawing me out of the spiraling anxiety. "Sit down, deep breath in and out." He puts my hand on his chest and the rhythm of his own breathing settles mine. My nose starts to itch, I feel the pressure that burns my eyes, and when I look at him again a wall of tears flood my eyes.

"You can't be here. It's not the right time. It's not ... not the right place ... I can't bear having you here. You, you are not, you are not ..." the sobs override my vocal cords.

"I'm not the father of Candice's baby. She made it up. She is with the real father of that child in the hospital right now. Ask Gretchen."

"It's true, Angelina. Candice is engaged to my ex, he's the father of that child. I met them yesterday." Gretchen leaves the table and comes towards me.

I collapse on Kai's chest. I feel his arms wrap tight around me.

"I'm sorry. I'm so sorry. This is crazy." I force a laugh. "I have news to tell you. You are the father of my baby." I take his hand and put it on my stomach. His eyes grow big as he caresses my body and he puts his other hand on it. He glances at Gretchen and Jenna who stay quiet looking at me and then back at Kai. I realize that I might not be in the right place and my news is revealed at the wrong time, but I am with my friends, the right people who will support me no matter what. Kai stays quiet, he swallows hard, and my heart picks up an anxious beat that this all might be too much for him.

"I'm sorry. I ... I ..." I choke as tears roll down my cheeks.

"Don't be sorry. I'm here. I'm here for you. All I ever wanted was an opportunity ... just give me a chance to be with you and take care of you and this, this, our little one." He looks up at me, and his eyes are glowing twinkles of happiness. I nod my head vigorously and throw my arms around him. He smells of nutmeg, cinnamon, and chocolate, a smell that promises a sweet spice of happiness.

## The End